The Princess and the Pauper

Also by Gwen Davis

NOVELS

Naked in Babylon

Someone's in the Kitchen with Dinah

The War Babies

The Pretenders

Touching

Kingdom Come

The Motherland

The Aristocrats

Ladies in Waiting

Marriage

Romance

Silk Lady

The Princess and the Pauper

POETRY

Changes

How to Survive in Suburbia When Your Heart's in the Himalayas

American Woman Loose in the UK

PLAYS

The Best Laid Plans

The Bridal Party

The Princess and the Pauper

An Erotic Fairy Tale

By Gwen Davis

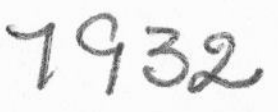

LITTLE, BROWN AND COMPANY • BOSTON • TORONTO • LONDON

FIRST EDITION

Library of Congress Cataloging-in-Publication Data

Davis, Gwen.
The princess and the pauper : an erotic fairy tale / by Gwen Davis. — 1st ed.
p. cm.
ISBN 0-316-17499-8
I. Title.
PS3554.A9346P75 1989
813'.54—dc19

88-37343
CIP

10 9 8 7 6 5 4 3 2 1

RRD VA

Designed by Jeanne Abboud

Published simultaneously in Canada by Little, Brown & Company (Canada) Limited

PRINTED IN THE UNITED STATES OF AMERICA

For my teachers:

Warner Berthoff,
who taught me Mark Twain, and

Ann E. Berthoff,
who taught me to write a simple sentence.
Or tried to.

Deeper meaning resides in the Fairy Tales told to me in my childhood than in the truth that is taught by life.

— Friedrich Schiller, *The Piccolomini*

But what about the frog? It, too, has to mature before union with the Princess can become possible.

— Bruno Bettelheim, *The Uses of Enchantment*

The Princess and the Pauper

1

ONCE UPON A VERY RECENT TIME lived a prince and a princess. Visiting royalty. The sweethearts the world needed to believe in. They had perfect skin and perfect smiles, and their bodies perfectly entwined, a graceful arcing of slender back against broad chest that seemed made to order for romance. But only in public. In private they could not stand each other.

Oh, it had been lovely in the beginning, being so sexily celebrated, the world waiting outside their bedroom, measuring the glow. If beauty was in the eye of the beholder, excitement was in the pens of the press. Like most people in the world the prince and princess believed the news: at the time of their courtship it was often about them. So having read how ideally suited they were, gloss being a great aphrodisiac, they'd discovered exquisite pains and exquisite pleasures that lasted only a moment. And burrowing into each other's secret places, imagined the feeling was love.

By the time they realized it wasn't, it was too late. Everyone, but everyone, had seen them get married.

They came from the tiny kingdom of Perq, in the Irish Sea, a place no one might have heard of were it not for the swath the royal couple cut, the tax benefits, and the tides. The island was washed with the same tropical flow of Gulf Stream that bathed the west coast of Galway, giving it mysterious purple sands, palm trees waving in salmon pink sunsets, making it an excellent setting for easy living and gambling. The last resort for those who had run out of them.

But for all the beauty of the young royals' native land, or at least the quarter acre consigned to their perpendicular palace, most of their time was spent traveling. Revving up goodwill, practicing their smiles. Their faces were frozen with insincere benevolence. Which was not to say they didn't feel goodwill. They just didn't feel it towards each other. And that was how the papers wanted them: nodding cozily, spirits interwoven. Everybody's dream of love.

Small as the kingdom was, and rich, it was secretly a debtor nation. The king had gotten into a crap game on the yacht of a Libyan arms merchant, and lost his hairshirt. The owner of the yacht, being (not surprisingly) a materialist, had refused to return the king's vestment for official religious remorse. In a desperate attempt to get it back, the king had gambled his country and lost. The merchant put up the capital to renovate Perq's gambling casino, and publicize the desirability of the island as a tax shelter and vacation spot. And it was he who had found Darcy, for that was the princess's name, and seen what a perfect match she was for Prince Rodney.

Everyone wanted to be a princess, to be admired automatically, to have everything everyone assumed other people wanted. Magic had vanished from the world. The closest thing to transformation was the lottery. People needed to believe there was still a little enchantment. There was no one who wouldn't want to be in her shoes, with the exception of certain feminists, who had written her letters suggesting she change her title to "Princeperson." So Darcy tried not to be discontented with her lot. She knew she had obligations, to women, her country, and her parents, who'd been given a condo in Marbella as payment for her, along with a subscription to *Newsweek*, starting with the issue in which she appeared on the cover. Divorce was out of the question. Perq was a country in which such things were frowned upon, most especially in royalty.

So she tried to swallow her malaise, and not read articles about countries where women were free, or thought they were. But since many such pieces appeared in the same papers and magazines as her picture, she couldn't help seeing them. Her appointments secretary always sent copies of the publications by private plane to the countries Darcy was goodwilling in, so she would have something to look at while she was under the hairdryer, which was often.

On this particular trip to the southwesterly tip of Wales, she found herself feeling more restless than usual. The goodwill here was especially intense, being not self-serving since there was nothing to be gained from the tourist trade. Wales was a poor country, and the Welsh were fiercely proud of their heritage, in spite of how little it had left them in the way of actual inheritance. But it was only a hydrofoil jaunt away from Perq, actually its closest neighbor.

Besides affording an opportunity for a show of friendship, the locale also boasted a particularly charming little tumble-down castle on a bluff overlooking Cardigan Bay. *Vogue* magazine planned a layout of Darcy in front of the castle, since, small as it was, even with its turrets crumbling, it was more a proper castle than the royal high-rise in Perq. Cromwell had said, "No one rises so high as he who does not know where he is going," which had certainly been the case with the architect who'd done the Perquian palace.

Darcy looked out the window of the inn where she was staying (there being no appropriate residence for royalty in Criccieth) at the sun glinting gold on the waveless, flat surface of the water, and the beach, so rocky with cobblestones it might have been an ancient street. And seeing the beauty of where she was, she wondered why she was so hollow as to feel sad.

At the same moment, just two windows down the road, a young housewife was watering her hydrangeas. They were fiercely blue hydrangeas, since everything in this part of the world was fierce in the very best sense; fiercely glad to be alive, fiercely proud of what it was, fiercely at peace. That was to say, everyone was happy there was no trouble at the present time, but remembered when there was, and told their children about it, and was ready to fight again if there was trouble, and couldn't help hoping that there would be maybe a little. Even the flowers grew as vivid as flowers could grow, as if reflecting the characteristics of those who nurtured them.

Shan, for that was the name of the young wife who watered her hydrangeas, had eyes as blue as they were, equally arresting. Her hair was the color of cornsilk, and fell in the same flaxeny manner, all in a piece, so it moved from side to side with the motion of her head. She was slender with high breasts, and her cheeks seemed freshly painted with a blush brush, though she wore no makeup, since her religion was Simplicity.

Her lashes were double-rowed, jet at their base, so they looked mascaraed, and her lips were crimson round the full outside curve, bright pink and wet from her habit of licking them when she felt excited, which she almost always did. There was nothing in her life that did not interest her, which made her galvanizingly alive. Boredom is a scorpion, turning on itself, filling the bearer with poison, killing those who try to kill it. But in Shan's case, there was only one pocket of her life that felt unfilled, and that was in her wish to see a princess.

She had heard for weeks that the Princess Darcy would be coming to Criccieth. Like everyone else in the village she had bought a share in the lottery, poor as she was. The prize was to be a royal tea party, with the mayor, the vicar, and one Ordinary Villager, whoever the winner was. She had pressed her young husband for a few pence to buy an extra ticket, so strong was her wish to smell the perfume of a princess.

At two the winner was to be announced. Leaning her slender neck to the right, curving her graceful body around the hydrangeas so she could see past the slate roof with its white painted legend, "TEAS," Shan noticed on the clock tower below the castle that it was just after one. There were royal guards standing outside the inn where the princess was staying. They were carrying staves and swords and little walkie-talkies, which went not at all with the red velvet, tight jackets, peplums, black belts, high white hose and brass-buckled shoes. Stationed just a few feet apart they nonetheless spoke to each other over their receivers: Shan could hear the signals crackling the air, the electronic sound of their reedy voices. It wasn't until she narrowed her eyes — no easy feat since they were so wide and large — that she saw how small the guards were, and wondered if they were midgets.

At the temporarily royal window Darcy sighed again, and pressed to her sweetly rounded breast the latest issue of *Cosmopolitan*, forwarded by her appointments secretary. It was all too bright for her, really: the day, the way people thought about her, the constant bowing and scraping of those who deferred to her, the beautiful places she traveled, with no uplift in her heart. Because always at the end of her day, her journey, her glance, was Rodney, whose private countenance was a glower.

That he was not with her this day, at least, seemed a special kind of pardon, an answer to the penance she did in secret for being unworthy, less than she should be, a woman. The royal hydrofoil had needed refurbishing, and as the official head of the navy, it was incumbent on Rodney to see that it was properly done. So Darcy had been permitted to make this trip alone. She had come on the queen's hydrofoil, which featured a sporting room in the wickedest sense of sporting, redesigned by a trendy London decorator for the particularly salacious tastes of the arms merchant who had won Perq, and along with it its queen.

Darcy sat down in the wing chair, outfitted now with pillows from all the fine houses of Criccieth, loaned by the better homeowners to make her comfortable. To hold the royal wardrobe, the closet was filled with plush, pink satin-covered hangers which the owner of the inn had bought for the princess's coming, at that summer's sale at Harrods. The room, even with its walls broken out and redone, as they had been for the royal sojourn, was still so small that her lady-in-waiting, usually at her elbow, had to wait outside. Darcy could hear her abiding breathing in the tiny hallway just beyond the door, the measured, deferential pulse of it: breath that was held to see what was coming, like life that hinged on expectations instead of being lived in the moment.

Darcy opened the magazine and read through the article about herself, how exemplary she was, exactly what the world needed in the way of a princess, with a quiz at the end for the reader: "Test Your Princess Potential." Frightened of taking the test, lest she fail and find out how unsuited she was, Darcy turned the page. The article that followed was entitled "How to Get Past Multiple Orgasms to Enlightenment," something that caught her full attention. On Perq they did not speak very often of enlightenment.

Since the king had lost his hairshirt to the merchant Rachid, the official religion of Perq had been canceled. Faith, which had come just after miniature golf as one of Perq's favorite diversions, had fallen into disuse, as had the miniature golf courses themselves. Rachid had begun a program of regularly rewarding those who showed the most self-interest. The one stubborn zealot on the island had announced on his regular television show that Sodom had been destroyed not for fellatio and anal intercourse, but because people didn't give money to the poor. Wrath swept through Perq like a hurricane. Those who said it was the language that offended them managed to close down the station.

So it titillated Princess Darcy past dreaming, all those words on the page about letting go and there being no enemy but the Self. Several prominent women in religion had been interviewed, besides Shirley MacLaine, and thoughts leapt out at her like "Beware of the temptation to perceive of yourself as unfairly treated." Darcy's head was absolutely reeling at the sudden assault on what the article called her "Belief System." Her breath came more quickly.

"Highness?" said her lady-in-waiting from the hall.

"Yes?" She put the magazine underneath her, as guiltily as if she had been caught masturbating, the subject of the next article.

"Are you all right?"

"Never better," Darcy said, adopting the attitude the article had assured her would create the reality.

"It's time for the lottery," said the lady-in-waiting.

Not quite a village square, more like a circle, curved the road outside the Moelwyn Inn. But for the occasion, the most special in Criccieth history, it served the same purpose: a gathering place for all the citizenry. They spilled over the sidewalks into the streets, the tallest villager with his cowlick scraping the bottom of the "Bed and Breakfast" sign, which hung suspended by chains from the white painted eaves. Where the road sloped downward towards the stony beach, children played on plastic tricycles if their parents had money, the poorer ones with balloons, the poorest with stones, flipping them towards the water, taking satisfaction from the sharp thwack of rock thudding against rock. There were squeals of celebration from infants in strollers, toddlers half-walking in red-braced harnesses, their steps alternating with the splat of their palms hitting the street. The brisk air, unaccustomedly warmed by the sun, streaked the children's cheeks with red, the same color Shan's were, caused in her case as much by excitement as by the special beauty of her skin.

She had put on her wedding dress, saucy with her grandmother's Irish lace running round the shoulders, squaring down to her cleavage, revealing the tops of her high, round breasts, setting her inside the frame of the creamy white costume like the picture she was. She had scrubbed all the grime from beneath her nails, and was wearing little white gloves, as she wished to be no less a princess in her way than the woman who would, she fervently hoped, be entertaining her. In preparation, she had practiced having Tea, elegant Tea, higher-than-high Tea, every day for a month. Coached by the local nobility, a pink-haired duchess, Shan had learned step by step, little finger extended, the way royals sipped and poured. At the same time the duchess, who'd been a showgirl in the twenties when Englishmen of good family still haunted stage doors, gave her pointers in posture and comportment, since she liked the girl and was always grateful when young people talked to her, and even more important, listened. The duchess (who was, in fact, no more than a lady, but no one checked such things in Criccieth) had turned eighty-eight in February, the cruellest month, no matter what T. S. Eliot said.

Pinky at the ready, stretched with anticipation inside white gloves, Shan stood near the rainspout by the entryway to the Moelwyn Inn. Flowers grew out of cracks in the walls, as well as the windowboxes. Red and white and purple impatiens bloomed out of the dirt by the curb, which a recent light rain had turned into mud. Shan was most careful not to step in it, since she was wearing her wedding shoes, white linen, with a touch of the garden where she'd been married a year before on the heels and the instep.

A roar went up from the crowd. From where she stood, Shan could not see exactly what was happening. But at the rear children were being hoisted on shoulders, so she imagined the front door was opening. Little flags of the nation of Perq were being waved; a golden phoenix rising out of a roulette wheel, Perq's national symbol as reconceived by the decorator who had done the queen's hydrofoil. Hawkers had hit the streets with them shortly after dawn that morning. As the flags whirled and pipes played and local buskers danced their button-vested enthusiasm, Shan could hardly contain her excitement. The mayor mounted a small platform to the front of the inn, the vicar close behind, holding a glass bowl with torn-off raffle tickets in it, which he offered him. The mayor picked one and handed it to the vicar.

"The winner of the lottery," the vicar said, his voice as rolling and round as one of his several chins, "and the one who will have tea this day with the lovely Princess Darcy, subsovereign of the Kingdom of Perq . . . our most esteemed neighbor to the slightly southwest . . . bathed by the magical Gulf Stream . . ."

"Will you get on with it?" said a woman in the crowd.

"Yes, dear," said the vicar. "The winner is number eleven."

"Oh, no!" said Shan, looking at the tickets clutched in her

white gloved fingers. Numbers ten and twelve. The first had been bought with money she'd saved, the second with coins given grudgingly by her husband, the winning one bought by someone else in the moment Shan had turned to Tom to plead.

A tear fell from her nearly always radiant eyes. Disappointment choked her throat. She leaned against the rainspout, letting the full flood of her shattered expectations pour over her, as the winner moved forward and the crowd began to disperse.

"Now, now, darlin'," said the duchess, placing a liver-spotted hand on her shoulder. "It's only a tea."

"But we practiced so hard, Your Grace. And all of it wasted."

"Good manners are never wasted. You can use them with me. Come to tea as usual with me this afternoon. We'll have scones."

"No, thank you so much anyway," said Shan, stumbling off in heavy-footed sorrow. But as she went past the doorway of the inn, she saw the princess coming down the stairs. Racing past the royal guards who, Shan now observed, were not midgets at all, but little boys, she called out the princess's name. The royal guards seized her from behind, and rudely pulling her away, flung her onto the sidewalk into the mud.

"That'll teach her to try and get past us," one of them said into his walkie-talkie.

"My dress!" cried Shan. "You've ruined my dress!"

"How dare you treat her like that!" Darcy chastised them. "You barbarians! Have you no feelings?" It was a rhetorical question: the standing army and the royal guard of Perq were made up of little boys, since they had the least mercy. "I shall see that you're punished for this," she said, and went into the street to help Shan.

"You poor thing," sympathized Darcy, noting the many runs in the young woman's stockings, before she pulled down her skirt. "Come inside."

Shan marveled even as she tried to regroup her shattered dignity: never had she been in royal quarters before. The mere presence of the Princess Darcy made the inn into a palace. Gingham curtains gave off a regal shimmer. The sun, dipping down into afternoon towards the mountains, irradiated the window, backlit the princess's perfectly shaped head, with its neatly pulled back golden hair. It seemed a veritable aura, as if she were not only royal, but holy. Shan was struck dumb with reverence, recognition of her own lowliness, and, thanks to the guards, filth.

"Did they hurt you?" Darcy asked.

"This was my wedding dress," Shan said sadly.

"I'll give you something of mine." The princess went to the renovated closet, bursting with royal garments on lush pink satin hangers. "I wish I had my wedding dress here. I'd be more than glad to let you have it. Why do we think the solution is getting married?"

She pulled a pale blue Saint Laurent afternoon dress from the hanger. "Here. You'll look nice in this. We have the same coloring. Your servants can take it in if it's too big."

"My servants?"

"You don't have servants?"

"No, Ma'am."

"But, who dresses you, then? Who helps you in and out of your clothes, and pulls your nightgown over your head at night?"

"Why, I have no nightgown, Ma'am. Tom says it would be a waste of money we don't have, when he likes me better naked." A dimple of what Shan was sure was wickedness revealed itself at the corner of her mouth.

"You shall have one of mine," Darcy said, a burst of generosity surging over the wave of envy she felt. She zipped Shan into her dress. "You have a pleasant manner, and you hold yourself well. Are you educated?"

"The duchess has been schooling me in manners, Ma'am, so I would be fit to take tea with you. For that was my only unfulfilled wish, to see a princess."

"Your . . . only . . . unfulfilled wish. All else in your life makes you happy then?"

"Oh, yes." Shan, seeing herself in the mirror, stepped back with a start. For in the dress she now wore, she looked amazingly like the princess.

"But what do you do for amusement?"

"Well, I walk by the sea, grow flowers, watch the sunset, sing songs, eat ice cream, drink beer . . ."

"Beer . . . ," said the princess covetously, since her only bubbly beverage was champagne, which soured in the belly when there was nothing to celebrate. "I should give my tiara to be able to drink beer. And to wear a dress like this . . ." She leaned over and picked up the cast-off, muddied wedding dress. Signaling Shan to unzip her, she took off her purple Valentino, and stepped into Shan's dress. "With mud on it! To be able to go out wearing something ordinary, and soiled, and know that *W* will not be taking a photograph, and writing about it, or think you're starting a trend!"

"*W?*"

"It's a fashion newspaper," Darcy said, waving her hand with a trace of the impatience she had had with people who were not as quick or sophisticated as she was, before she'd read the article and learned that everybody was connected. Suddenly, she caught a glimpse of herself in the mirror. "But it could be you! We look so alike! If you had a little more makeup . . ."

"And you had a little less, if I may say so, Your Majesty . . ."

"But you may and you have," said Darcy, and giggled, as the two of them set about transforming each other, Darcy with a mascara brush in her hand, Shan with a washcloth. That done, they took hairbrush and comb to each other. Finally, Darcy stood with her hair flowing free and cornsilky while Shan had an elegant chignon. And they were each metamorphosed into the other, with tears in their eyes: Shan because she had never dreamed she could look so royal, and Darcy, because she had never imagined, after all the articles in *Bazaar*, that she could seem common.

Simplicity tugged at the princess, a wish not only to have read the article, but to have assimilated it. To relate in the fullest sense to her fellowwoman. And be excited again about going to bed with a man. "Oh, I would give my ring, and my Rolex to be able to be you for just a little while. . . ."

"And I would give all that I had — if I had anything — to be you, Your Majesty."

"Shall we do it then?" asked Darcy.

"Oh, I never could get away with it," said Shan.

"Of course you could. I wouldn't know you weren't me, if I weren't me. Just speak as little as possible, and seem as though you mean well. Whole nations are run by people who do just that." She took the ring from her finger and put it on Shan's, and was switching the watch from her wrist to the girl's just as delicate one, when she noted the bruise on Shan's forearm.

"But who did that to you? Was it my guards, those sadistic little twerps?"

"I'm afraid so, Ma'am."

"I shall see that they're strung up by their thumbs." Flinging open the door, she ran down the stairs, calling out, "You, guard! Get over here!" But before she could reach the landing, the two little boys in their red Gainsborough outfits, brandishing their swords, were waiting.

"How dare you treat anyone like that!" Darcy cried. "I shall see that you are thrown in the tower!"

"Get out of here, trash!" said one of the guards, tripping her. The second laughed in merriment as Darcy hit the floor. "And that's for getting me in trouble with the princess," he said, kicking her mud-spattered rear, arcing her out in the street with the force of his foot, which he had strengthened through soccer practice and abusing cats.

"You fool!" Darcy said, landing in the mud. "I'm the princess!"

"And I'm the archbishop of Canterbury!" the little boy guard said, doubling himself over with his wit, as his partner laughed, and the two of them slammed the door to the inn, and bolted it.

* * *

Shortly after two-thirty, the princess's lady-in-waiting came to get her for the magazine shoot at the castle. Shan could barely control her shaking. She imagined if she were discovered she would be flung into the Tower of London, providing the tower were still in use, which she wasn't sure it was. True, it was traditionally only for those of very high birth, but she was sure they would make an exception for one who dared to counterfeit royalty. They'd send her there without turning a hair, once they discovered the impersonation, which, she was sure, would be very easy.

It was to her great amazement then, that the lady-in-waiting seemed not to notice anything amiss, simply bustled about collecting hairbrush and comb, and the various accessories the people from *Vogue* might not have remembered. Then she put a shawl round Shan's shoulders, since a cloud was passing over the sun, and the two of them went down the stairs to the limousine parked at the curb.

"But you have the posture of a professional!" the lighting director of *Vogue* said, as he adjusted the reflectors to catch her just so.

"A professional what?" Shan said. To her surprise everyone laughed, imagining wit where there was only innocence. She was oddly at ease in the shadow of the castle, having played there since she was a little girl. It was the highest point in Criccieth, this bluff above the bay. Where long ago sentinels had stood to mark the coming of hostile ships or landed armies, twentieth-century children lifted box kites with shining streamers, strands of red and yellow and blue, to catch the friendly but impressive winds. So it was a dance to her, really, being in this place where she had played all the young days of her life, and come back to kiss by moonlight.

"A professional model, of course," said the lighting director. "If you ever decide to get out of the princess business, you could have a great career. By your leave . . ."

She nodded. He moved her back a little, hardly touching her

arm, and that with much deference. Her shoulders brushed against the stones, familiar reddish buff rocks set in their perfect circular design, looking all in all more like a sand castle than those actually made of sand. A troop of young Welshmen and women sat in the shadows cast by the crumbling turrets, on benches set up in the open courtyard. One of them looked agonizingly familiar to Shan, like one she had kissed in this place by moonlight.

"I think we need a man in this shot," said the director, and turning, peered into the group of observers. "You there, villagers!"

"We are ac-tors, sir," said the handsomest of them, in roundly Burtonian tones, getting to his feet, whipping his cloak around his shoulders, like mystery. "Here to rehearse a play for the festival next Saturday."

"How tall are you, Ac-tor?" the director asked, marking the fine reddish curl of his hair, and the black brightness of his eyes.

Backed against the wall, Shan trembled. Unless she was much mistaken, the young actor was none other than her childhood sweetheart, Miles, not seen by her or even his own kinsmen since he'd run off to London to join the theater.

"As tall as the situation demands," he said. "A giant Macbeth for Scotland, a crookback Richard for England." He bent himself over nearly double to illustrate.

"How about for a layout in *Vogue*?"

"Your six-foot servant," said the young actor, and bounded up the stone stairs. "Miles Griffith at the ready, sir."

"Over there," the director said, "by the princess."

"With the greatest of pleasure," Miles said, and tossing his cloak, right arm over left shoulder this time, spun himself towards her with a flourish. The ruddiness of his complexion deepened as he came close to her. "Your Majesty," he said, and bowed.

She held out her hand, as the duchess had shown her. He kissed her fingertips, held them for a moment too long, stared into her face, seemed to turn it over in his mind.

"May I have my hand back?" she said.

"Forgive me." He let her fingers go. "It's just . . . For a moment . . ."

"Yes?"

"You look so much like someone. . . . A girl . . . long ago. Before I left this village."

"Did you love her?" Shan said.

"I wasn't sure. I only knew I loved the theater."

"Did it love you back?"

"From time to time."

"A woman would have been more faithful."

"Only if kept under lock and key."

"All right, children," the director said. "Let's use the light."

Now, meanwhile, what of the real princess? It had been a long time since Darcy had been allowed to roam about on her own, and she had pretty much lost the knack of setting off in a direction that had not been charted for her. This, combining with her discombobulation at having been so rudely treated, muddied, and, in fact, bruised, served to conjure up in her an actual sense of terror, bright as was the Criccieth afternoon, peaceful as the little curve of bay looked set against cobblestoned shore. So long had Darcy been honored, she'd forgotten what it was to be befriended, so her feeling of isolation bordered on panic. She had not a penny with her, nor any of her credit cards. Looking down at her mud-spattered skirt, she could not imagine anyone's wanting anything to do with her. So the smiles that the villagers proffered her, the little nods of amity, seemed to her insincere, cloaking disdain, rather than being the full-out neighborliness they were.

What had appeared in her fantasy as an adventure, a lark, now took on dark crow wings, screeching to her of sorrow and potential disaster. So black was her brainpan — for, since most of the women in the world thought in terms of rescue, the ultimate rescuer being a prince, and that was exactly what Darcy was fleeing — she could imagine only the worst. She sat on the concrete stairs leading down to the rocky beach, her forehead against the metal railing, cooling off the feverish thoughts, her vision of her poor, wasted, badly dressed body floating out to sea. So when the skeletal fingertips touched on her shoulder, she gave a start so enormous that the old lady whose hand they belonged to was nearly knocked over.

"My dear!" said the duchess.

"I'm dreadfully sorry," Darcy said, and stood to help her.

The duchess held her hip with gnarled fingers, on each of them a ring, amethysts circled with seed pearls, cabachon emeralds curved into mounds like a green pudding. "What a terrible reward for my wanting to ask you to tea."

"Tea?" Darcy fairly cried, for so profound had been the fear in her heart, that she had been unable to feel the gnawings in her stomach. Now, reminded, she felt how actually hungry she was.

"I am not who you think I am," said Darcy, comfortably settled in front of the duchess's fireplace, in the center a gas heater that took tenpence pieces. Porcelain animals paraded on the mantel above, with wicker monkeys hanging by their tails, and little stuffed tigers and leopards on safari near brass andirons.

"Of course not, dear," said the duchess. "We are none of us who people think we are. We are creatures of Infinite Light whom history has sent into the shadows, and it is only now that we are starting to emerge."

"Double cream, please," said Darcy, slightly fascinated, and wildly hungry. It was an exciting feeling, really, actual hunger. "And two sugars as well."

"Well, I see where your brush with royalty has given you richer tastes."

"It was not a brush with royalty. I am myself royalty."

"And all along I was afraid you didn't listen," said the duchess. "Yes, it is true. We are each of us a Queen of the Universe, created by the Goddess, to bring affection and succor to this planet laid waste by men. And we must come back, over and over, till we get it right, and effect some change for good."

"You really believe all that?"

"Believe?" said the duchess. "I *know*."

It occurred to Darcy that the duchess, odd as she seemed, had perhaps also read that issue of *Cosmopolitan*, and was on the same track as the other women interviewed by the magazine. So maybe it was not so much that she was dotty, as that she was in tune. For something most strange and wonderful seemed to be going on in the consciousness of women, besides wanting to get laid. The truth of it was, in spite of the fact that men were in charge, women seemed to be more interesting. Especially once you realized, even capturing the prince, that that was all he was.

For men were stuck in their roles even worse than women were, defining themselves by what they did, and not by what they thought, or were, or aspired to. And all the poor prince knew — did she pity him? had distaste been tempered by compassion? had the transformation really begun that was more than a change of clothes? — was that he was an emblem for their state, and that he had to seem beneficent and help flood victims, and see that the hydrofoil floated. But what did he think of in the rainbow borderline between dusk and dreaming, when people wondered what their lives meant, if anything?

"Scones?" asked the duchess.

"Oh, yes, please," said Darcy, delighted that the doughy edges were fretted with currants, tiny and dark, like an assault by flies. The scones were warm to the touch. She broke one open, and watched a puff of steam rise from the center. Secret heat. She understood about that. Taking a pat of freshly whipped butter, she placed it on the soft inside of the crispy scone, and watched with delight as it melted. Having been so sated with sophisticated pleasures, it had not been her lot of late to observe the simple joys. This, she could not help thinking, was really great fun. She could hardly wait for the jam.

"You have come a long way, dear Shan, for your age and education. Now you must make something of yourself."

It was a pretty conceit, really, a princess as an ordinary person, trying to make the ordinary person into something.

"Do you suppose I could?" she asked, as Shan, even while Darcy wondered what she would have made of herself had she not been a princess.

"Of course. It's a new world out there for women. And your husband isn't the lout he pretends. They're all like that. Even Lord Mayberry, my dear late husband, tried to be less than the dictates of his soul. But he couldn't fool me."

"I would imagine anyone would have a hard time fooling you," Darcy said, starting to enjoy the duplicity of her situation, abandoning plans to tell of her true identity. And since there was no need to play the part of a princess, she actually let the butter run over her fingers and licked it off. It tasted more delicious than butter ever had.

"Lucky you're taking tea with me instead of the princess. That would never do," the duchess remonstrated, even as she smiled at the girl's obvious pleasure. "No, you musn't underestimate your husband. There's a lot of sensitivity in Tom."

"Tom?" Darcy said.

"I know it sounds like wishful thinking, but I've caught glimpses of sensibility in him. You can lift him. Raise him from the mire."

"How?"

"By lifting yourself. Then you will have the leverage of angels." The duchess smiled her long-toothed, slightly yellow smile, jaundiced more deeply by the contrasting redness of her lips, painted bright as they'd been when she was still a showgirl.

"All very abstract," said Darcy.

"Very well, then, I will channel," said the duchess, rolling her eyes up into her head. And turning slightly crimson, a shade darker than her hair, she spoke with the booming voice of an Afghan, one who had just finished fighting the British in the Khyber Pass.

"Shan, hear me, Shan," said the booming voice. "Plant seven seeds in the windowbox, and eat them as they flower. The blossoms will serve as an antidote."

"What kind of seeds?" asked Darcy, amazed by the voice, but not very impressed by what she recognized as the trick, since whoever it was didn't know she wasn't Shan, so how psychic could they be?

"These," said the Afghan, and seven seeds cascaded from the pink crystal chandelier into Darcy's lap.

"How did you do that?" Darcy asked. But the duchess had opened her eyes, and seemed to remember nothing.

Meanwhile, the bogus princess, too, was having tea, as had been promised, with the mayor, the vicar, and the winner of the lottery, whom she had hoped would be herself, never dreaming she would be the princess the winner would have tea with. The winner, as it turned out, was one Samuel Stroll, a good-natured fellow who ran Criccieth's souvenir store, filled with maps and shells and fold-out picture postcards of Criccieth, plus some rather rude greeting cards manufactured in England, of a type very popular in such seaside resorts as Blackpool. The English, reticent as they were to discuss anything that smacked of human feeling, had an endless appetite for raunch, and loo jokes, which had translated into bawdy greeting cards, distributed everywhere in the U.K., including Wales. Englishmen came to Criccieth in summer and sent them to other Englishmen that they wouldn't dare ask "How are you?" for fear the answer might be "Mother died." Of course no Englishman or -woman worth his or her salt would say anything that direct, no matter what the facts were, prefacing their answer with something like "Oh, quite well, and how nice to hear from you, you sound in very fine shape which I suppose I am too, considering what happened to Mother."

Besides his seasonal business with the tourist trade, Stroll cleaned the beach every morning that the sun was bright, and even when it wasn't, sharp, long stick in his hand to pierce what could be pronged, large garbage bag slung over his shoulder for what had to be picked up by hand, like cans and cast-off bottles.

For this he was not paid, since you couldn't pay a Welshman to do that kind of work. He did it because he loved his land, especially Criccieth, and wanted the beach to be pristine, rocky as it was on that shore, which seemed to him more beautiful than sand.

As it was a small village, everybody knew each other, and, as they were Welsh, more deeply than the average inhabitant of the United Kingdom, being aware of each other's histories and misfortunes, and childhood loves. So Shan was most especially nervous that Samuel Stroll, having sold her what few postcards she had sent in her life, would instantly see through to her true identity. But like the vicar and the mayor, so impressed was he to be in the presence of what he assumed was royalty that no trace of suspicion hardened the edges of his total acceptance and joy that bordered on drunkenness, as though there were intoxicants in the tea. True, Stroll was a very trusting, loving man to begin with, or he would never have cleaned the beaches out of simple caring for his place of birth. But even in those trained in guile, as politicians and churchmen were, she raised not a hackle of skepticism.

In fact, Shan quite nearly convinced herself, so well did she pour, so correct was her conversation. Trained in the right manner of taking and offering tea by the duchess, who had spent considerable time in England, she filled their cups with just the right amount of dark fluid before adding milk, and filled her queries with nothing that could possibly embarrass them, or touch an emotional chord. It was all so civilized, she almost didn't have to be there at all.

But at a certain point the mayor said what a shame it was the princess's stay was so short, since there was a great Welsh pageant to take place that next Saturday, and a troop of gifted players rehearsing a tragedy in the original, still-treasured tongue. And then they spoke of Miles, and how talented he was, and how all the village had been charmed by him since he was a little boy, and how he had loved a local girl, before he ran off to join the theater.

"Oh, yes," she said. "I met him when we did the photo session at the castle. Who was the girl he loved?"

The vicar smiled. "Ah, it's good to see the interest of women travels a universal wire, even to the island of Perq. For men are here for their careers, but women are here for love."

"Are you sure?" Shan said, for she was lately into wondering what she had been born for, besides her daily pleasure at being alive.

"Well, hear your own question, Highness," said the mayor. "It is love that captured your full attention."

"Well, what is more important?" said Shan, and bit a piece of sugar, which was not good manners, but she desperately needed a crack at something sweet. The meeting with Miles had quite unhinged her. For much as she'd come to care about Tom, there was something about first love that pulled at the deepest place in woman.

"The girl was a lovely creature. Still is. Shan, by name. I christened her," said the vicar.

"And what happened to her?"

"She married a nice enough fellow."

"Is that all he is? Nice enough?" It was a query Shan was really addressing to herself.

"He's a miner," said the mayor.

"Well, not all of us are lucky enough to be able to sell souvenir postcards," said Samuel Stroll, and with that proffered a packet of them to the (he thought) princess.

"Is a man what he does?" Shan asked. "Or what he is?"

"An interesting query," said the vicar. "Lucky for you that your husband's a prince." He chortled, quite pleased at himself, as the others laughed with him. Including Shan, her head tipped back, as she ha-ha-haed in the tinkling way the duchess said was ladylike.

But when the time came to go, to leave Criccieth, Shan's legs got weak, and her nose started running, and there were in her eyes something quite like tears.

"But Your Majesty's caught cold," said the lady-in-waiting, as she finished packing her things. "It'll be good for you to get back to Perq."

"Are you sure?" Shan asked. "Are you absolutely sure?" From the window of her room underneath the slanted eaves, she could see two blackbirds having an argument on the slate roof opposite. The wife was railing and squawking and screeching, and, much as the male tried to turn a deaf ear, he couldn't avoid her. She pursued him, relentless. So it went, Shan supposed, marriage; no matter how low down on the evolutionary scale. She owed it to herself to see firsthand what it was like, being married to a prince among men.

2

SO OUR BOGUS PRINCESS zipped towards Perq on the queen's hydrofoil, making hardly a ruffle on the clear, calm surface of Cardigan Bay. You can imagine how busy were her thoughts, usually as serene and still as that body of water, not from any lack of depth, but from the bliss of allowing things to be the way they were. Now, however, she was muddled with fears and doubts and wonderings and worries, a veritable crashing surf. But she had made her decision and there was no way out of it, except to confess her perfidy, a foolish thing to do before she had satisfied a little of her curiosity. For how often did a real woman have the chance to explore the unreal?

Back in Criccieth, the sham Shan concluded her luxuriant tea, the first in her grown-up recollection where she'd eaten everything she wanted; scones with jam and cucumber sandwiches and two and finally three sugars in (she could not even remember how many) cups of creamy tea. Her stomach felt absolutely awash, like a ship that had taken on water belowdecks, and was listing slightly to port, which the duchess had also proffered, Darcy had said no to none of it. Besides enjoying the unique opportunity to overindulge, which she never did — in case her lady-in-waiting was making notes on her behavior to one day leave her service and write a scandalbook — Darcy was afraid to stop eating and drinking because the hospitality might be concluded, and she had absolutely no idea where she was supposed to go. Having decided to keep up the deception, it would certainly not do for her to ask the duchess where she lived.

The seeds that had fallen from the pink crystal chandelier, with its pink spun glass angels dancing around the periphery, were deep in the pocket of the soiled wedding dress. Every once in a while Darcy would finger them and silently count to herself the seven, making sure that none of them had fallen out. But when she asked the duchess what she supposed they were for, and where they had come from, the duchess looked at her with blank, watery blue eyes, and seemed quite dazed and ignorant, as if she hadn't been present for that part of the afternoon.

"Well, I have enjoyed this more than I can say," trilled the duchess, when the clock struck six.

A tiny hook of panic caught Darcy, deep in her belly, where there was a little room in between the cakes and the sandwiches, and she wondered, for an instant, "What will become of me?" This was a standard question in fairy tales, but in fact Darcy had never asked it, since she had never had a chance to feel anxiety or self-pity, so painlessly had her life unfolded. She'd lived in a balmy climate, always had plenty to eat and comfortable clothes, parents who doted on her, school subjects she could master, sharp ice skates and polished skis for winter vacations in Zermatt, which was where Rachid had found her on the slopes. She had been barely seventeen at the time, and the angst available to young men and women with insane relatives or advanced algebra requirements or the longing to catch joy as it flies (understanding how fleeting joy is, and accepting that even while struggling to hold on to it) were denied her. She had never had pimples, bandy legs, or, in fact, an orthodox adolescence, since she had been beautiful from birth, and had never gone through an awkward phase, instead making everyone else feel awkward that they were not Darcy. She was extraordinarily graceful, extraordinarily flexible (the only one on the ski slopes who never had to do knee stretches). It had seemed inevitable, really, when Rachid found her and scooped her up to be a princess.

"May I help you tidy up?" Darcy said, the words not coming easily. Naturally she had not lifted a finger to clean or set plate in dishwater for all the years she had been princess, and in fact had not done so for as long before as her parents had intuited her pampered possibilities, when her mother had started doing everything for her, so her hands would stay soft. In truth, the mere sight of dust or garbage of any description irritated Darcy. She had always liked everything in its place, with no effort from her. Still, she considered doing dishes rather than going home to an address she didn't know.

"How kind of you, dear. But the cats and I can manage." There were about ten of them that Darcy had spotted during the afternoon, piled up like cushions near the fireplace, and propped behind the duchess's back. She wore a ginger one now like a fur around her neck as she walked Darcy to the door. "I wouldn't want Tom angry with me that I'd kept you too long."

"Tom," Darcy repeated, as if reinforcing her brain with his name might actually make her know him.

"Remember what I said," said the duchess, opening the door on which hung fifty or so bells, some of them inoperative, being made of paper and gilded foil, metal ones, a few with their clappers removed, but all those made of crystal ringing, and very clearly. "Lift him. You can do it. You'll see."

Darcy peered out into the street. A light mist had come in from the bay, so the street was slightly shrouded, hints of Rippers in every shadow, benign though the village was supposed to be.

"Which way?"

"Any way you can," said the duchess. "It will come clear to you as long as you speak the truth and act out of love."

"I mean which way do I live?"

"According to the tenets of your heart."

"I mean where is my house?" said Darcy, somewhat impatiently, as philosophy had not been one of the requirements for becoming a princess, and she had very little patience for it, except predigested as it had been in the magazines.

"Why, just down the street there," the duchess said, not the slightest bit suspicious, since lately she herself had sometimes needed to be pointed in the right direction. "The white house with the blue hydrangeas in front."

"Thank you for a lovely afternoon," Darcy said, and started to hold out her hand to be curtsied to, but remembering who she wasn't, leaned forward instead, and kissed the old woman's cheek.

"And thank you, dear," the duchess said, "for making me feel less alone. For though we are none of us alone, it's easy to feel lonely, and think that we're the only ones who can't remember where we live."

So Darcy was by herself for the first time since that time on the ski slope, before she'd been found by Rachid. Skittishly she set off to cross the street, looking both ways as she hadn't had to do since childhood, since traffic where she walked was usually cordoned off. A motorcycle bumped up the cobblestoned road. The driver, the ends of his cloak tucked up beneath him, slowed.

"Shan?" he said. The muted, mist-broken light carved out the features of his face, with its high forehead, angular cheekbones and fine, strong nose with a slight break in it, just below the bridge.

"And what if I am?" she said.

He trailed his foot, and put the motorcycle in stopped balance.

"But it's Miles," he said.

"What's that to me?"

"I don't blame you for being angry," he said, and parked the scooter by the curb, dismounting it as though it were a horse, and him just home from the joust. "But if it does any good, I want you to know I never stopped thinking about you." He touched her upper arm, the soft inside part next to her breast. "Except during *Hamlet*, but it's a very hard part."

"So you're an actor?"

"Nothing else would have taken me away from you. . . ." The fingers of his other hand moved across the tender part of her throat just above the collarbone.

His hair was red and curly, and his eyes were wide set, heavily lashed, and black. No one had looked at her with eyes so filled with longing before, not even Rodney in the beginning. It was unabashed hunger. She longed to have someone feel about her like that. His fingers on her throat were expert and gentle. She tilted her face to catch more of his touch, this time closer to her ear.

"I heard you married," he said.

"Tom," she reminded herself, and came out of her tilt.

"Do you love him?"

"What difference does that make to you?"

"If I could have taken you with me, I would have," he said earnestly. He pressed her back against the trellis, flowers all around them, roses she could smell, and lilac, all the perfumes on her mirrored tabletop in Perq, missing only Opium. "I swore the minute I had some money I'd come back for you. But it isn't easy getting started in the theater. I slept in cellars, places with no heat, no light. And all I could think of was you. That gave me heat and light." He moved in closer. His lips were very close to her neck, and then they were on it.

"Stop," she said, hoping he wouldn't, but he did. It shocked her that the touch of a man she didn't know could so move her. He had a scent that was stronger than any of the flowers she pressed against, slightly metallic and musky, like an after-shave lotion some promoters had once given Rodney, in the hope that he would endorse it. But it had been too heavy for him, as was their approach, and he had poured it in the royal sink. Darcy had gone into the other half of their double toilette and smelled it lingering there. A kind of drunkenness had come over her, something lost and Proustian, a recollection of a past passion she hadn't actually had, might never have. She'd very nearly swooned. Now, smelling it, and on Miles, she felt dizzy. She wondered if women were so without ballast that a smell, a touch could make them light-headed, if the key to their secret door could be opened with chemistry. It did not occur to her that it might be only herself who was so affected, since she was no longer a princess, but a simple girl who had been jilted.

She took it quite personally, since she and Shan were identical to the sight, so she knew he could have found no one prettier. And how Shan must have loved him, if his touch to a stranger were any indication of the heat he could engender, and they'd had all that young time in the shadows of this village, with its secret places, its flowers, its castles, its double cream. So added onto Darcy's unsure footing at not knowing where her life would lead even in the next half hour was a light coating of umbrage at this most attractive man's leaving her counterpart. Insecurity and resentfulness combined to stiffen her spine, and sent out little warning rays that made Miles back off.

"I'm sorry," he said. "I forgot myself."

"Quite the contrary," she said. "I would wager you never forgot *yourself*. It was me you forgot."

"Only during *Hamlet*," he said, and smiled again, boyishly.

"I have to be getting home," she said, and tried to move past him, hoping she would not catch another whiff of him. It was overwhelming, not because he was overbathed in the scent, but because she had never been so struck by a man's smell. It resonated in her, like history, and flashed other times, and she wondered if perhaps women who wrote of men who were lovers in previous lives were speaking the truth, and not just covering up their wish not to seem roundheels.

"Will you come and see me in the play? We're rehearsing all week. The performance is Saturday at twilight. At Criccieth Castle," he lowered his eyes, as if the locale were a candle that sputtered memory.

"What play is it?"

"*Hamlet*," he said. "I've retranslated it into the original Welsh. So the poetry sounds as he meant it to sound, the Welshman who actually wrote it. Will you come?"

"Perhaps," she said, moving past him, hoping he would try to bar her way, wishing he'd throw his arms up and pin her back against the wall, swallow her with his lips, nail her like a butterfly. But, actor though he was, he was still a gentleman, and let her pass.

The front door to the house was open. Darcy turned the handle gingerly, half-expecting it to resist, like the burglar she supposed she was, although of course she wasn't looking for profit of the jewels and cash kind. Still, she was intruding, and moved warily, exploring, noting.

The living room was covered with old wallpaper, peeling around the edges from moisture, dusty pink, with tiny tea roses and ribbons running up and down in lines, so it looked like sentimental stripes. The place was quite small, made smaller by the paper. She herself would have called in the painters to strip it and paint it white. There was an old brown sofa, frayed at the seams, its stuffing coming out, with a sad, sweet little pillow, embroidered "Home, Sweet Home." A footstool, also worn, with dwarfed Chippendale legs, ball and claw, stood a few feet away, the impression of boots (they must have been boots, the markings went so deep, and were so dirty) still on it. Electrified Victorian candelabra, enclosed in dusty glass (her counterpart was less than meticulous, she could not help thinking), hung at intervals along the walls. When she went to switch them on, she ran her finger over the glass, and saw that the dust was in the grain. So there was that, at least: Shan was tidy. But what a pity she was so poor. What a drain it had to be to look at such sorry paper all day, and read books (there were many) from the *library* (Darcy checked the ex libris).

A narrow staircase led down to a tiny kitchen, with an old gas stove, an icebox (it was truly an icebox, small, with a block of ice inside on which lay a fish, eye staring up at her) and an ancient sink that was more like a washtub. The floor was green linoleum, which looked newer than anything else in the house, but was badly laid, buckling at the edges. Certainly poverty had no magic to it. Darcy could not imagine coming into this room with a light heart.

She flung open the tiny window, with its little white shutters, paint peeling, and took a deep breath of the misty air, as much to rid herself of the claustrophobic feeling as to fill her lungs. The windowbox outside, like those on the front of the house, was lush with blue hydrangeas, like snowballs played with by schoolboys with inky fingers. She remembered the seeds in her pockets, and ferreting out a bent spoon from a drawer, scooped seven little holes in the dirt, and started putting in the seeds. She was nearly finished when she heard the door open, and heavy boots thudding in the hall.

"Here I am, Shan darlin'!" she heard the voice call out. It was a nice voice, not as deep as the actor's, and a bit more grainy. But cheerful. "And where are the fine smells of dinner cooking?"

"I got a little behind," Shan said, quickly covering up the last of the seeds, and closing the window.

"Oh, I wouldn't say that." He bounded down the stairs into the kitchen, and his hands were on her buttocks, squeezing the round underedge of her cupped into each palm.

She fairly jumped because he was such a big bear of a man, she could tell without even turning around. But she did, and a bear he was, but more teddy than grizzly, with sandy hair, a flat, happy pie of a face, round, green eyes, button nose, and a low-slung mouth, bottom lip bigger by half than the one that topped his broad, innocent smile. A man with no deceit in him, she could tell that right away, and people with no deceit had no suspicion either. So she was not afraid of him.

"I would call it ample," he said, and squeezed. "Better than ample. A great honey apple of an ass." He grinned and snapped at her nose playfully with small, pointed teeth, left front buckled slightly over the right one. "What's for dinner?"

"Can't we go out?" she said.

His face darkened. "Out? Are you not feeling well?"

She didn't have time to answer. It was as if he saw her, suddenly.

"And what are you doing in your wedding dress?"

"I went to see the princess."

"Did you girls have a mud-wrestle?"

"The guards," she said. "The nasty little guards. They threw me into the street."

His eyebrows lowered. The teddy bear was gone, in its place a fierce creature with breath waiting to explode. "I shall go have a chat with them."

She pulled at his arm. "They've gone back to Perq. And I'm all right, really."

"Ill-mannered bastards. How dare they touch you." He grabbed her and held her very tight.

She could feel his measured, angry breathing through her breasts, mashed against his chest. It was not gentle, but it was comforting. Only as she looked directly ahead at his big bullish neck did she notice the grime in the creases of his skin, the light patina of gray dust. Quite involuntarily she recoiled, since never in her life had she been touched by anyone dirty.

He looked at her, hurt around the edges of his puzzlement. "But what's wrong?"

"Nothing," she said. But seeing his hands, his palms slate dark, the fortune telling part of them, life lines, love lines, mounds and valleys, tracked with his day's work, she could not help but look disapproving. "Maybe you should wash your hands."

"And maybe you should try and remember who I am. And that's your husband who works all day in the slate and the soot to see that you have shelter over your head and food in your belly and *why isn't it ready?*" His green eyes were flecked with the yellow of anger.

"I'm sorry," she said, and, to her credit, meant it. She had not intended to wound him, to trigger this volcano of pride.

"Oh, it's all right," he said, and hugged her again, as if he were more angry with himself for the outburst than he'd been with her. "I just knew it had to happen, that's all, if you got to be with the princess. I knew it would upset you. Make you hate the life you have. That's why I didn't want to give you the money for the lottery ticket."

"But I don't hate this life," said Darcy, sincerely. "I find it . . ." She struggled for the right word, since the duchess had told her to speak only the truth in order to lift him. Visitor though Darcy was, temporary as her sojourn might be, she saw no reason not to whisk through his life and do a little charity. She already liked him as well as she did the children in hospital wards. "Interesting," she concluded.

"Are you mocking me?"

"No, I mean it."

But his eyes were pained, as if he did not quite believe her, since he knew it was not so for him. Interesting was the last thing he would have said about the life he had offered her. Passionate, yes, filled with occasional beauty, and when they could afford it, music. But he was, after all, a Welshman, so he knew that life was a trick, giving those with the biggest hearts the greatest chance to have them broken. He had long ago set aside the finer aspirations of his soul, abandoned even his own sense of loss and frustration at having daily to enter the darkness of the mine, take elevators deep down into the shafts, feel the chill and know that hell was only hot in the good legends. What hell was, really, was a cold place, where the spirit could not be renewed, in the absence of light.

"Make dinner," he said, trying to seem as unfeeling as she had to be at this moment, to make such fun of him.

Now what to do? There was poor Darcy, left alone in the tiny kitchen that was hardly a kitchen, she who'd been in her own only rarely, to tell the chef what to prepare for state dinners, and then, after having the menu planned by her staff. A flush moved from her chest up to her forehead as she stared back at the fish staring at her with its flat eye, that seemed the judgment of the universe. She turned it over so it wouldn't be looking at her, but there was the judgment again, on the other side.

Getting to her knees, which she'd done only in the presence of the queen and the king before he'd disgraced himself, and the archbishop when he'd blessed her marriage to Rodney, she began to forage through the cabinets underneath the sink, looking for a pan. Once, on a beach, in a seaside resort in Italy in the early days of the marriage when it was still fun, she and Rodney had actually watched a fish being cooked, so she knew it was done in a pan. She found one finally, set it on the stove, and, after puzzling for a bit, opened one of the jets. Setting the fish into the frying pan she put it on top of the burner.

"What's that smell?" Tom called in from the living room.

"I'm cooking," she said, a little giddy, and actually impressed with herself, because unless she was very much mistaken, that was what she was doing.

Tom was in the doorway. "For God's sake," he said, throwing the window open. He turned off the jet, and waved the gas-filled air out the window. "What's the matter with you?"

"Matter?"

He stared at her for a moment, let the air clear, whooshed it away. Then he lit a match, and turned on the burner.

"Oh," she said. "You use a match."

He leaned back against the doorjamb, arms crossed, and looked at her. A furrow of concern lined his brow, little fillips of disbelief pulled down the corners of his mouth.

"I can't do anything with people watching me," she said, which was not quite the truth of her experience, since there was almost nothing she had done since she was seventeen without being watched.

"Well, if I promise not to watch, will you use butter?" he said.

"I was just going to do that," she said, and looked around, desperate.

He opened a cabinet just below the window, cooled by the night air, and took out butter in a covered dish. He handed it to her without speaking, one bushy brown eyebrow raised.

"Thank you," she said.

"Are you sure you're all right?"

"I'm fine," she said. "You may go."

"I may, may I?"

"Yes," she said. When he was gone, she put the butter, all quarter pound of it, into the pan, and watched with some pleasure as it sizzled and melted.

In her youth, in her childhood, she had been in the kitchen while her mother cooked, on the rare occasions when a maid or housekeeper wasn't there. She remembered little of it, except that her mother had seemed frazzled and discontented, not at all happy. Nothing of a menial nature seemed to come easily to members of their family. So it had been with great relief that her parents had welcomed her becoming a princess.

But watching the butter turn brown, and the fish start to fry, Darcy felt something quite like satisfaction. There was a feeling of control in cooking, once you had the handle and the jet turned on, and the match struck. The fish that had lain there all slimy and scaly crisped up in the pan. And even the awful eye that had stared at her so coldly, scorched on its surface, seemed less disapproving. In truth, she began to feel in charge. If not of her life, at least of the fish.

"Would you like me to set the table?" Tom asked from the doorway.

"That would be nice, dear," Darcy said, falling quite easily into the conviviality she imagined all truly well-suited couples enjoyed.

He'd lit a candle, set it on the small table to the side of the living room, raised the leaf, and put two plates and the silver (which was tin) on the mats. "Will you have a beer?" he asked her.

"Oh, yes, please," Darcy said, excited at the thought, really. This was it, now, she was really getting into it, the parts of Shan's life that kept her going, and happy: the little pillows of simple pleasure that made ordinary people comfortable.

Carrying the pan, with its well-browned fish (she remembered that from the Italian shore, the crispness of skin that had looked so delicious, and finally tasted so) into the living room, Darcy set it on the table. Tom was studying her over the candlelight with a look more intense than the flame. She tried not to seem awkward or unsure, or in any way proud. For if a cat could look at a king, a miner could certainly look at a princess, especially if he had no idea that was what she was.

She lifted the fish onto his plate, so the tail and the head hung over the edges. "Aren't you having any?" he asked.

"Why don't you take what you want and give me what's left," she suggested, with the hope it would seem like humility, and not as if she didn't know how to cut a fish.

He started to halve it, when a spurt of innards caught him in the eye. "What's this!" he shouted. "What's this!" He threw down his knife and crashed fork against his plate. "You didn't even clean it!"

"Clean it?" she said, puzzled.

"Have you gone mad?" he cried. "I knew this would happen when you went to see that spoiled bitch."

"Spoiled bitch!" she cried. "Why, she's no more spoiled than I am!"

"Taking on airs!" he said. "Not even having my dinner ready. Ruining your wedding dress!"

"Well, what's so special about this dress? It's not like I'll be needing it again!"

"And I suppose you're sorry about that! I suppose it seems old-fashioned and foolish that people should marry once and it should be for a lifetime."

"No, I'm not sorry," she screamed, sorry, but not that she was married to him.

"I suppose you would rather it was Miles you married. Miles who ran off and left you. Miles who dreamed only of *his* dreams, and never of you."

"You don't know that!" she said, furious now, because anger was a self-starting engine that needed only the ignition turned, and not even a foot on the gas. "He thought about me all the time, except during *Hamlet*."

"So that's it, then." He got to his feet, "It isn't just that bitch princess that's made you go all fuzzy in the head."

"Stop calling her a bitch!" Darcy said, getting to her feet now, too, breathing up into his face.

"I heard he was back," Tom said. "I heard he was around here, sniffing out old fantasies of glory."

"Who says they're fantasies?" she cried, because the truth was, she understood why Shan had loved Miles. Why, little as she knew him, she could almost imagine she loved him herself. Not like this lout, who expected her to know that the inside of a fish was supposed to come out before cooking it. Was a woman born with this knowledge?

"Do you want him then? Have you been with him? Is it back to that?" The rage was tempered now with sadness.

Something quite like pity touched her. How deep did his feeling have to go, this miner, the slate dust still in the wrinkles of his young neck, for his eyes to look so sorrowful? How did a man love like that, with such fear of loss? Was that what separated ordinary men from princes?

"I have been faithful to my husband," Darcy said, which was the truth, as the duchess might have wished, and the disgusting fact of it.

"Then get upstairs," he said gruffly. "See if you can remember what to do in the bedroom better than you did the kitchen."

"I don't feel like . . . ," she started to say, but seeing the angry longing in his eyes, she realized it would be a mercy. In its way, a highly moral thing to do. Spiritual, really, if such things still counted, as they no longer seemed to in Perq.

"You will wash first?" she could not help asking.

"No, I will not wash," he said, heavily. "I will wash myself in you."

"But . . ."

"Get upstairs," he said firmly.

"But . . ."

"Not another word." He rousted her up the stairs, his fingers jabbing at her fleeing bottom, as he laughed, and touched, and reached around for the underneath of her, and, finally, getting her to the landing, picked her up and carried her into the bedroom.

Tossing her onto the bed, he raised the skirt of her wedding dress, threw it up over her head, and unzippered his pants. Then, coarse as he was, he did something amazingly subtle. Stopped, and felt her with his eyes. There was still plenty of light: summer evenings in Wales made up in brightness what they lacked in warmth, and she could see him studying her there. He spread her legs and stared inside them, his look grave and hungry and slow, checking every inch of her, unhurriedly, like an explorer about to descend into uncharted terrain. So thorough was his scrutiny, so leisurely and deliberate, that she felt more heat than if there were fingers tracing her, slowly trailing. She wondered in a sudden spurt of panic if he saw it was unfamiliar, if there, at least, she was a different color or size than Shan. But there was only ardor in the way he eyed her, not the least lurk of suspicion. An electric connection between the juice in his gaze and the syrup starting to flow from her.

And then he was inside her, his thickness gliding along her inner walls, scaling them. So consistent was the gentle onslaught, so steady and comfortingly steadfast ("He'll never let you down," she could hear some grandmotherly Welshwoman promising) that Darcy felt the ecstasy of relaxation. Not the orgasms described in glossy women's magazines, but a real sense of being filled up. Touched to the top by his tip. She did not so much climax as breathe.

Shuddering, he came to rest inside her, without a tender word. The crude, unpolished ruffian. She absolutely loved it.

They were waiting for the princess at the dock in Perq, and only she knew she wasn't the princess. It was hard for Shan not to gape at the splendors that awaited her, the queen standing there in her daytime jewels, a tiny brass band of Nubian dwarfs playing the national anthem on instruments that were bigger than they were, one of them sinking into the soft ground under the weight of the sousaphone.

The hydrofoil made its way into the harbor, more a yacht marina than a place for proper ships. Besides having the lowest taxes on the planet, Perq offered maintenance for privately owned luxury vessels, at least cost, as well as crews who were willing to give up their lives (which weren't all that exciting) for smart enough uniforms. A local publication had been established by an entrepreneur who had failed in Beverly Hills, called "*S*," which stood for "Sailor," and everybody who worked on the yachts, or owned them, subscribed. In fact, it cost the publisher almost nothing to produce it, since he'd brought the cover logo with him from Los Angeles, where the "*S*" had stood for "Superficial." The paper had not failed for that reason: no one in Beverly Hills took umbrage, since in order to have your feelings hurt, you had to have them. It had gone under simply because in order for a newspaper to survive, people had to read, and those who could afford it (nearly everybody) had somebody do their reading for them.

So on either side of the water lane, where the hydrofoil made its way (sideways) and on all sides of all sides of that, great yachts were anchored. They had clever names in many languages, and sails and motors, and great masts, since some yachtsmen fortified their sense of high-living by buying tall ships of the antique kind for the annual tall ship regatta in Saint-Tropez. The weather in Perq was not dissimilar to that of the Mediterranean resort, because of the quirky flow of tropical stream. Actually, it was more balmy in winter than the south of France. Besides catching the Gulf Stream, the island sat in the center of a mysterious energy Perquian scientists labeled the Bermuda Circle, where cares disappeared like blips of lost aircraft on a radar screen. It was, in layman's terms, the eye of the calm.

Powerful though that energy might have been, it was not so affecting Shan, who felt almost literally beside herself. As the hydrofoil sidled up to its berth, she could see the queen (she knew it was the queen because her lady-in-waiting murmured, "But the queen's come to meet you. How odd . . .") standing so tastefully bejeweled in her opals, flashes of iridescence on her ears, underscoring the electric violet-blueness of her eyes. She was wearing a pale green suit that emphasized the trimness of her figure, except for her melon-sized breasts, which were insured by Lloyd's of London as one of Perq's national treasures. For the occasion they were tastefully half-bound in a tight pale green silk blouse with a huge opal drop surrounded by diamonds bobbing in her cleavage. Her once-again black hair (she had gone to frosting, but her subjects hadn't liked it, any more than *People* magazine had) was wrapped in a turban, of the same pale green silk as her blouse. Only her shoes with their not very high heels were a neutral color, the only thing about her that was not overwhelming. Shan could hardly breathe. What could she possibly say to such a dazzling creature?

"Why is it odd?" she asked her lady-in-waiting, wondering if there was perhaps some secret feud between the queen and the princess she was supposed to be. In Criccieth she had not had a single enemy, since to have an adversary you would have to hold yourself apart from other people, and Shan knew she was simply a part of everybody else.

"I would have thought Prince Rodney . . ." The lady-in-waiting lowered her eyes, as if she'd spoken out of turn.

"Yes?" Shan prodded her.

"Well, I'm sure he has some important affair of state, or he would be here."

The hydrofoil shuddered against the pier, and came to rest, and the royal gangway was lowered, as the trumpeter in the brass band blew a fanfare, slightly New Orleans. Shan felt oddly comfortable, suddenly, put in place by the music. She and Tom loved American jazz of the old kind, and had a good if sometimes warped collection of 78's.

"Thank you," she said to the Nubian who had trumpeted her down the gangway. Then she curtsied to the queen, deep, in the manner the duchess had taught her, right knee nearly touching the ground, arms back like a ballerina, gracefully trailing the air with a wisp of wrist, forehead almost to her bent left knee. "Majesty," she said.

To her surprise, the queen looked angry. "Get up," she said, and turned on her not very high heels, walking quickly towards the limousine, as the little royal guards, with their walkie-talkies, searched the cheering crowd for signs of violence.

Once seated inside the back of the Rolls, the queen pressed a button, closing the window separating them from the driver, and turned to Shan. "I don't like your ridiculing me," she said, violet eyes aflash.

"But what did I do, Majesty?" Shan asked.

"And cut the 'majesty,'" the queen said. "To you I'm Isabel."

"But what did I do, Isabel?"

"I hate it when you play ingenue. You know very well what you did. All I asked was that you keep up appearances with Rodney, and remember your place, and the place of this nation. Not that you jeer me with curtseys."

"But I didn't mean . . ."

"It isn't easy to be queen," Isabel said, and looked out of the window. "I'm doing the best I can."

"I'm sure," Shan said, although she wasn't.

"No marriage is easy, for God's sake. You ought to understand that."

"Oh, I *do*."

"Thirty years with him. You think I've had fun? You think it's a buggy-ride being with a spineless royal twit?"

"Probably not."

"You think Rodney's difficult! Where do you suppose he got it from? Certainly not my side of the family. All I ask is for you to remember your place, and not make fun of mine."

Outside the window mountains sat directly next to the sea; palm trees waved between pine. As they moved inland, the scenery dipped into valley and riverbed, all in the twinkling of an eye. Great waterfalls cascaded where a moment before there had been a meadow. It was to Shan's eye not unlike Wales, except for the brilliance of the climate. But the intensity of Nature's changing spectacle was exactly like that of her homeland, such a small country that everything vast and inspiring seemed to be crammed into its confines, like a very brief life that included all the passions known to man. She was overwhelmed by the beauty of the place, and the anger of the woman who sat beside her.

"I'm sorry if I offended you," Shan said, because she was.

"Don't be a simp," Isabel said. "Just be decent to him in public, and do your duty, and pose for the Christmas cards. The king and I won't be in them this year. The world might see from the size of his nose what a drunkard he's become."

The perpendicular palace where the royalty of Perq held sway did just that: tilted slightly and blew in occasional high winds. There were thirty-two rooms, four to a floor, and no elevator. Those with the strongest hearts were assigned to the top. EKGs were regularly administered not only to the king and queen and prince and princess, but also the staff, to make sure there would be no disruptions of affairs of state, no interruptions of service at a state dinner, for example, by anything so unseemly as the chef having a coronary. As a result of the king's last physical, which showed his liver to be distended, his breathing to be irregular, and his nose to be an embarrassment, his quarters had been changed to the ground floor. Shortly afterwards Rachid had had him moved into a dungeon in the cellar which he told the king was for his own protection in the event of nuclear war. And he'd told the queen the king had gone to a sanitorium in Switzerland.

The chains which held the king were also said to be for his own protection. He was shackled daily after five in the afternoon when the sun had passed over the yardarm; otherwise, as everybody in the inner circle knew, he would reach for a drink. For all the control Rachid exercised over Perq, its queen on a sexual level, the king on a tyrannical one, Rachid did not like to see any human being in real agony, unless they had insulted him personally, which the king had never done, saving his cries of "swine" and "scuzzball," until the merchant was out of earshot. Rachid would regularly descend into the deco dungeon (the cellar was done in high-tech stainless steel) and blow some cocaine up the king's nose, so he wouldn't have to deal with reality.

Rachid was in the process of doing just that, when the word came down that the princess had returned, with the queen. He was somewhat startled by that intelligence, since he was a man who, apart from his basic villainy, was passionate when it came to love. He was sure the princess did not love Rodney, more probably loathed him. Rachid considered her a young woman of some spirit, and so had encouraged her to go on this trip alone, half-expecting she would run away. Women could not live without some tickles of lust, or at least the best of them couldn't. Best of all of them was the queen, his queen, and often as he had her, and well, he intended to have her in public. That was to say, as soon as he had dispensed with this despised king, and his weak-willed son, he would crown himself king in the cathedral which had been converted into a jai-alai court.

Rachid was fairly subtle for an arms merchant and a Libyan, his character as individual as his looks. He had thick blue-black hair that waved around his head like a sinister halo, and aqua eyes, as palely blue-green as the Straits of Bosporos before pollution. Iridescent eyes they were, shining and full of humor, like his smile. That there was nothing funny about anything he did was nearly beside the point, so good-humored and handsome did he seem. And, as noted, he was artful for somebody heavy-handed, and did not intend to seize power blackheartedly, obviously. It was for this reason he had not allowed the king to drink himself to death, because it might humiliate the queen. Instead, he had invented the fiction that the king was drying out in Switzerland, and was drying him out, in his own way.

"She came back?" Rachid murmured aloud to himself, when his adjutant reported news of the princess.

"You see!" said the king, his beady eyes bright. "You were wrong, Rachid. You may have taken control of Perq with your filthy lucre. But you don't know human nature. She *does* love my son."

"She loves your son as much as the queen loves you," Rachid said, contempt edging the bright white porcelain of his smile. "Their marriage will end in disaster. The people will turn away from him, as they've turned away from you. And I will be more than the great benefactor of Perq. I will be its king!" He blew another blast up the king's nose. "See you tomorrow, Highness." Athletically he bounded up the stairs.

"Swine," the king murmured into his beard. "Scuzzball."

Oh, she had known they were going to be the quarters of a princess. But majesty imagined could not touch on majesty in fact. Teddy bears with pink plumed hats, seed pearl necklaces, bracelets, and seed pearl earrings (two on one ear — were they punk teddy bears?) lined the pink abalone-shell-inlaid headboard of the bed. She took one of the bears and held it to her throat. The feathers caressed the underside of her chin, like acceptance. The teddy bears, at least, would not mind her being an impostor.

The pillows, all trimmed with lace, pink ribbons threaded through them, likewise received her, unresisting. She was expecting softness from the mattress, but instead was surprised to have her collapse stop in midrelax. There was a sound nearly as hard as the resistance against her back. Leaning over the edge of the bed, she lifted endless layers of lace dust ruffle, and saw the board underneath the mattress. So this was how princesses slept, she noted. This was how they kept up their regal posture, constrained even in sleep.

The door opened, and her lady-in-waiting carried in a strapless gown, its bodice all rhinestoned (or were they diamonds?). "Pardon me, Your Highness," she said. "Your gown for the Christmas card layout."

"Thank you, uh . . . ," Shan said, wishing she knew the girl's name. She felt most impolite and distant not to be addressing her directly.

There was a knock on the door, a kind of woodpecker's rap, really, fast and determined and, it seemed to Shan, impatient. The lady-in-waiting opened it. "Your Majesty." she said, and curtsied.

Standing in the doorway was Prince Rodney.

He was much better looking than he appeared in photographs, which made him seem heavier, with his eyes closer together than they actually were, and emphasized his nose, Roman and definite, a really important nose. But he was quite as tall as the photographs showed him to be: six feet two at least, Shan thought she could tell he was, even with her head half under the bed. She sat up somewhat primly, smiled what she hoped was a princessly smile, looking directly at him with eyes that were just a shade lighter than his own. Steel blue eyes she characterized his as, the color of cold winter nights at sea, probably from all the service he had given the navy.

"Would you leave us please, Junella," the prince said. The lady-in-waiting sped by him, with a murmured, "Certainly, sire."

How powerful it was to be a princess, Shan thought. One had only to have the wish (hadn't she just a second before wished she knew the lady-in-waiting's name?) and it was granted, even if you weren't truly the princess.

"How was your trip?" Rodney asked, when the door had closed behind Junella.

"Oh, it was fine," said Shan.

"You're looking lovely," he said, in a peremptory fashion, not really looking at her, as though compliments made him uncomfortable, or the truth of her looking lovely did.

"You're looking very well, yourself," she said, because he was. Quite handsome, really, fair haired, pink skinned and lean and long. A world away from her Tom.

"It's kind of you to try and be civil," he said. "But I know how you really feel."

"You do?" she asked, puzzled.

"I've spoken to Mother, and I'm sorry. But she says it's impossible. There's no way we can divorce."

"I see."

"We have to stay together for the sake of the children."

"We have no children," she said, authoritatively, having read perhaps every magazine story about the prince and princess.

"That's the next thing," he said, and moved towards her, taking off his sword, his royal jacket with the braids and the epaulets, starting to open his belt, with the phoenix, national symbol of Perq, taking wing from its golden buckle.

"Wait," she said. "No!"

"It's your duty," he said. "This isn't about you and me. It's about the survival of Perq." And he was beside her on the bed.

"But I can't." Just thinking about how unlike Tom he was had made her remember Tom. She tried to roll away from him.

"This is nothing personal," he said, and kissed her breast.

"No," she said, and leapt from the bed. "I'm not Darcy. I'm not the princess. My name is Shan. I come from Criccieth. I changed places with Darcy as a lark. There's nothing royal about me at all. I'm just an ordinary girl who happens to be wonderful looking."

He stared at her with eyes that were pained. "I see," he said.

"Oh, I'm so glad you understand."

"I understand," he said, "I understand perfectly." He got up from the bed and picked up his jacket and his sword. "There's nothing you won't think of as an excuse. Desperation has made you *most* inventive."

"But it's the truth," she said. "You must believe me."

"I *must?* I *must?* Well, maybe you're not truly the princess, but I am truly the prince. And nobody tells me what I *must* do. Not even *you*, Darcy!"

"I'm not . . . ," she said.

But he'd slammed the door.

3

SO OUR DARCY AWAKENED with joy in her heart, her limbs, and between her legs. For though her counterpart might have been experiencing the fulfillment of a lifelong fantasy, what it was to be a princess, the actual princess was experiencing a fantasy she hadn't known she had: to be thumped and bumped and whumped by a powerful stranger. And he had been powerful, Tom, filled with reined-in rage and despair: she had felt the sorrow underpinning the thrusts, a kind of animal melancholy, that this was all he could do to dominate her. But how she did love being dominated!

Outside the walls of the little white cottage blackbirds were berating the dawn, chiding the slivers of morning that broke above the horizon. Darcy sighed a great, contented sigh, and, eyes still shut, ran her hands over her breasts and rib cage and belly to see what she had slept in. And there it was, skin. What an amazing thing was life, that a young woman who had everything (so the world thought) could discover a pleasure so basic as her own bare flesh. It felt satiny against her fingertips, as the coarseness of the sheets scraped into her awareness. But even that roughness, unaccustomed as she was to it, was exciting, as Tom had been. Quite without meaning to (how would she excuse herself for being a hussy?) she reached for him.

But the bed beside her was empty, just the warm impression of him beneath her hand. What a curse for the romantic heart, to be a member of the working class. For now she understood, firsthand, that it meant he had to go to work. She was half-expecting a honeymoon.

Disappointment tweaked her edges and she sat up, cross. It was a first for her, really, abstract sexual excitement. It seemed to her it would have been more decent if Tom were still there to inspire and share in it. Having those longings come from nowhere but recollection and who knew what else felt somehow unladylike.

And what was she to do with a day that hadn't been planned for her? That which had seemed such a merry prank the day before (and such a good choice in his burly arms during the night) now offered her a platter of inquietude. Still, she had determined to discover the joys of an ordinary life, so she had faith (a little) that there were some.

Bounding out of bed (the room was quite cold), her feet coming to rest on a patch of blue carpet, a fuzzy edged floor sample from a showroom it looked like, she wrapped the eiderdown coverlet around herself, and made her way to the bathroom. It shocked her, really, the ancient sink, stained with the brown markings of infinite drops of water from the leaky tap, the bathtub, peeling, standing on claw-footed legs. There was an old rubber plug on a chain. She closed the drain with it, turned on the hot water, hoping to steam up the room. She pulled down the toilet seat. (Well, there was that connecting them all, anyway, prince and miner, the seat left up, the true brotherhood of man.) The seat beneath her was icy cold. She shivered.

Still, she was feeling everything, and that was an improvement over callouse. So much of her life in recent times had been just rushed through, parading, that she'd hardly even lived it.

She washed her hands with the sliver of soap on the sink, and saw herself in the mirror above. An unaccustomed peace seemed to sit on her countenance, the furrow of fretting between her brows she'd noted in recent months vanished. And to her most pleasant surprise, the selfsame dimple of wickedness Shan had revealed when she spoke of sleeping naked with Tom appeared to the right of Darcy's mouth. How becoming it was, being satisfied.

She leaned over and ran her hand through the bathwater: it was still freezing cold. Only then did she note the heater on the wall, with its slot and the cup of tenpence pieces on the stool. Remembering the duchess's fireplace, she put in a coin, and smiled as she heard the clink of metal against metal. The bath, when filled and warm, seemed veritably earned, something she had won by induction. She relaxed in it as though it were praise.

In like manner she enjoyed the texture of the towel she dried herself off with, and putting on Shan's only other decent dress, that hung, freshly washed and pressed, in the very small closet. The prospect of making the bed, however, unstrung her as cooking the fish had done the night before. So she simply put the pillows where she thought they belonged and covered it all with the quilt.

There was a five pound note on the sideboard in the kitchen, and a scrawled reminder from Tom that he'd like chicken for dinner. Darcy tucked the money into her pocket, and opened the window. The sky was pale blue, a dollop of clouds around the edges, thick as double cream, as if the day were starting with dessert.

Leaning forward over the windowbox, she Eskimo-kissed the hydrangeas, feeling the flutter of soft blue petals against her nose. Touching their base (she did have the experience of *endless* garden shows) she felt how dry the earth was, remembered what Shan had said gave her pleasure: growing flowers. Darcy looked around, found a watering can, filled it, and watered. As she did that, she remembered the seeds. Giving a thorough soak to the soil where she'd planted them, she was astounded to hear something quite like a swallow. "Glub," went the earth.

"Excuse me?" Darcy said.

"Glub," went the earth again. There was a slight shift in the soil, a bubbling, and to Darcy's amazement, a tiny sprout appeared above the surface.

"But I must have a green thumb!" she said, delighted.

Buoyed by her first personal achievement, she set out to explore the village. Shopkeepers nodded to her as she passed their open doorways, and she smiled, and waved, as she usually did from limousines and carriages, a flutter of hand displacing a ripple of air. The scent of freshly baked bread beckoned from the open hearth of the village bakery. Pulled by the fragrance, she went inside.

"Good morning, Shan!" said the man behind a display case filled in neat lines with pastries and muffins. "What can I do for you?"

"I'd like one of those," she said, pointing to a cornet.

"Make it two," said a resonant voice behind her.

Never in her life before had Darcy understood that there was marrow in her bones. But she knew it now, thrilled to the marrow as she was, by only the sound of his voice. What kind of woman was she, frolicking with a stranger as she'd done in the night and, not even a moon later, being that excited by another man's voice. "Good morning, Miles," she said, not even having to turn because she could smell him.

"Better for having you in it."

She turned and looked at him. He was wearing Elizabethan costume and leotards, so she could see how fine was the shape of his calf, the straight line of his leg, the fullness of his thigh, and what was above. He looked at her as though she were pastry. "Still the flatterer's tongue," she said. Surely it was a good guess that he had always been a flatterer.

"Ah, but a flatterer doesn't mean what he says, and says it only to inflate the vanity of the one he flatters. I mean what I say, and you have no vanity."

"I don't?" she asked, surprised, because if she had looked like Shan, and she did, she would most certainly have been vain.

"You have always been modesty itself. A swan that never preened, not dreaming it was a swan."

"Two cornets," said the baker, watching them both with interest.

"Thank you, Roger," said Miles. "Many's the morning I woke up wishing I had a bite of your bread."

"Not to mention a taste of Criccieth's other delicacies," Roger said.

"I suppose everyone in Wales knows how you ran off and left Shan," Darcy said, once they were out in the street, making their way along the narrow sidewalk. He brushed her with nearly every step, the outside of his thigh whisking alongside hers.

"Don't speak of yourself so impersonally," Miles said.

"Well, how should I speak then? With affection? The same affection you showed?"

"Will you have me on my knees, penitent?"

"Yes, I think so," Darcy said, and grabbing his arm as he started to buckle, added, "But not here."

The actors had come up from London in a number of vehicles, private, and belonging to the repertory company. Miles, as leading player and adaptor, was permitted to borrow the finest car, a vintage MG, bright red, with an assortment of chrome and brass accents, all highly polished, ranging from a huge radio antenna to an old bugle horn soldered to the driver's side. He beeped at the sheep by the side of the road, less in warning than in greeting, waving his hand above his handsome head when he caught their eye, which wasn't easy.

"I missed the sheep," he said, as they sped through the countryside, with its winding lanes and slightly wider roads.

"Why didn't you take them with you?" Darcy asked. "You could have eaten them."

He looked at her out the side of his eye.

"I could have eaten you," he said. "Gobbled you up and made you my nourishment, my sustenance. But that wouldn't have been fair."

"Why do men always pretend their motives are for the good

of women? I'll tell you what isn't fair. What isn't fair is assuming you know what's best for us."

Pine trees cloaked the hills surrounding them, great swatches of dark green velvet on the morning. Miles turned the car right, suddenly, between a break of wooden fence enclosing a meadow, filled with grazing sheep, onto an unpaved road no wider than the car. Reeds brushed Darcy's face as they bumped along, feathered her cheeks. How very in charge he was, she thought, taking turnings invisible to the uninitiated, driving down a road she hadn't even seen was there, cutting through the nodding vegetation as though his very presence were a machete.

"Well, granted we don't always know what's best —" he said. "But the least of us knows what's wrong for a woman. And that's deprivation and hardship and uncertainty about the future."

"Everybody's future is uncertain," Darcy said. "All we can do is fully appreciate the present." She'd read that in the article.

"Exactly what I'm doing," he said, low in his throat, and parked the car.

They had stopped by a river, a crystal place so still it seemed not to flow at all. The surface of the water shone like mirrored slate, reflecting the trees surrounding. Along the mossy banks, foxgloves grew, purple bells majestically dipping from either side of each tall stem, tens of blossoms open on every stalk.

"Has it changed?" He helped her out of the car. "Our river Dwyfor?"

"I don't suppose so," Darcy said. "Rivers don't change."

"On the contrary." He opened the car trunk, took out a plaid blanket and a sack. "Rivers never stay the same. That's what makes them rivers. You can't bathe in the same water twice."

"Are you sure?" Darcy said.

"Well, I suppose if you swam fast enough downstream . . ."

"Or turned back the clock," she said, wishing she could do that. Wishing she could change the time to when Shan had been his first true love, and switch places with her then.

He looked at her hard. And then his hand was wound through

her elbow, and they were making their way along the grassy banks as socially as if they were walking in the King's Road. Only instead of interested passersby watching them, there were sheep, lounging in the shades of trees, staring with eyes as black as Miles's, but passionless, sanguine. Like parents who'd agreed not to interfere, but weren't too trusting.

By a grassy place where the river had moved away from the bank, leaving a bed of moistly glistening rocks, Miles spread the blanket. Darcy could hear the quiet rush of the river now, where there had seemed to be only silence, a gentle bubbling, nearly indistinct. It was so peaceful, so calming, she had all she could do to feel annoyed. But irritation had to be there, if she was to be true to Shan's feelings. He *had* left her, after all. The least she could be was piqued.

"Nice that you're prepared," she said, as he knelt in his Shakespearean costume, breeches and doublet, straightening out the corners of the blanket. "Were you so sure I would come?"

"Yes." He opened the sack, taking out a bottle of champagne, and glasses, setting them out beside the bag with the two cornets. "Come." He patted the blanket in front of him. "I have to be back for rehearsal. We don't have much time."

"What kind of woman do you think I am?"

"Wonderful. Full of understanding and forgiveness."

"Maybe I've changed. Maybe I'm like the river. Maybe I only look the same."

"Maybe." He patted the blanket again.

"It's just that I'm tired of standing," said Darcy, and dropped to the blanket beside him. "You're not to take it as meaning anything else."

"All right," he said, and smiled.

"Because when a man finishes with me, I've finished with him," she said very proudly, as that was exactly how she imagined she ought to feel if a man left her, which none ever had, since she'd had only the one. That is, until the night before.

"I never finished with you," said Miles, and started to unwind the wire from around the champagne bottle top. "I had things I had to do to be worthy of you."

"Oh, then it was me you ran off for? Me you were thinking about?"

"Always," he said. "Except during *Hamlet*," they said together, and laughed.

The cork popped, and the champagne spilled out, Miles catching it in the glass, filling it and offering it to her. He filled his own, and toasted. "To the prettiest woman in the world."

"Well," said Darcy, clinking glasses, and smiling. "One of them, anyway."

The royal shoot was planned for eight o'clock that morning. Everyone apologized for the earliness of the hour, from the kitchenmaid who brought Shan her breakfast in bed, to the royal hairdresser who came to tender to the royal hairdo, to the designer of the dress for the royal Christmas card, who entered with Junella, the lady-in-waiting. The two of them zippered the princess into the jeweled sheath, making sure all the crystals and rhinestones (or were they diamonds?) were sparkling enough.

"But you look divine!" said the designer, as she hooked the back of the dress. "Check out those shoulders! I'm so glad we decided to go bare!"

In the photography studio, the scenic designer and his assistants (dressed like elves: it was, after all, for Christmas) were spraying the edges of the leaves with crystalline frost. The leaves themselves were tied with invisible threads to silvered twigs and white painted branches imported from Switzerland, where winter came every year, as opposed to Perq, where there had been only one winter in recorded history, and that when an evil sorcerer had tried to lay waste the kingdom. That had been in a long-ago century, before there were photographs, though there were paintings of that time, since Perq had always managed to produce a few artists. But no one took the paintings too seriously, showing as they did hills and valleys covered with snow, streams frozen, waterfalls caught mid-drip, looking more like limestone crystals on the ceiling of a cave than the usual Perquian splendors. Most observers assumed that the painters had gone slightly mad, as painters often did, and that, like Mark Twain's death, reports of Perq's winter had been greatly exaggerated.

Winter was a season of the mind, the chill that came when the imagination cells dried up. And nothing like that ever happened, according to the Tourist Bureau across from the entrance to the castle. "Here there is no winter!" the brochure proudly proclaimed, even as the kingdom prepared its annual frosted Christmas card.

Rachid had taken objection to the planned usual greeting, saying it gave the wrong impression of Perq to make it look like everyone else's Christmas. He had suggested palm trees and waterfalls, to underscore the verdant beauty of the place. But much as the people feared him, there was still a stubborn clinging to tradition. The Ruling Fathers, a council that met several times a year, had overturned his suggestion for a more tropical card, along with the request that the holiday be renamed Rachidmas. Several of them had died quietly in their sleep, so the Fathers remaining had agreed to make a second, less seasonal greeting card.

But it was the frosted one, really, the one with the illusion of snow and silver bells and leaves crusted with ice, that the citizens of Perq loved, and waited for, and hoped to receive in the mail. And just as excited were those who helped prepare it, with devotional ministrations, holding spray cans, crystalling leaves, hanging snowflakes from the ceiling. Christmas bells played over the loudspeaker to inspire them, so wild and sweet and clear, several of the (costumed for the occasion) elves wept. Only the hardhearted didn't love Christmas, in a world where department stores decorated for it before it was even Halloween.

A white antelope, with silver-painted antlers secured to his head, stood with dazed eyes blinking against the lights in the middle of a mound of papier-mâché snow. Chubby babies outfitted as cherubs, with phosphorescent wings, in silver and white tutus, stars on their heads, hung harnessed to Lucite rods, while their anxious mothers stood on the sidelines. The door opened, and everyone oohed and aahed as the purported princess entered, slender and honeyskinned, in her jeweled dress.

"You look like a snowflake, Your Highness," mewled the scenic designer, clapping his hands together soundlessly. "This will be quite the most beautiful Christmas card in Perq's history. Where's the prince?"

"He's on his way over from the palace," said one of the security guards, his voice changing in midsentence, a deep blush suffusing him as he perceived the coming of his adolescence, and the end of his career.

"Well, tell him to shake a royal leg," said the scenic designer, and laughed at his own boldness, just a little nervously.

They moved Shan to the glitter-painted white royal carriage standing in the snow. White liveried footmen helped her climb. The room felt cold to her, in spite of all the bustle, the people, and the angels hanging from the ceiling. It did not occur to her that any of it was artifice, since she imagined that privilege and power carried along with them the ability to have things exactly as you wanted. So as far as she knew, above her head were angels and beneath her carriage was snow, so actual it chilled her.

Colder still did she become as the door opened, and Prince Rodney walked in. He was all in white, his epaulets, the stars of his royal rank on them, silver, with silver buttons and silver buckle on his belt, the phoenix rising from it, gold. His sword was sheathed in silver and ivory. His boots were all white leather with an elevated heel, so he looked even taller than he had the night before. Sorrow pulled at the corners of his mouth, which hung a little slack, and he avoided her eyes as he climbed into the carriage beside her.

It struck her as terribly sad that such a fine-looking fellow, a prince after all, should be so discontented. That he and the wife she was supposed to be had discussed divorce. She had always imagined that only ordinary people had cares and troubles, and had to get over them because that was how life was. It had never occurred to her that the high and mighty got in higher and mightier traps. Poor people imagined that money was the solution for everything, and yet here were Rodney and Darcy, caught in their pricey web, unable to get out in spite of who they were because of who they were. Oh, wasn't the world full of ironies.

"Closer to the princess, sire," the designer said, as the photographers started loading their cameras and changing their lenses. There were two of them assigned to the picture, the official royal photographer and his upstart apprentice. He had been dismissed from the royal service because of his upstarting, but was reinstated by Rachid on receipt of several compromising photos of the merchant with the queen on her hydrofoil, taken through a telephoto lens.

Rodney stiffened, and moved closer to Shan. She could feel his mortification, the awfulness of his plight, more touching because she had always thought it was only women who had plights. Never a man who was suffering, caught in an emotional dilemma. Oh, certainly she'd understood that her Tom was a little dark-browed and melancholy. Their country's troubles, lack of work, the pointlessness of great aspiration in an economy that couldn't support even little dreams, were shadows lining his heart. But good men made do: that was what made them men, they had courage to rise above. But how could a man rise above having risen above?

Compassion warmed her, softened her stance, and she reached for Rodney's hand, like the friend she thought she'd like to be. He looked at her, puzzled, having expected only scorn, seeing eyes that looked at him with interest.

"Oh, that's perfect, children," the photographer said, snapping away. "Let loose the cherubs!"

Someone pressed a button, and, like a carousel rig, the Lucite rods began to turn, and spun the chubby babies through the air. Music played. The antelope bleated.

"Oh," said the scenic designer, holding his long-fingered hands together in ecstasy. "Don't you love love? Don't you love Christmas?"

By late morning the babies were crying and the antelope had lain down, his muzzle between his forelegs, as if he had seen enough. Everyone agreed (but the upstart apprentice) that they had plenty of shots from which to choose. "That'll tie it up here, Majesties, darling," the scenic designer said. "Let's boogie over to our other location."

"I could use a few more shots," said the upstart apprentice.

"We have more than enough," the royal photographer said.

"Well, maybe for an *old*-fashioned card," the apprentice said contemptuously, snapping a picture of his former superior in extreme close up, focusing on a particularly deep wrinkle.

"Why are there two of you?" Rodney said, coming down from the carriage, his princely confidence apparently restored. "Why isn't it just you, Kostia, like always?" he asked the royal photographer.

"There have been some changes, sire," said Kostia, not really looking at him. "My apprentice, Adrian, has been ordered to submit a second set of photos, in direct competition to mine."

"But that's ludicrous," Rodney said. "Insulting. Who gave such an order? It could not have been my father. And certainly I never suggested such a thing."

"It was the regent, sire," said Adrian, bowing.

"What regent?" Rodney said. "Perq has no regent."

"The honorable Rachid, sire," said Adrian. "He has been proclaimed regent in your absence."

"But I haven't been anywhere," said Rodney.

"Perhaps Your Majesty needs a higher profile," said Adrian. "We all could have sworn you were gone."

"Watch your tongue, upstart," said Kostia. "Or it will not be long for your mouth."

"You have no power over me, *old* man," said Adrian. "I am

under the direct protection of my liege. And he has pledged me to his personal service, for the greater glory of the kingdom, and its publicity department."

"This is outrageous!" Rodney said. "Kostia has been the official court photographer since I was a boy."

"Exactly," said Adrian. "And while some of us have grown, others of us have merely gotten taller or older."

"Throw him in the tower, Majesty," Kostia said.

"We don't have a tower anymore."

"Then build one!" said Kostia.

"Boys, boys," Shan said, coming down from her princessly carriage, somewhat startled by her own boldness. But a strange thing had taken place during the photo session. By her warmth, or just the suggestion of it, towards Rodney, she had taken away his gloomy edge, emboldened his stance. The slump had gone from his shoulders. The downcast expression, which makes people look shorter and fatter with their eyes closer together, had vanished from his face. As little ego as Shan had, as little conceit, and as humble and truly out of place as she had felt at the start of this adventure, she was not blind to the effect she had upon people. It was clear she had brought about some kind of healing in Rodney, just by the gesture of friendship, touching his hand. She did not imagine for a moment that change was simply because of her, but knew it was the caring. Nobody in the world failed to respond to caring, especially from one they thought didn't care. If she was going to seem to be Darcy, there was no reason not to use it to do a little mending, of fences and hearts.

"Look around you." She waved her honeyskinned hand towards the sugar-frosted branches, the winged babies, wailing openly now. "This beautiful setting, this wonderful season . . . is this the time or the place for anger?"

"We still have a hundred and twenty shopping days," said Adrian.

*   *   *

So it was that they moved the shoot to the second locale. Rodney was silent in the limousine as they drove deep into the country, which, because of the smallness and density of the island kingdom, took only ten minutes. He watched Shan thoughtfully, studying her profile. She could feel his eyes and his attention, and tried to keep her head up in the way the duchess had assured her was royal. But she was wearing a crown and the diamonds on it were as weighty as problems of state. She imagined that that was the reason for the head that wore the crown lying uneasily.

"You were wonderful back there," he said finally.

"I don't think I did very much good," she said. "They kept quarreling."

"I don't mean with Kostia and Adrian," he said, swallowing. "I meant with me."

She looked over and saw how very open his face was, made more vulnerable by the translucence of his skin, the little shocks of pink on his cheeks, as if one were seeing through to the blood flow. His eyes, steel blue as they were, seemed quite dark against that paleness, and the mouth that appeared so stiff and despondent at the start of the session now looked relaxed and even — no doubt about it — sweet.

He reached for her fingertips. "I thought you despised me."

"How could anyone despise you?"

"I admit I haven't been the most fun husband in the world, but I'm willing to change, Darcy. I'm eager to try."

"I know Darcy will be happy to hear that," Shan said, and patted his hand.

"Is that the reason you acted kindly to me? Because you're trying to make me think you've gone mad?"

"I'm not trying to make you think anything. I'm not Darcy."

"It would be easy to go mad, with things the way they are," he said sadly, looking out the window, as the limousine approached the great waterfall. "Rachid and his henchmen taking over everything. Father too ill to come home from Switzerland."

"What's he doing in Switzerland?"

"Mother's sent him to a clinic . . . for his health." He looked at her. "But you know all that. Don't pretend. You know how he drinks."

"I'm really sorry," Shan said, and was. For her own father had died of drink, and his father before him.

"Don't be sorry," said the prince. "I'm sorry enough for both of us. The three of us, I suppose I should say. You and I and this other girl you claim you are. What's her name?"

"Shan," said Shan.

"Well, this will be fun," said Rodney. "Perq's never had a multiple personality before."

Where the layers of gray shale came together with the schist, and the earth had been torn by great volcanic eruptions, vomiting up black boulders that ringed the lofty pines, was the great waterfall, Pandemonium, of Perq. It cascaded from a height of two hundred feet, the highest waterfall in its time zone. Those who had trekked in the Himalayas, or seen Victoria Falls, or visited Yosemite when there weren't many tourists (though these were a vanishing breed) had been exposed to that kind of majesty, where one had to look up and up and up and sideways and down. Shan herself was awestruck by the sight of the falls, the crashing sound, the fresh smell, as though the water washed the air in its descent. Tumbling over rocks and coursing across boulders, it came to churning comparative rest in a sylvan pool that coddled the water on its way downstream. By this puddle of peace the scenic designer had set the second royal photo, placing Prince Rodney and the princess with the waterfall in the background, and the lush green trees all around.

They had been recostumed for the second shot, Rodney all in his earth color royal wear, beige uniform and sword sheathed in brown leather and gold, gold epaulets and gold stars showing his rank, brown boots with golden buckles, and, of course, the national symbol of Perq, gold phoenix, rising from his belt. The princess had been rebedecked in flowing pale green, so she looked like a woodsprite, except for her crown.

They stood for over two hours, Rodney and the bogus Darcy, while Kostia and Adrian snapped them from every angle, sometimes taking pictures of each other by mistake. There were fewer members of the royal entourage present than at the first locale, since many of the staff were loyal only to the adornments of royalty, its paraphernalia and embellishments, and didn't have much appetite or liking for nature. Democracy had made inroads in Perq only insofar as privileges, not rights, were concerned. A privilege all members of the royal entourage enjoyed was not to have to go anywhere they didn't want to, except to the grave and charity dinners. So the royal junket at this juncture was composed of minimal staff, fewer and fewer as the day wore on and they disappeared into the woods.

"But where is everyone going?" asked Shan at last, when there was hardly anyone left but the photographers and two security guards whose testosterone levels hadn't started increasing.

"There's a myth about this waterfall," Rodney said. "It's supposed to be an aphrodisiac."

"I don't know what that is," Shan said because she didn't, but was most curious. Her inquiring nature brought animation to her already lively eyes, which seemed almost to dance in her face. Of course women's eyes are bigger than men's to begin with, their failure to grow facial hair making them appear more childlike, and it's been suggested this may be designed to evoke a protective response from the male, but certainly by no one who's ever written a fairy tale.

Still, Rodney found his heart quite close to melting. It had been so long since Darcy looked at him with anything other than loathing, that this innocence, feigned though it might have been, moved him to his royal core. "That means it arouses people," he said. "Makes them fall in love."

"But in order to do that they would have to be free," Shan

said, a little frantically. Because something about this man touched her deeply, this prince whose wife didn't understand him. And he cut such a tall, fine figure in his uniform.

He looked at her gravely, his eyes exploring what he considered the familiar face. "Leave us," he said to the security guards.

"Yes, sire," they said, and went off, holding hands and their walkie-talkies.

"Leave us," he said to the photographers.

"I don't think the regent —" Adrian started to say, but Kostia pulled him off by the seat of his trousers.

And they were alone in the woods, the prince and the girl he took to be the princess, with the crashing of the water, and the sighing of the wind in the leaves, like moans, as if the air itself had fallen under the spell of Pandemonium. He took her by her fingertips, and led her closer to the falls.

And they were standing close to each other, separated by only a breath, and that coming rather fast. The waterfall splashed them. And soon their clothes were soaked through. The fabrics clung to their fine young bodies.

"You've never been more beautiful," he said. "Whoever you are."

A little torrent of water fell between them, and he caught it in his mouth, and then swooped against her mouth, giving it to her to drink from his moist, parted lips. And they were all wet. And he was a prince. What could she do?

And his lips glided like the waterfall itself down the side of her neck and to her bosom. And gentle though his fingers were, tapered and long, royal like the rest of him (all of him? — well, she supposed she would see, and soon), there was a certain crisp efficiency in the way he went at taking off her clothes. Starting with the catch at her throat, which he had opened in an instant, probably from all his experience unhooking fishnets, an adjunct of his training in the Royal Navy, to the buttons down the side of her skirt, there was a brusque, businesslike quality to it, almost as though he were getting state matters out of the way, so he could enjoy the banquet. And enjoy it he did, his mouth suckling her nipples until they stiffened, the tip of his tongue making deft little circles around the hard points of her, while his fingers lifted the tight elastic of her pants and found her other button.

And she sighed against him, and opened her mouth as he slipped off his sword and unloosed his private weapon, which even now rose radiant from its sheath. And she moaned aloud as he entered her, partly because she was so sorry to do this to Tom, whom she truly cared for, and partly because it felt so good, so sleek and long and fine inside her, and yes, there was no doubt about it, yes. Royal.

The champagne that Miles poured for Darcy was terrible, sweet and fruity, without the least dryness or nutty overlay. Under ordinary circumstances, she would have spilled it out, turned up her already turned-up nose with its flaring nostrils at it, treated it with the contempt she usually saved for social climbers and used-book drives. But cloying as the flavor was, she didn't mind it at all, edged as it was with Miles's fragrance, the hand that had offered the glass with its invisible fingerprints still impressed on the rim, the smell of him wafting into her nose.

"I've missed you," he said.

"And I you," she answered, not insincerely. For if she had known him before she most certainly would have missed him, longed for him nightly. Even knowing him now for the first time she expected it would be hard to let him go. Little needles of attachment sewed at her heart, and she wondered if there would be a way to take him back to Perq. Make him perhaps the head of the National Theater, which hadn't been started yet, but she couldn't think of a better time to get it rolling. "Is it so wonderful, the theater?"

"Well, it gets in your blood, like a woman," he said, and slipped off her shoe. He lay on his stomach, elbows propping him up, and, lifting her foot, kissed her bare instep. "It isn't just the smell of the greasepaint. It's the smell of the cream that takes it off." He smiled at her and reached into the sack, took out a white lidded jar, uncapped it, and held it under her nose.

It was that smell. His smell. "Yes," she said, closing her eyes, swimming in it. "I understand."

"Do you?" he said, and started massaging her foot with it, rubbing it in between her toes, tracing the valley of skin between big toe and next with his finger, stroking it back and forth. Never before had someone touched between her toes. Even the royal masseuse, who gave attention to feet, had only squeezed the tips of her toes, not explored in between. It was quite the most sensual feeling Darcy had ever experienced, one she had not even read about in *Cosmopolitan*. She sighed aloud with pleasure.

"That's right," he said. "That's good." He began the same on her other foot, smiling as she suspired her contentment.

It was as if Darcy realized for the first time she had feet, never having been aware of them before except in the negative sense, on too long journeys, where she'd trekked for sociability or the press, or through hospital wards. Never had she imagined that feet could be a source of ecstasy.

"Oh, how shall I ever be able to walk on these feet again," she sighed.

"Don't," he said, smiling roguishly, and carried her to the river's edge, and washed them.

"How shall I ever be able to go back home?"

He rubbed them dry in the curly tangle of his reddish hair, kissing them, toe by toe, nipping at the fleshy part of her sole. "Don't. Run away with me."

"But what will happen to . . ." Rodney, she didn't say, and, really, now that she thought about it, didn't care. "Tom," she said.

"Why he's a big strong oaf of a fellow, with a good bullish head on his shoulders. He'll survive."

"And what will become of . . ." Perq, she couldn't mention. Loyalty tugged at her, because she was not completely selfish, just spoiled, which you would probably be too if you were a princess. But she was intelligent, and as rich people go, sensitive, so understood a dream that went deeper than a woman's waking one. "My country," she finished.

"Well, granted Wales is small," Miles smiled at her, kissing the palms of her hands, in between words. "And doubtless you're as wondrous a creature as it has produced. But it, too, will go on. Come with me to London."

"I don't know what to say . . ."

"Then say nothing," he said, and kissed her. His mouth was as soft as his hands on her feet had been strong, and reassuring. And she felt as much a part as if this were, indeed, an old love rekindled, and not the first great flush of new love that it was to Darcy. She envied Shan, her past, what sweet initiation there must have been by this river. Not a royal honeymoon, tented at night for the world press who went along.

"I must go," he said against her mouth. "The queen and the king await me."

"Me, too," Darcy said, and smiled.

"Will I see you later?"

"I have things to do," Darcy said, wondering where she could learn how to cook a chicken.

"I'll be at Criccieth Castle rehearsing if you want me."

"Oh, I want you," she said. "But there are more important things than our desires."

"Name two," he said, and picked a stalk of foxglove, nodding purple in his hand.

"Duty," she said.

"What nonsense. We're supposed to be happy."

"Not at the expense of other people," she said.

"And what's the second?"

"Love."

"What are we talking about here?"

"Not the same kind of love. Love of country. Love of the planet. Love of life."

"But what's it all mean if we're not with the one we love?"

He had her there.

"Come," he said, and held out the foxglove. "A wish." He put the tip of his finger in the center of a petaled bell, and closed his eyes. Opened them. "Now, you."

"All right," she said, and put her finger inside, and thought, "Let me do what is right."

The butcher on the main street was a little surprised to see Shan coming in to his shop. Small as Criccieth was, it supported two meat-merchants, not because there was a need for them, but because they were father and son and had had a falling out some ten years before. The father had said all sons thought they were smarter than their fathers, and the son had said that in his case he was correct. So the father, whose name was Geoffrey, had thrown his son into the street, and the son, whose name was Archibald, which perhaps contributed to his feeling of superiority, had raised his fist to the sky and proclaimed he would be more successful than his father, and at the same trade. The entire town was divided in its loyalty, those who sided with youth, being all young themselves, the patrons of the son, no one trading with both except Archibald's mother, Geoffrey's wife, who had in secret fact staked her son to his own business with money she had pilfered from her husband.

So it was with some astonishment that Geoffrey greeted Shan, who never in her young housewifely career had bought anything from him. "Why, Shan," he said. "What a pleasure to see you in my store."

"A pleasure for me, too, friend," she said, not knowing his name, for all it said above the awning was "Meat Market." She more or less avoided his eye, so busy was she looking through the plate glass at the fish and the cuts of beef, and the chickens, all pale and featherless, heads dangling off to the side.

"I thought like the rest of the youth of this village, you only did business with my son, that stubborn wreck of a young adult, as you people now call yourselves."

"Well, anyone can change," she said, wondering if the chickens had insides, like the fish did.

"Not Archibald. Not for all the years that I raised him did I imagine he would turn on me. He was such a nice little chap. Watching me with what I thought was admiration. Little did I dream he coveted my business and didn't even have the decency to wait till he inherited it."

"Are these regular chickens?" Darcy said.

"Well, they show no signs of being constipated." Geoffrey chuckled.

"I mean, are they what a man would expect when he asked for a chicken?"

Geoffrey looked at her curiously. "Has Archibald promised you bigger ones?"

"No. Nothing like that," she said. "How would I prepare it?"

"You would say, 'Chicken, get ready to meet your maker!' " He laughed again. "You want to stew it, bake it, roast it, or broil it?"

"What's easiest?"

"You young people are all the same. Broiling," he said.

"Do I do that in the stove?"

"Under the broiler," he said, looking at her carefully now, wondering if indeed she was playing some kind of trick on him, if Archibald hadn't sent her to test his patience, or make him seem like a fool. "Are you pulling my shank?"

"I've had a very hard day," she said. "Aren't there times you can't think?"

"Almost all of them," he said.

He took a chicken, halved it, lopped off its head, cleaned out its innards, and gave it to her, all nicely laid out. "Just put that under the flame."

"Thank you," she said and paid him. "You've been very kind."

"Why not? I have nothing against you. Youth must be served, except not necessarily lamb chops."

Just before it was time for Tom to get home, Darcy opened the oven, and finding the right place, struck a match and actually got it to light. (It wasn't easy.) Then she put the chicken on the metal rack and slid it under the flame.

"What's burning?" Tom said, as he came in the door.

"Oh," she said, so pleased she had gotten the oven to go on, she hadn't thought about turning it off.

"What's happened to you?" he said, as he beat out the flames. "Have you lost your head?" He carried the rack, with its charred burden, to the sink, holding it with a towel. "It's him, isn't it?" Tom looked at her with raging, sad eyes. "He's made your brain go soft. You've been with Miles, haven't you?"

"Nothing happened," she said, realizing to her surprise that nothing, really, did. You couldn't be unfaithful with feet. Could you?

He grabbed her, embraced her roughly, and kissed her hard. She started to fight him, because though it hadn't happened yet, she belonged to Miles already. And she was a faithful woman, she was, she was, she was almost sure. "No," she said. "Don't. Let me alone."

"Alone!" Tom said, and swept her up in his arms, whisked her towards the stairs. "It wasn't alone you were! It's not alone you'll stay!"

He carried her up the narrow staircase as easily as if she were a twig, threw her on the bed, and himself on top of her. "NO!" she screamed, and wailed and hollered and fought. But he pinned her flailing arms, pressed her twisting mouth with his own, suffocating her cries. And he had her in spite of all her tears, her sobs, her passionate resistance.

She absolutely loved it.

4

"WHAT IS THIS?" Rachid said, his aquamarine eyes suddenly bathed in fire like a dragon's breath. He fingered the prints that Adrian had brought him of the Christmas layout, contact sheets, sixty-four photos per glossy leaf. In each of them Darcy was looking at Rodney with what to Rachid's horror could only be described as interest. Good grief, even — could it be? — admiration? "But she despises him. Why is she looking so friendly?"

"Wait," said Adrian.

"I hate Christmas," said Rachid, his darkly handsome face etched with swarthy misanthropy. The very sight of the light in the photographs, the twinkle of crystalline twigs, the subtle sparkle of angel hair clinging to branches discomfited him, gouged little rivulets of irritation in his liver. His own quarters, recently refurbished by the decorator who'd done the queen's hydrofoil, were a comforting dark. Heavy rosewood, brought in at enormous expense from Hong Kong, filled nearly every inch of the room, so that bed (a four-poster, the posts elephantine) was adjacent to chair, and chair barely slipped under oversized desk, with a bust of Napoleon on it, and a map of the world. Yellow exes marked the elegant resorts, red circles Club Meds; these were the only bright colors in the room. The walls were draped with burgundy velvet. Burgundy Roman blinds closed off the day. Burgundy velvet canopied and cloaked the four-poster bed. He himself was dressed in black to reinforce his love for the murky underbelly of human nature.

"I knew it was a mistake to allow them that winter setting," he scowled, as his thickly lashed eyes skimmed the photos. His jaw clenched at the chubbiness of the cherubs. "Frost makes people so sentimental."

"Wait," said Adrian again.

"Stop telling me to wait," said Rachid, opening the top button of his black silk shirt, loosing the pointed silk collar, easing the choke in his throat, allowing a tuft of black chest hair, touched with silver, to spring free. He had the same color hair as the queen, this woman that he lusted after so it shook the very foundations of his villainy. For he understood well that to be a completely successful blackguard no one else's needs or wants could come into play. It was a testament to his own weakness that he cared about her, wanted her to be happy. But only with him, so he hadn't let his spider nature down completely.

"You won't have to wait long," Adrian smirked, and reaching over to the sheaf of contacts, turned to the sylvan setting, with the waterfall and the palms. And there they stood, Rodney and Darcy, looking at each other with undisguised longing. Adrian turned to the final sheet.

"What?" An apoplectic tremor locked Rachid's tongue against the roof of his mouth, and his eyes rolled editorially. "What is this?"

"Well, Your Reverence must *know* what it is. Sex is the same in Kuwait."

"I am not from Kuwait, greenhorn. Only my ships are from there. And stop calling me 'Your Reverence.' There is no more religion in Perq, even for those of us who deserve to be worshipped."

"How shall I address you, then?"

"A simple 'Your Greatness,'" said Rachid, his thick black eyebrows knotting above the finely carved bridge of his aquiline nose, as he examined the photographs. "I don't believe this. Do you have a magnifying glass?"

Adrian handed him one. "And a raincoat for your lap, Your Greatness."

"Nobody likes a smart-ass." Rachid waved the raincoat away. "How could this have happened?"

"The wind in the palm trees, the gentle crash of the waterfall, two hearts that beat as one, wet skin . . ."

"Shut up," said Rachid. "This is a disaster. . . ."

The burgundy velvet curtains at the foot of the bed parted, and the queen stuck out her head.

"What disaster? Is the Red Cross coming?" She saw Adrian, and quickly closed the curtains again.

"It's all right, precious. It's only Adrian."

"Only Adrian," Adrian murmured, seething. "I knew my mother should have named me William."

"We must do something," Rachid hissed, pushing Adrian towards the doorway, pressing the contact sheets into his hands. He waited until they were outside the room. "They cannot possibly feel this way about each other."

"The camera never lies," Adrian said. "A picture is worth a thousand words. The proper study of mankind is pornography."

"Meet me in the dungeon at five. And you better have a plan to nip this in the bud," said Rachid, slipping back into his room, locking the door. "You can come out now, priceless. He's gone."

"How could you let him come here?" Isabel raged, as she slid from between the curtains, setting a silver-slippered foot on the Chinese rug. "How could you invite him to be witness to our intimacy?"

"He already had telephoto shots of us on the hydrofoil. How do you think he wormed his way into my confidence?"

"You should have him put away," she said, and drew her silver peignoir tighter about her impressive breasts. "I wish we still had a tower. Or a dungeon." Glittering silver ribbons pulled her thick black hair away from her face, beautiful in spite of the earliness of the hour, and the lateness of her day. "I hate it when you can't punish people."

"Isabel." He moved towards her, smiling. "You have to have more faith in my ability to wreak revenge." He kissed her neck.

"You shouldn't touch me in the morning," she said. "It gets me off-balance for the whole day."

"Then perhaps you should lie down." He placed his hand on her shoulder, pushing her gently backwards onto the bed, and pressed his face between her breasts.

"Oh, why am I so happy?" she said, tangling her fingers through his hair, which felt as soft as her own, and without conditioner. "How can my heart be so joyful, when I am betraying everything that women are supposed to stand for?"

"No one says you have to stand for drunkenness, for sloth, for public degradation. You've done the only thing you can." He ran his tongue along her collarbone. "Sent him to the best sanatorium in Switzerland."

"You think they'll help him?"

"If anyone can."

"Let's call him." The queen sat up. "See how he's doing."

"You know the rules," said Rachid. "No visitors. No phone calls. No letters."

"It seems so extreme. Poor Quirin."

"And no pity. Drunks feel sorry enough for themselves."

"But it isn't his fault he was born spineless. It runs in the family. My poor Rodney. It's a miracle he's as strong as he is."

"A miracle," said Rachid, unenthusiastically.

"I think they're going to be all right, now, Rodney and Darcy." Isabel got up from the bed. "Darcy seemed somewhat . . . subdued, after her journey. Much less contentious than before she went away. She's not a bad girl, you know, just a little willful. But then she is an Aries."

"Let's not talk about Darcy," Rachid said, loosing one of the ribbons in her hair. "Let's not talk about anything."

"Why do you have to be so attractive?" she sighed. It was not an idle question. Just as she appraised the basic decency of Darcy, she was always examining her own worth, or lack of it. And it was a source of genuine anguish to her that she didn't have a stronger character, that her sexuality overrode her basically moral instincts. She was always the first one at earthquakes and landslides, had been named Woman (Queen) of the Year by the International Red Cross, actively concerned as she was with natural disasters. But what of the disaster that Nature had wrought in women, the weakness that dislodged their underpinnings when men were involved?

She knew very well that Rachid was less than a hero, ambitious, driven, self-serving, short on charm except for the oily kind, amazingly lacking in humor (when was the last time she'd had a good laugh?). How singularly lacking in poster boys for the species they were. Not many representatives who, plastered to the wall of the mind, would make you think of sacrificing for them, because they were noble, inspiring. As little interest as Isabel had in women, there was no question more was going on among them, more questing, more aspiring, more attempting to understand their own nature and the nature of life itself than seemed to be happening among the men she knew. Yet when there was the *one*, the singular set of fingers that unlocked the combination to the earlobe, the voice that sent a tremor through the knees, the lips that loosed the hinges of the brain, rational behavior went out the proverbial window. So no matter how foolish you thought a man was, thought was no longer the keynote. All became hunger and longing, and, finally, relief. Was it a built-in joke on the part of the God no longer officially honored in Perq, to construct such a complex machine, and leave such a simple screw loose?

She supposed that part of her pique was at herself, for being so needy. She had more or less come to terms with the woman she was, being in her fifties. She knew she was bright. Her mirror told her daily she was still the fairest in the land (for a dark person; Darcy of course would have won for the blondes). And she understood she had a good heart, because, the honor of having been chosen by the Red Cross aside, she *did* want to help those who'd been in catastrophies: her stomach did clutch when the earth churned and planes crashed and she realized that there but for the grace of God (who wasn't anymore) went she. And if she could help wipe out the blight of terrible diseases, she would. She would do anything. Even now Perq's scientists worked day (and night, she presumed) on any number of research grants she herself had been responsible for getting them. So it was not as if she had no conscience, no compassion for humanity as a whole. Not as if she mistook her privilege for something that set her really above, and apart. But there was no way, even working at optimum humility, that she could see herself as low. Why was she so willing to settle, then, when it came to passion? Why did she not make the same demands of a man that she would have made of a friend of the same sex, before allowing her into the circle of the heart?

She supposed, like most good women in the world, she should really blame her mother, who had always flattered and paid obeisance to men as a caste. Her mother had raised her not to aspire to her own distinction, but to set her sights on the Most Eligible Man, taking her identity from whichever of them she would belong to. The queen mother-in-law actually thought like that, as if women were truly vassals, even the royal ones among them. She had paraded her like a float through the courts of Europe, until she caught Quirin. All the more painful, then, was the realization of the king's weakness and inadequacy, his sense of his own failings, that drove him to drink. How terrible to be a king, and know there was nothing kingly about you: and how devastating for a really smart woman, a natural survivor, to have landed a fish that couldn't swim.

Still, she had tried to make it work, for the sake of the state, for the sake of her son, whom she adored. The only area of a woman's life that was more irrational than her sexual longings was her maternal ardor. Nothing would interfere with the happiness of the prince. So she had stood by Quirin's side, and lain in his bed, and propped him up at public ceremonies all the time that Rodney was growing up, and being schooled, and learning how to be royal. It was only after he himself had married and begun what she hoped would be his mature life that she'd allowed her exasperation with Quirin to move between her legs. Disappointment and irritation transmuted itself into sensual appetite, and there being no disasters in the world for some weeks, as though Nature had declared a moratorium, she had nothing to do but be vulnerable to Rachid.

She was mad at all of them, really: Quirin for being less than what she hoped, her mother for making her settle for less than what she needed, Rachid for being less than she deserved, and herself for being so hot. Once on a goodwill visit to the United States she had made a tour of Christian Science Reading Rooms, and engaged in conversation with the ladies behind the desk at the time of one of that country's quaint Supreme Court decisions, something to do with breaking in on homosexuals, and the illegality of oral sex (one of her favorites). And the women both said they thought that law was quite right, since sex was only for procreation. Isabel had asked if that was so, why women still had sexual longings after their childbearing years, and both women answered "They don't." So she felt very guilty, ignorant as she understood the women were, because her own hungers were paramount now, as they'd never been in her youth. It was as if she'd discovered a new toy to give her juice in her middle years, something that made her nights of consequence, fuller for his visits inside her. There was a positive edge to her life now, a little buzz to her day. Every sunset seemed more beautiful with someone to share it with. Not like the king, who had just been waiting for it to go over the yardarm.

She felt remorseful about him, too, and her gross infidelity. Even in a sanatorium as he was, he was still her husband. She was disgusted with herself for being so bestial, so lascivious, wrote notes at teatime to Mother Teresa asking if she could use an assistant. Nothing would have pleased Isabel more than to be truly selfless, a beacon of virtue, to have one of Perq's surgeons open her up and remove the bawdy, run an IV through her system and drain out all the lickerish. But things were how they were, and she would tear the notes up, and run to find Rachid in time for the sunset. Snuggled into her mindless, adulterous passion as the world grew dark, she did, too.

Still, with his soft, curly hair in her cleavage, she forgave herself. And as he burrowed his furrowed brow between her breasts, she soothed him, tried to ease what she was sure were his cares and his worries, even as she prayed he had some. Because it would have been just too disgusting, too unconscionable, for him to be enjoying all this without being a little racked, a little torn, as she was.

Pleasure without pain to measure it against, joy without sorrow to rebound from, ease without difficulty overcome, made life insipid, half of what it should be. Outlawed as God might have been in Perq, Isabel was sure the world was of His design. And in the guilty feelings He gave to women, at least, He was Jewish.

Now Darcy woke once again all covered with warm and lovely feelings, like a quilt. The actual quilt that lay over her in the bed where she had slept (oh so well!) with Tom was raggedy in comparison to the one that satisfaction had wrapped her in. What an adorable brute he was! How deep his feelings had to go, for a man of such limited experience and unsophisticated dreams. She had heard him in his sleep, crying "No!" "Back off!" "Get out of here!" to a dragon, she imagined, or an invading army, or Miles. How much he must really have loved his true Shan, to fight for her the only way he knew how, with the strength of his body, using it not to defend her against marauders, those who would run off with her (were there more besides Miles?) but to try and conquer her, subdue her.

She understood from articles in various magazines that rape was an act of violence against women, and not of desire. But what had occurred the night before had seemed less an assault than a seizure, a kind of sexual epilepsy, because he loved her

(Shan) more than he could control. So he had laid claim to her, in a manner of speaking, staked her out, in a sense, as his own. Never dreaming or suspecting that she was not his Shan, and that the real perfidy was not Miles's but hers. And that he could not keep her, because he had never had her, except in the biblical sense.

But how Darcy enjoyed wallowing in lust! How she relished a man's going mad for her, even if he thought she was someone else. Her whole body was tingling, an aliveness she'd never suspected existed in her, marching through every corpuscle like a brass band, fully uniformed, a spectacle she felt tempted to cheer. "Oh, I am having such a good time!" she could not help crying out aloud as she sprang from the bed.

Once again, the other side of it was empty, she noted with just a little pang of discontent. Strapping as Tom was by night, she wondered what he would have been like in the morning, when her resistance was less, when she awakened benign and receptive to what doubtless would have been his advances. Would he have been gentle, bear though he seemed? Could he have been sensitive, if he weren't fighting off specters, taking the cudgel to the ghosts of the past, the part of her life he couldn't control? It seemed quite unfair (oh, there it was, the way it had said in the article, the thought that she was being treated unfairly) that he had to go to work, not giving her a chance to explore other levels of her sexual feeling. But if the magazine had been correct — and how could she have any doubt, popular as it was — everything in life happened so you could learn what you needed to learn, so maybe she didn't need to learn what Tom was like in the morning.

Seeing herself in the bathroom mirror, she noted, once again, how very placid her brow seemed, the worrisome crease gone from it now, erased as with heavy makeup. How pretty she was, really, even with her features naked as they were, certainly with her body naked as it was. How she wished they had a bigger mirror, so she could look at herself full-length, with all her unsuspected majesty (as opposed to the official kind) exposed.

Never in her life had she imagined that there could be such delight in simplicity. Just waking up, when one was pleased with oneself, was a happy experience. She dressed in her clean dress (later in the day she would have to wash the soiled one) and went down to the kitchen, reading with some trepidation Tom's note ("Try *meat*" was all it said), throwing open the window to greet the day.

To her surprise, it was overcast and gloomy, not at all what she'd expected, as if the very day should reflect her mood, be designed for her. Didn't the sky see how happy she was; shouldn't it respond in kind? For the world was just a reflection of how people saw it, she was sure. And lovely as she was, young, and fresh, and felicitous, that was how the world should be too, lifted by her very presence in it.

She started to pout at the clouds, disapprovingly, to make her displeasure evident, when she noted the hydrangeas in the windowbox. They looked much more vibrant for the grayness of the day, their color brilliant. And she wondered if perhaps the brightest flowers needed their share of dreary days to grow, and whether it was the same with people.

Just then, she remembered the seeds she had planted, and checked the earth for her sprout. Yes, there it still was, all closed in its bud. She went to the sink (still with the charred chicken in it), reached underneath for the watering can, filled it, and watered the windowbox.

"Glub," the earth went again. To her amazement, another sprout shot up at once, as the first bud began to open.

And in front of her very eyes bloomed a beautiful flower, that looked not unlike herself. A radiant halo of pale yellow, the color of her cornsilky hair, edged the top petals. In the center of those petals were dots of cornflower blue, like her eyes. As she peered into the heart of the blossom, belled like a foxglove, she saw what seemed to be tiny little breasts, and a slender waist, honey gold hips and thighs. And she wondered if perhaps there was a flower fairy inside, if the seeds had sprouted more than their share of enchantment.

She struggled to remember what the duchess (or perhaps it was really the Afghan) had said. And she recalled that he had directed her to eat the seeds as they flowered, and that the blossoms would serve as the antidote. But the antidote to what? she had neglected to ask. Nor had she thought there would be anything like a person inside them. Eating a flower would not be totally new to her, as in the beginning of her marriage to Rodney, when it was still fun, and they had been to Italy, where she'd seen them cooking a fish, she'd also eaten *fior di zucchini*, delicate zucchini blossoms, deliciously coated and fried. As it was early in the morning, she thought she'd best eat this one raw, especially as she had yet to learn how to cook. But what if that was a fairy inside it? Eager as she was to absorb the magic that had come to her from the chandelier (had it been a trick?) she wasn't prepared for cannibalism.

"Is there anyone in there?" she asked the flower. "Hello? Hello?" But there was no answer, and Darcy was hungry. So she ate it.

A gentle warmth seemed to flood her insides, emanating from the area of her heart. And there was the sound of a bell — quite a clang, really, as in an amusement park, when someone struck the hammer to the pin with the strength of a champion.

She felt actually incandescent. Her dress, a faded red and blue plaid, seemed to her to be glowing, as though suddenly spun with luminous numinous thread. She ran back up the narrow stairway, the wooden steps creaking beneath her feet, and, racing into the bathroom, looked at herself in the mirror.

But whatever she was expecting — radiance, transformation — she was very much surprised. For instead of having changed into a creature even more resplendent, she was exactly as she'd been before. And now that she saw herself again, she realized that although she was as pleasant to look at as ever, none of it had anything to do with her. It was only the package she'd come in. Nothing to feel proud of or conceited about. Bereft of ribbons and rings and Rolex, she was just a pretty girl, which was not in any way her doing. All that she had felt vain about were things for which she deserved no credit: the way she looked, what had come to her through nature, what had come to her through Yves Saint-Laurent.

She touched her cheek, the translucent skin, which was none of her design, and puzzled aloud: "But what's happened?" And she wondered why she had ever thought she was better than anyone else.

Well, there was chicken to clean (it was easier to clean up than to cook, she was pleased to discover) and a bed to make (it was simpler today; with the sheets all pulled out and askew from the night's activity, she could start from the beginning). So though it was a bit of a struggle (certain corners hung out, till she figured out how to tuck them in), she managed.

She very much missed her maids — she remembered what attractive young women they were, and how she had never looked at them really, recalling how gracefully they fluffed the pillows, leaning over the royal beds with a certain slender fluidity that she tried now to emulate. But she finished the job quite commendably if she had to say so herself, which she no longer would, having eaten the blossom that cured Vanity.

Then it was off to her friend the butcher, who sold her a fine cut of lamb at half price, so pleased he was to have the custom of someone so young and so humble. He told her how to prepare it the easiest way, for modest as she'd become, she told him she was not a very good cook, which she hadn't been even when she wasn't modest. But now she had the virtue of being able to admit her shortcomings, the humility that came with shedding Vanity, like a prize in a box of Cracker Jack.

Unassuming as she newly was, she walked with her head slightly bowed, the royal posture still proud, but in a compliant way. "Good morrow," said the gently booming voice, the vowels rotund, mildly overfed. And Miles moved out of the doorway of the inn dressed in his Shakespeare, looking like the likeness of the poet himself, all puff-shouldered, brown-velveted, and narrow-waisted, brown tights showing his splendid legs, with their bulging calfs and muscular thighs and the rest of his glory.

Like the hydrangeas, his color seemed more brilliant against the gloom of the day. His reddish hair looked as though burnished by firelight, glinting orange as he cocked his head, and smiled at her, and savored her with his eyes.

"Good morning," she said, hardly able to look at him, not so much out of maidenly modesty as panic. For in spite of her growing affection for Tom, and her strangely burgeoning loyalty, she was so excited at the sound and sight (and the smell? was he too far away? did she only imagine that fragrance on the air?), she could barely breathe. Losing vanity doesn't mean a woman's going to get smart.

"Have you had breakfast?" he asked, falling in step beside her, taking her under the elbow with his gauntleted hand.

"I had a little something," Darcy said, wishing she could tell him about the flower. But all she knew about this man, really, was that he was an actor, and blissfully attractive, and probably gifted, if the resonance in his voice was any indication. But she knew a number of people in the entertainment industry, making tours as she and Rodney did, being invited everywhere as they were, sponsoring command performances to raise money for Queen Isabel's charities. And she understood about actors that their currency was deceit — not necessarily ill-natured. But deception was how they earned their living, pretending to be what they were not. So although she would not have lied to him, there was no point in being *too* honest, sharing with him the fact that she had breakfasted on magic, and was partially transmuted.

She knew it was better to keep something of herself in reserve, since courtship required secret weapons. Having set aside vanity, she was clear-eyed about ego, and recognized that, splendid peacock that he was, he would be jealous if someone else had showier feathers. And in truth, there were no brighter plumes than magic in a windowbox.

"How beautiful you are," he said, moving his face indecently close to her cheek, considering it was only late morning, and the middle of the street.

"It's only the way I look," she said, and, hearing the words fall from her tongue, was surprised at them.

"Have you made up your mind to run away with me?"

"I don't know." They had reached her doorway. The paper-wrapped package of butchered lamb had blood starting to seep from its corner. "I have to put this in the icebox."

"Would there were an icebox for the passions of man," Miles sighed. "A place where we could cool our glands and chill our gonads, so this too too sullied flesh would melt, but only in the sun of real love."

"I'll go along with that," said Darcy, and went inside.

He was right behind her, his knees practically bending into the backs of her legs. He watched over her shoulder as she put the meat away.

"I don't think you should be in this house," she said, feeling a spurt of fidelity rush through her veins. True she owed nothing, in reality, to Tom. But she knew how proud he was, how deeply he loved, how fiercely he wanted to possess. And she felt connected to him, in the most basic way. "Someone will tell Tom."

"Then so should I tell Tom. So would I come and face him direct and tell him I've come back to claim what was never his and was always mine, body and soul."

"Only feet," said Darcy, primly.

"Can you claim you don't want me?" he said, turning her around and holding her by the shoulder, looking deep and hard and gravely into her face.

"No. I'm not a good enough actor for that," she said.

"And what is that supposed to mean?"

"It means I don't believe you. It means that lies are your stock in trade. It means you can tell me from now till tomorrow how much you care for me, how much you want to do for me, how deep is your need for me. It means you can tell me from now till tomorrow that you love me, and I won't be sure who you don't love better is yourself."

"Well, who's more deserving?" said Miles.

"Oh, she was right to marry Tom," said Darcy, disgustedly, and moved around him.

"I was just joking," Miles said, and smiled, and wheedled with his breath in her ear, hugging her around from behind, squeezing her so hard her breasts came together. "There's no one I love better than you."

"Will you tell me from now till tomorrow?" she asked.

"I have rehearsal," he said.

In spite of the flower having healed her of Vanity, Darcy felt something quite like a prick in her spirit balloon, the explosion of disappointment when life is not what we expected. For it is the dream of young girls and even old ones, that when a man says, "I love you," he will act accordingly, give up his own wants and desires as a woman would, and doesn't just mean "I love you for the needs of mine that you satisfy," and "I'll come through when I can."

But unfortunately there are not enough magic flowers to go around, and it is harder for an actor to set aside his own ego than it is for a rich man to pass through the eye of a needle. And although Darcy knew it was not about her, since she wasn't even who she was, she could not help taking it personally.

Still, there were six more days he had to be in Criccieth, and six more seeds that would burst into flower. So perhaps by the time he left, she would know whether to leave with him or not, whether he meant what he said or not, and whether there was any romance in the world that was not of a woman's making.

There were trees that grew near the southern shore of Perq as singular as the climate itself, their idiosyncratic charm caused less by the tropical flow of the Gulf Stream than something strange in the earth. Perq's scientists, several of whom had won Nobel prizes — not the ones given in Sweden, but one established by a local candy store owner named Harry Nobel, who didn't think foreigners were always objective — had worked hard and long to isolate the chemical in the soil. Something between a nitrite and an aphrodisiac, it had given rise to species with erectile tissue in its fronds. Thick gray trunks spiraled upwards as in ordinary palms, which were everywhere along the shore. But in this particular genus, the branches twisted around and inward, giving rise to leaves standing up phallic in all directions, like gigantic bouquets of cigars, fortunately without the aroma.

It was said if you bathed in sap from the trunk of that tree, it would heal not only sexual inadequacy, but the fear of it, something that ran rampant in the sophisticated capitals of non–third world countries, where men had time to worry about such things. Although Rachid's origins were primitive, he had anchored his yacht in enough blasé basins, so that the scent of sexual panic had gotten into his nostrils. In spite of his natural propensity for lust, the inspirationally voluptuary nature of the queen, a full library of Maurice Jarre music, and an impressive collection of erotic art, he still awoke sweating some midnights, or later, that he would not be able to perform. So he bathed every teatime, after a strong massage, and a workout with a Jane Fonda lookalike, but with big breasts, in the oil of the bark of the Fescennine tree. For so was it called, after the ancient town of Fescennia, in the long-ago country of Etruria, noted for obscene jesting and scurrilous verse, some of which Rachid collected, along with its pottery.

The tub in which he bathed was a dark red marble, stained with the blood of centaurs, according to the Italian who'd sold it to him, spigoted with gold from the teeth of satyrs, and jets pumping hot air from the words of politicians. Luxuriating in it now, his head eased back on a plastic pillow shaped like a woman's ass, Rachid allowed the oil to permeate his pores, and the myth of its magical properties to permeate his subconscious. "Speak to me of love," he said to the court minstrel, a thinning-haired fellow with long, slender limbs, who looked like a youth shot through a tunnel into middle age, unscathed by evil or any particular maturity.

"Love," the minstrel sang, plucking the strings of his ancient instrument, the only part of him that had aged. "Lifts us and sinks us and whirls us about in a maelstrom at mealtime . . . And makes us all join Overwooer's Anonymous."

"What a silly song," said Rachid.

"Thank you," said the minstrel, who had long ago learned the consequences of substance in poetry.

"Your Greatness." One of Rachid's lackeys, a former security guard from a London disco appeared in the doorway. "It's nearly five."

"My towel!" Rachid ordered. "And you, minstrel — turn your hand and your head to something a little more inspiring by this time next week," he said, as his lackey held the towel out for him, and helped him from the tub. "Or your days are numbered."

"I'd like a Tuesday that's a five," said the minstrel.

"What a fool you are," said Rachid, swaddling himself in burgundy terrycloth.

"Thank you," said the minstrel, who had also learned what happened to most bright people in the world.

To get to the dungeon, that secret part of the palace that even the queen did not know existed, so crafty had been Rachid's decorators (known officially in interior designers' circles as The Architects of Doom), one had to pass down a secret stairwell. A huge wooden butcher's block in the middle of the second kitchen, where family dinners were prepared, had an invisible spring which, when pressed, moved the butcher's block aside to reveal the trapdoor opening to the stairs. So it was that in order to keep the knowledge strictly among those in his inner circle, Rachid had been forced to take into his confidence Rhea, the assistant chef, a formidable woman who, in her youth, had been nursemaid to Prince Rodney.

Though seemingly mild in voice and manner of speech, Rhea was in every way a virago, a hot-tempered woman who suppressed her own rages by making an inordinate number of curries, and putting hot peppers in most dishes including scrambled eggs. Working closely with Perq's nutritionists, who had determined that there were fewer stomach diseases in countries where people ate chiles, it allowed her to punish the palates of those who took her for granted, which was everybody, while selling them the myth of improved health.

There was tremendous loyalty on the part of the royal family. So when Rhea's nannying days were over, they'd given her her new post, after a ten-week sabbatical in Paris where she'd taken a Cordon Bleu course and failed it.

Intrigue, however, was mother's milk to her, something for which she had a natural aptitude. The coming of Rachid, this Middle Eastern Macchiavelli, had stimulated her as nothing had since the accidental drowning of the woman her husband had run off with, a seaweed-haired creature who'd come into their lives like Venus on the half-shell, rising from the wreckage of a yachting accident, tangling Orin, Rhea's husband, in her sexual web, and then, fortunately, her hair in another yacht's anchor. Orin had come home, penitent and lost, taking the mishap as a direct finger from the gods, abasing himself on the linoleum of the kitchen, begging Rhea's forgiveness. She had only pretended to pardon him, and fed him a diet heavy in meat, eggs and butter, cheesy sauces, and shrimp, in the hope of hoisting him on his own cholesterol. But he stayed as healthy as she stayed angry, and loved her all the more for the richness of his diet, saying he had found the only woman who understood true conciliation. For if absolution came from the milk of human kindness, why shouldn't exoneration be coated in cream? So it was that he grasped the nature neither of nutrition nor of women. But it is amazing how many men live a long time without having a clue to either.

Even now she was fixing him a deep-dish pizza for his afternoon snack, in the walled brick oven Rachid had built for her in exchange for her silence. "I'm expecting Adrian," Rachid said, as the butcher block moved aside, and he reached for the bolt that opened the trapdoor.

"He's already down there," said Rhea, moving the cheesy pie deeper into the oven with the long flat shovel.

"What ambition," marked Rachid.

"Maybe he just likes dungeons," she said.

"Well, Quirin," said Rachid, as he bounded down the stairs. "How's it going?"

"Toad," said the king. For though he had once saved his expletives for the moments when Rachid was out of earshot, he was tired of being a prisoner and not expressing his feelings either. He had long held his tongue thinking it would make Rachid more merciful. But the cocaine blown so regularly up his nose had sharpened his irritation, and what was left of his intelligence showed him clearly that pity was not this shitheel's long suit. "Newt."

"Sticks and stones, Your Majesty. Sticks and stones. And a frog may sound like an insult to you, but it is swampy music to my ears, for I will remind you that a frog may be transformed into a prince. And thenceforward, to a king."

"Never," said Quirin.

"Cocktail time," said Rachid, loosing the blankets that held the king to the prison bed, raising him to his unsteady feet, and chaining him to the wall. "A little of the best Bolivian. Nothing's too good for the monarch of the realm." And, so saying, he blew some cocaine up the king's nose.

"Adrian," Rachid said, blowing. "Have you come up with any ideas?"

"I have, my liege," said Adrian, his sycophantic smile brightening. "The problem as I see it is that your plan depends on the marriage of Rodney and Darcy collapsing."

"Precisely," said Rachid. "The entire world press is waiting for that event. Humiliation at supermarket checkstands all over the world. Oh, it warms the cockles of my cockles.

"For when the people of Perq in the absence of their ailing king understand that the prince and his consort have no love for each other, so shall the kingdom have no love for itself. And the people shall lose faith in romance and tropical breezes and palm trees and everything but profit. And they will offer me the crown."

"Never!" said the king.

"I'll make you a side bet on it," said Rachid. "I'll bet you the one share you have left in the Perq casino, that you didn't already lose to me."

"I've given up gambling," said the king.

"A little too late," said Rachid, and blew some more powdery substance up his nose.

"All well thought out and doubtless psychologically correct, Your Greatness," said Adrian. "But as you saw from my photographs, the prince and the princess seem to have fallen back in love."

"I knew it! I knew it!" said Quirin.

"We must get them back to the vale of mutual loathing," said Adrian. "If Your Greatness is to become king."

"You have an idea?"

"More than an idea, I had the audacity to already set a little something in motion."

"Audacity in your book might come dangerously close to impudence in mine," Rachid said, stiffening. "You know the punishment for impudence."

"If this does not meet with your approval, I shall be very surprised."

"As will your skin, when we peel it," said Rachid.

Adrian reddened. "You underestimate me."

"Perhaps. And perhaps your skin is just a little thinner than it should be to succeed in the chicanery business. You're too sensitive for your own good, Adrian, and certainly for mine. What is your plot?"

"Since there has been this untoward change in the princess's affection, we obviously can't count on her turning against him. So I have found another girl, a woman made to order to look exactly like the Princess Darcy." He opened a model's portfolio and showed Rachid pictures. The young woman looked so much like Darcy even Adrian, who had photographed Darcy (or at least thought it was Darcy, not knowing about Shan) was convinced it was Darcy.

"But where did you find this person?" asked Rachid, astounded at the likeness.

"Through a friend of mine — a plastic surgeon in California who specializes in making people into celebrity lookalikes. He is most famous for transforming the top male rock and roll singer into the woman he most admired, which took some doing. This young woman was easier, since he didn't have to break her cheekbones. But is she not, as they say, a ringer?"

"Astounding!" exclaimed Rachid.

"It is my plan to have this girl, in the guise of Princess Darcy, make a public spectacle of herself, slutting about in the pleasure spots of Europe . . ."

"Flirting openly with ski instructors!" said Rachid, getting into the spirit of it.

"Lingering in doorways with jazz musicians."

"Rock and roll," Rachid amended. "Jazz has a certain elegance."

"And the citizenry of Perq will deplore her behavior, and be disgusted with the prince for not being able to control her. And by Christmas —"

"Christmas . . . ," said Rachid, hating the very sound of it, the word, edged as it was with bells, ringing in his ears like the happy noise of children laughing, believing in Santa Claus, who was almost as loathsome to him as the God he had had outlawed.

"By Christmas there will be a dishonor so great that the very soul of the kingdom will be degraded, and people will demand her exile for life, and the prince's along with her. Siberia will seem too good for them."

"And what is this debasement? Better make it good!"

"The Princess Darcy — or so it will seem — will be the Christmas Centerfold in *Playhouse* magazine. I have already gotten a guarantee from the editors, if I can deliver."

"You are insidious beyond measure," said Rachid. "I'm really impressed."

"My friend the plastic surgeon is standing by for the finishing touches," Adrian said. "So must we sneak into Darcy's chambers as she sleeps and get impressions of her breasts and bellybutton. Because it wouldn't do for someone to look at the photos and say, 'Are those the breasts and bellybutton of a princess?' "

"How would anyone know?" asked Rachid.

"We just mustn't take a chance," said Adrian. "I'm for total authenticity."

"You worm," wheezed the king. "You give the word 'slimeball' new meaning."

"I didn't know there was an old one," said Rachid. "Well, Adrian, my truly gifted. When I am king, I shall see that you are properly taken care of."

"I'd like that in writing, Your Greatness."

"Certainly, certainly," said Rachid, and took out his pen. "You have paper?"

"My lawyers are drawing up a deal memo, even as we speak. As soon as it's signed, I will deliver the impostor."

"You've thought of everything," Rachid said, not quite with absolute pleasure.

"And what will happen to the real Princess Darcy?" asked the king. For blitzed as he was, he was a king, and paternal, and concerned, and asked good questions.

"Why, there's room for her here, right next to you." Rachid struck a second set of metal cuffs in the wall near the king, clanged them against each other so there was a kind of knell, insidious. "The family that flays together, stays together. Has a certain ring, don't you think?"

Sometime during the night, drugged as she was (for Rhea had put a sleeping draught into the royal cocoa), Shan felt something warm and wet sliding over her breasts. Too groggy to struggle her way up into wide-awakeness, Shan smiled in her sleep, imagining it was just another wonderful erotic trick on Rodney's part. So clever for a prince, so unleashed in his imagination, once he knew someone cared. What a lucky girl she was!

For he had changed completely, just in the short time since the waterfall, by his own confession to her in the now steamy nights in their royal bedchambers, and on the royal floors, and royal balconies, in darkness, except for the moon. Changed from the lily-livered (by his own description) prince that he had been, to a fiery man of the earth.

So primed of late by his eroticism, Shan dreamed that the wetness now sliding over her nipples was the oft-aroused Rodney's ingenious tongue. As villains made plaster impressions of her aureoles, she sighed with delight. Thus women are seduced by their own imaginations, even in the presence of slime and cement, which men sometimes can be, as well as use.

5

THE GREAT SANDSTONE BLUFF on which Criccieth Castle stood was, in truth, not very great. But as it rose several stories higher than any other part of the village or its structures, including the tearoom, with its white painted legend "TEAS" on the gray slate roof, it was great enough, as decent men seem heroes in a villainous world.

The castle itself dated from around 1200, during the reign of Llewelyn the Great, which was probably also relative. It was hard to imagine, looking at the edifice, that battles had raged and fortunes changed and men had risen and fallen, and honor been lost in such a place. Even when viewed from not very far away, Criccieth Castle seemed less historical than postcard. No waves crashed against the cliff at its edge, falling down to still, shallow water, clear enough so one could look down and count the pebbles on the sea floor. So serene did the castle stand, and small, that it could best be described as a darling castle, an adorable castle, precious adjectives with a tendency to primp, that have no place in what is monumental, even on a tiny scale. But, in this case, the descriptions were most fitting. The flags that waved from its slightly crumbling turrets were green on a field of white, fluttering in a current more zephyrlike than harsh, as if the wind took its cue from the castle and could not begin to bluster.

Now in the tower where once the rebel leader Madog had been held hostage, where the Black Prince had marked the approaches of armies and ships that had chosen their sea-lanes not too well, the nightwatch trembled in fear at the coming of the ghost of Hamlet's father. In the courtyard, the actress playing Gertrude sipped her tea and wondered how her life would have been if she'd listened to her mother and chosen a man or a profession she could count on. Recently divorced, she speculated on what subtext she could give the queen, other than voluptuous gratitude, since the actress knew firsthand how few men were out there, and it seemed to her not such a big deal, Claudius's being a murderer. In fact she was pretty annoyed with all men, including Hamlet and Shakespeare, since she found particularly insulting Hamlet's speech in which he told his mother that at her age the heyday in the blood was tame, which proved how little young princes, and Shakespeare, knew about women.

An interested ring of children watched the rehearsal, captured by the spectacle of tall men whipping cloaks about their shoulders. It was a fairly windy day, so the children had come with colorful kites to fly. Although they deferred to the director who'd invited them to stay and watch if they were quiet, a certain sad surrender was boxed in with the kites under their arms and pressed to their chests, while they studied how grown men played. The children were uniformly beautiful, towheaded and rose-lipped, a slightly melancholy cast already in their young, wise eyes. They listened to the glottal sounds of their ancestors' tongue, which had become, once again, the language of their lullabies, as their mothers stubbornly reclaimed them for Wales, making them Welsh in their speech and their dreams, preparing them for a world that had nearly forgotten about them.

In the midst of their wide-eyed congregation sat Darcy, imagining herself to be invisible, struggling to ferret out the substance of the play, to hear past the harshness of unfamiliar tongue to its drama. Having lost Vanity, she did not imagine for a moment she was any kind of critic. But she was determined to see if Miles was gifted, as part of her decision whether or not to run away with him. For it was the first time in her life she had options, or seemed to, and now that she was a free woman, albeit poor, she wanted to choose intelligently for herself, or the girl she was supposed to be. And running off with just anybody simply would not do, as exciting as the idea did seem to her.

Miles, for his part, was also trying to be inconspicuous, at least for a young actor in the showiest part in the history of the English language, which of course Hamlet was not being done in at the present time. Miles's personal tendency to bombast, the natural grace with which he leapt and bounded and had scaled parts of this castle in his youth, were kept strictly in check, as he had determined his Hamlet should be neither athletic nor brooding, but simply a young man who didn't trust women.

It was an attitude that everyone seemed to be able to relate to. The one constant throughout the time of the building of the castle, the writing of the play, and probably the original struggle as it took place in Denmark, was men's suspicion of women. Minor though their role might have seemed before the so-called elevation of their sex and the struggle to equality, as little place as women had in history books except as the bearers of sons and occasional Virgin Queens, there was no doubt that men had always been fearful of their mysteries.

Darcy herself, though far from a student of human nature, had chaired one charity ball to raise money for an anthropology grant in Perq, to study man-woman differences. Naturally she had considered herself only a figurehead. But the anthropology study, once established, was something she checked in on from time to time. And the basic facts of human beginnings and development, that man was the hunter because he could run faster, while woman had to stay home so her hips could widen to give birth to a creature of such a huge brain, seemed to indicate to Darcy that it went deeper than unfair; it was simply the way it was. Men had always admired warriors, women had always admired men, which only showed how peculiar was human taste whatever the sex.

"Can I sit on your lap, Shan?" said a little boy in a red rain slicker and black Wellington boots, dressed for the storm that seemed to be coming. He was yellow-haired, with small teeth on either side of an impressive gap, and his eyes were pale blue and pink-rimmed, as though he had been crying.

"Why, of course," she said, pulled by some instinct of neighborliness and compassion, imagining that the girl she was supposed to be undoubtedly knew him, probably liked children, and had room on her lap. In truth as he scrambled upwards onto the promontory of her knees, and settled himself comfortably in the curved trough of her thighs, she realized she had been a little cold and that his small, bony body warmed her.

"You look right with a child on your lap," murmured Miles, from a few inches away, while on the platform the king exhorted Rosencrantz and Guildenstern to spy on the prince and report why he was crazy.

"Do I?" she said.

"Though we shouldn't have one right away," said Miles. "After all, there's a whole world of exploring you'll want to do in London."

"Are you going to London?" the little boy asked her.

"What's your name, son?" Miles asked.

"Jackie."

"Now, Jackie, do you understand what's going on here?"

For a moment Darcy was afraid that Miles was about to teach the boy the basic tenets of seduction. Understanding as little as she did about male networking, she imagined that the civilians among them, those who were not princes of the realm or rulers of nations, could not wait to exchange sexual gossip, since it was the only real power they had, dominion over women.

"Up there . . ." Miles pointed to the platform which local carpenters, under the direction of the Criccieth Tourist Association, had constructed for the presentation of the play. " . . . a great drama is unfolding, while down here" — he circled the air with his finger, including himself and the boy and Darcy — "a little romantic comedy is being played. All of it about secrets. The king . . ." (he pointed to the stage again) "has very dark and evil secrets. Shan and I, on the other hand, have very bright and sweet ones."

"Why is it a comedy?" Darcy asked, trying not to be too offended. But Vanity cast aside notwithstanding, she was still the star of her own show, and didn't see anything funny about it.

"Is she going to London?" the little boy asked again.

"Why, we don't know, and anyway it's all pretend, and we lose the game if anyone tells. So you will keep the secret, Jackie?"

"You have any candy?" said the boy, who had already learned what it was to have an advantage.

"I shall get you some during the break," said Miles.

"Why a comedy?" Darcy said again.

"Because there is no tragic hero with a fatal flaw," said Miles. "Because there is nothing grave at stake here, and no one will die."

"Nothing grave at stake?" she said. "And what is the heart of a woman? What is her life?"

"At least it would be a comedy if girls knew how to have a better time," Miles said, tweaking the boy on his nose, and dashing up to the platform for his entrance.

"But how could I even consider running away with him, when his only concern is himself?" Darcy said to the blackbird outside her open window; the bird stared back at her, beady-eyed. "Imagine his implying that the fault is mine, when there isn't even a fault yet! Setting me up to take the brunt of the failure when it happens, because it always does, because it has to. There isn't a love in the world that can last. And isn't it amazing how they blame us before it even has a chance to go wrong?"

The blackbird, cocking its head as though taking it all in, stood for a moment on the white painted fence near the windowbox, and then raced up to the eaves of the roof opposite, pecking in what seemed a visible show of impatience, until another blackbird came out. And then the first blackbird began railing in a tone not unlike that Darcy had used, while the other bird tried, vainly, to get away. She chased him, unforgiving. "You tell him," said Darcy.

In the kitchen, to her sort of surprise, all was more or less in order, the charred chicken having been disposed of, the lamb for that evening quite neatly prepared and waiting to be cooked, salted and peppered, as the butcher had instructed, with some diced mushrooms on the side for making it even more special. The wedding dress soiled by the royal guards (did she feel at all like returning to Perq to see that they were punished? was revenge as savory as freedom?) soaked in the deep, narrow tub at the side of the room, the mud they had thrown her in floating to the surface of the water like fat in gravy. Darcy had never before seen dirt actually lifting from fabric, something coming unsoiled. In its way, it was actually interesting, like the domestic version of one of Dante's circles of hell. The unknown, no matter how simple, was still the unknown, and, therefore, fascinating as it unraveled. So a feeling of accomplishment was setting in for this young woman whose only previous achievements had been laid out for her by the state: nodding, giving the royal imprimatur to certain events, lifting the spirits of those who wanted to see a princess. But as she had not in her young adult life so much as closed a button on one of her dresses, much less washed it, there was an undisguisable feeling of virtue in what she was doing.

A distant ancestor of Darcy's had been a Pilgrim, watering her way to the New World on the *Mayflower*, armed with one family jewel and the Protestant ethic. No one knew what had happened to the jewel (an emerald) but once a year, without fail, Darcy would get a printed card from the descendant, exhorting her to remember the pleasure that came from a day's work well done. Always it had seemed to her a kind of recrimination, a finger pointed at her privileged shortcomings. But now that she had actually done a day's work — or half of it: the lamb had still to be cooked, the dress to be hung up and dried — feelings of well-being and self-esteem percolated in her.

She checked the progress of the bud in her windowbox, gave

it an extra slug of water for good measure, waited for the sound of the "Glub," which came, but not so thirstily. And feeling so much a part of the life she now lived as to be proprietary and even jingoistic, she went out to explore her (well, who would know it wasn't) birthplace. There was a bank and a post office, pharmacy, and shops, and most touchingly, for her whose people had lost it, a nine-hole miniature golf Pitch and Putt course, where, gloomy though the day was, people played. Oh, how sweet were the freedoms people took for granted on the shores of Snowdonia.

For though the Tourist Information Center across from Memorial Hall might have seemed a bit boastful of its tiny brochure, in which it spoke of Criccieth as "The Pearl of Wales," Darcy thought it was not really inappropriate. A pearl was simply something lovely that had sprung from irritation. She was having the best experience of her life as a result of having been annoyed with her lot. Privilege, real privilege she considered now, was a day in which you could do anything you wanted, once the laundry and marketing were over with. So she practically skipped along the High Street, low as it might have seemed to those who had danced at royal balls.

Still, enthusiasm being a new avenue for her, it was not long till she exhausted her exploration, the High Street having come to an end. Her inner resources being freshly pried open, as a can of sardines with an old-fashioned key, one that breaks off as the lid is peeled halfway back, a light cloud of "What to do now?" blew over her. This combined with her budding lust, and her very short memory, which all women have when it comes to infatuation. So forgetting she was angry with Miles, in quite quick order she found herself back in the courtyard of the castle, heart racing, which could not be accounted for by what was, according to the most perspicacious appraisal of the CADW (Welsh Historic Monuments), a very short climb.

And there was Miles, soliloquizing, his infatuation with the language (as he had translated it) and the gifts of the original poet carrying him to greater heights than would Criccieth Castle.

Darcy had seen the play in nearly every language of every country she had visited, including a Polish *Hamlet*, and a production by a troup of touring lesbians, who had presented *Hamlet, Princess of Denmark*. So she recognized that he was doing the "To be or not to be" speech. In her inner ears, she could hear the rush of her own blood, the drumming of her pulse, the words, translated, becoming "To flee or not to flee." Having discovered freedom, should she abandon it? For to place herself in the pocket of an actor would put her no less in thrall than she had been with Rodney, except without the wardrobe.

"Are you going away?" Jackie, the little boy in the red oilcloth slicker asked, his freckled face shiny, tilted up to her. His eyes were welling with tears.

"Oh, but Jackie, I haven't made up my mind. And what would be so terrible if I did?"

"You mustn't go," he said, and the tears spilled over. "Dad said my mum only went away because she had to. He said no one else was going to leave me."

"But I wouldn't be leaving *you*," she said, and wondered all at once whom she would be leaving. If it would be only Tom, or maybe also the woman she was just starting to be. "Come," she said, and took the boy up on her lap, felt the knobbiness of his flat little bottom, wondered if perhaps one day soon she could buy something to cook that would stick a bit more to the ribs, and whether she could invite him. "Let's watch the play."

But the boy turned his head away from the stage, and looked across the battlements towards the bay. He shivered, and fear yellowed his pale eyes. And the shiver became a tremble that shook him, from toe to head. And he pressed his face against her breasts, and hid his eyes.

"What's wrong?" she asked, putting her arms around him.

"It's out there," he said.

"What is?"

"They said it might come back," he whispered. "And it did. It's out there. In the bay."

* * *

Now did the lovely bogus Darcy awaken late, and with the oddest feeling in her breasts. Since Shan's coming to Perq there had been any number of formal events, official duties, the posing of the romantically fateful Christmas cards, and various other princessly activities that had precluded a sleep-in. But this radiant morning for some reason (none that she could know of, since Rachid had gotten Rhea to spike her cocoa, and after that importuned the entire staff to let the princess rest undisturbed) Shan had been allowed to loll, and loll she did, moving up to wakefulness in quilted little steps. With a sigh here, and a deep inhale of luxuriant pleasure there, she stretched and yawned her way back to her blissful, incredible reality, rubbing her shoulder blades exquisitely against the royal blue satin sheets, turning over and doing the same for her breasts.

Her nipples felt stiff. It was a most peculiar sensation, one she was used to having brought about by the fingerstrokes and (crafty little prince that he was) tongue caresses of a lover. So to have it built in, and in the morning, with her supposed husband absent (lovely as it was between them, he always slept in his own quarters) gave her a bit of wonder. Why, she speculated, should her breasts be in any way sore, when passionate though the prince was, he was always so gentle? Faithful as she'd been to Tom, once Miles had vanished from her life, she was used to a man's love being rough, without subtlety. But her prince came to her all silkily swathed, from his nightclothes, to his fingertips, to his aristocratic member, which seemed satin-cloaked, as though presented with documents tied with ribbon, proving its pedigree. That which rose from its royal sheath seemed less a snake than fine baton, about to conduct a classical symphony.

And oh, if excitement and innovation were the rubies of romance, then crowned she was in more places than one. For it was as if he were discovering her for the first time (which he was, but he couldn't accept that, still worrying that she was trying to deceive him, telling him she wasn't Darcy). And nothing he could do, or imagine, or try to imagine doing, was too much, when it came to this girl that he adored. That was what he said, all the time, against her hair, between her breasts, in the crook of her elbow, and everywhere else there was room for him to speak into. "I adore you," he would say, and proceed to demonstrate how he did. But always sweetly, nothing of the Welshman about him, fierce, albeit in a loving way. He was gentleness and gentry incarnate — fitting and proper for him, terribly joyful for her. Good girl that she was, and raised well, faithful wife that she had been, hardly even dreaming of Miles, she loved making love with her prince. With gusto and surprisingly little guilt. For Destiny had placed her in the royal bed, and she was supposed to learn, and she was in the art of love an avid scholar. It seemed to her, quite without making excuses, that if her body so warmed to a stranger, perhaps women were not built to be with just one friend.

Still, it puzzled her that her nipples would be sore. She rang for her lady-in-waiting and told Junella to draw her bath. On the threshold of the tub Shan took off her royal wrapper, and noted the strange, powdery gray residue at the tip of each breast. Slipping into the low pink marble bath, she watched with surprise as a piece of gray plaster floated up out of her bellybutton.

"Are you using a new toothpaste?" she asked Rodney, sotto voce, at luncheon. It was more or less a family gathering, consisting of the prince and the (purported) princess, Queen Isabel, and Rachid, who had taken to openly holding the queen's hand at mealtime, and sometimes, it was unavoidably concluded, her knee.

"Why no," he said, lifting his crystal water glass and sipping.

"It's just that I found this . . ." She waited for Isabel and Rachid to seem immersed in each other's conversation before saying very softly, ". . . peculiar lint in my bellybutton."

But quietly as she spoke, Queen Isabel heard. "Darcy dear, there are some things we do not discuss at table, if we've been well brought up."

"It's like farting," said Rachid.

"We who have been well brought up do not even say *farting*," said the prince, contemptuously. "Had you not been raised in a sewer, and had you had the good fortune to spend quality time with my father the king, you might have made off with his manners, instead of his country."

"Rodney, dear, please. We who have been well brought up do not discuss usurping at table."

"And why not, madam? Nostalgia is always in good taste. I remember when you had a consort who elevated you with his affection, instead of one who rolled you in the mud."

"Mud is very sexy," said Rachid, picking his teeth with a gold toothpick.

"Rodent," said Rodney.

"Pay no attention," Isabel said to Rachid. "He isn't himself."

"I am very much myself. It is the head of the table who is not himself."

"Perhaps we should call in the doctor," said Isabel.

"The doctor is not himself," said Rachid.

"Oh, all this talk of those who are not themselves," said Isabel.

"Including you, madam," said Rodney. "For were you yourself you could not cavort with this slug who is not fit to fill so much as my father's toilet."

"Rodney, please . . . ," said the queen.

"I am sore to the heart that you are my mother, even though you can't really be my mother since you are not yourself."

"Anyone else?" said Isabel.

"Well, there's me," said Shan. "I am most certainly not myself. That is to say, I am myself, but not the myself you think me to be, since I'm not Darcy. So of all those here who are not themselves, I am the one who is most genuinely not myself, being just a simple girl from Criccieth."

"I'm tired of this game," said Isabel. "I like it better when we play charades."

"But in my case, it is not a game, Majesty," Shan said. "I am not now nor have I ever been a member of the royal family."

"Don't let her give any interviews till this has passed," said Isabel. "That's all the press has to find out — that Darcy has gone crackers. I can see the headlines in '*W.*'"

"The fashion newspaper!" said Shan, with some pleasure, since she did so love accumulating useless information and being able to give it back unexpectedly.

"And how would you know that, being a simple girl from Wales?" said Isabel.

"Why Darcy told me, just before we changed dresses."

"Keep her away from the press," said Isabel. "What have we got for dessert?"

"Chocolate soufflé," said Rhea, coming in from the kitchen, carrying the soufflé. "But the center's a little caved in. The eggs weren't fluffy enough."

"Probably," said Rachid, "the chickens weren't themselves."

After lunch, Rodney took his princess into the royal gardens, to feed the swans. Rhea had given them what was left of the somewhat collapsed soufflé, as the swans were particularly fond of rich desserts and not known to be overly critical. They glided in figure-eight patterns on the pond, which was itself figure-eightish, because Rachid had had all the waterways in the kingdom, with the exception of the Falls, redesigned. He disliked round bodies of water, since he was trying in every way to escape the dogmas of his youth, especially that which had filtered into the Middle East and his family, of karma. Simplified, it boiled down to "What goes around comes around." The mere idea that what you sent out you got back terrified and affronted Rachid, since that was no consciousness for a villain. So he had had lakes and ponds and fountains recast in the form of an "8," according to the ancient Cabala, the number for overcoming subconscious forces, which in his case was the conviction that he'd be punished for his wickedness. Any man who could change the course (even *still*) of nature had nothing to fear from a spiritual principle. So it was that the swans had to sail in a figure-eight-shaped pond. What a far-reaching villainy was this that set even a handsome prince and his lady by the side of a pond that wasn't a pond exactly.

Still there were slender-stalked reeds, and moss and marguerite daisies on the banks for them to sit in, as they tossed little pieces of chocolate to the eager, rapacious swans. The day was penny bright, copper around its edges, warming to the skin.

"Oh, I do love being here," Shan said, resting her head against his knee. "I do love being with you."

"Then why do you want to embarrass me?" Rodney said. "Why make me look like the fool?"

"But I don't. I haven't."

"What do you think it does when you tell them you're not Darcy?"

"But I'm not."

"It's a terrible game you play, Darcy, and a dangerous one. I love you better and deeper than ever I have, and you know it."

"I know you love me well and deep for now. But I have no comparison from before."

"Why do you stubbornly stick to that story?"

"Because it's the truth," she said.

"But the truth does good, and there can be nothing but harm come from such a tale. People will think you don't love and respect me and you don't care about Perq."

"But I do. How could I not?"

"Then just be a quiet, good girl," he said, and patted her corn-silky hair, cupped his hand to the back of her neck and soothed the pain that women have, the strain of wanting not to seem needy, even though they are. The effort of trying not to look as though they crave comfort, when they do. All of it compromising their natural excellence and the muscles at the tops of their shoulders.

So what was Shan to do now? For it was clear to her in a diffused way that she had fallen into a tub of buttery romance. Good girl that she was (it rather annoyed her to have Rodney imprecate her to be what she'd always been), she knew what her moral obligations were. Those were clearly to her husband. But was not Rodney now her husband, and more her husband than he'd ever been Darcy's, from the way he told it? And was she not in fact saving him? For if indeed the prince she had met that first day was as he seemed, he'd been dangerously close to wimpdom, that crashing loss of masculine strength that any man needed for even a dog to look up to him, much less a populace. So wasn't she doing a good greater than her own desires, even though she desired him? Wasn't she putting a nation at the top of her priorities? Wouldn't his collapse, if she failed to be there to love him, result in the fall of Perq? Who was there but the loathsome Rachid to take over, since the king was a sot, and in Switzerland. Why, it was a case of complete self-sacrifice, or would have been if she hadn't been having such a good time.

And what was wrong with a woman's doing what made her happy, especially if it was lifting everyone else? Well, almost everyone else. She felt in her heart that Isabel didn't really like her, and knew Rachid's turquoise eyes glittered black at the sight of their being so happy together.

And then, of course, there was Tom. Dear Tom. She hadn't even thought about him, so caught up was she in her adventure. Her sweet, good husband, dismissed from the mind like a terrier sent to the kennel while the family went traveling. What was he doing without her? Or, was he not without her? Was Darcy as good a replacement there as Shan was being here? Maybe you could best fill the needs of those who didn't really know you, and you didn't really know, because you came to them fresh, with the enthusiasm of an explorer. Perhaps all love needed to be love again was not being taken for granted.

Oh, it was all such heady stuff, headier for being not connected to the head at all, but the heart and the loins. For nothing made any sense in love, but love itself. Sense was the very last post in the fence, really, the least essential ingredient in romance. Sense mattered little when what really counted were the senses.

And how she did drink him in, the stateliness, the elegance, the subtlety, the silkiness, and not least of all the gratitude. For there was something so touching in seeing a royal humbled, noting how mindful he was of her contribution to his restored confidence and horniness. For a man who was not loved, whether prince or commoner, had only his calling to measure himself by, which was not the same as a pair of eyes that exalted.

And she'd been so busy! Why, she hadn't had to do a thing with Tom, except be there, ready when he was. Making love with Tom was like riding on a bus: all she had to do was get on. Tom was in charge, Tom would see they got to their destination. But she had so much to contribute to Rodney. As delicious to the touch as he was, he was fragile, the sad example of his father, perhaps, having undercut his belief in himself, whatever the circumstances had been with the real Darcy lopping off what was left of his hardihood. He had come to Shan that first night when she turned him away a broken young man. What a joy it was to know that with a few movements, a kiss, a well-applied pressure, you could restore what a man needed most, to feel he was a man.

It was all so *interesting*, besides passionate. With all that the duchess had managed to pass on to her of correct conduct, and pouring tea, she had said not a word about making love among the royals. And in Shan's most humble opinion, that was absolutely key. For they were in the sheets (satin or not satin) only creatures of the flesh, and vulnerable. It was a restoration she was doing, really, as valuable as the ceiling of a chapel. Artful. Saintly, perhaps. Maybe even God's work, if God had had the patience of a loving woman, and not so many crises to deal with in a day.

"Oh, I do love you, Rodney," Shan said, for his fingers had reached the back of her neck.

"Then you will say no more that you aren't Darcy?" he said, and leaned to kiss her.

"If it pleases you," she sighed. And they kissed and she thought how very like were men and women in that neither of them wanted to hear what wouldn't make them happy. Longing for intimacy, but only insofar as it would make them physically intimate and not reveal what they didn't want to know.

"Now this is what I call a proper dinner!" Tom said, exultant.

He had scrubbed his face and his hands on coming home to a house that was not disordered, brushed his hair, wet it, parted it neatly on the left, so he looked quite a bit like the schoolboy

Darcy imagined he had been when Shan first met him. There was a sweetness about him, so, with his hair all slicked back, and his collar properly buttoned, as though he were paying court to her for cleaning up and presenting a meal that wasn't burned. So would men always be thankful for what they previously considered their due, if only women would be smart enough to hold out on them.

"What's in the bay?" she asked him as she lit the candle on the table, the roseate glow softening their faces, and the food and drink between them.

"Water."

"Don't play with me, Tom. What's out there?"

"You've lived in this village long as I have. You know the stories same as I do. It's just superstition. Those fools with their boats and their nets dragged Loch Ness last summer, and what did they find? The same that's in Cardigan Bay."

"There's a monster?"

"No more a monster than was found in the Loch. Poor son of a bitch, and what did he ever do to hurt anybody? And what would have happened if they found him?" He skewered a forkful of meat, and tasted. "This lamb is perfect."

"Thank you," she said, and felt herself blushing to the very roots of her hair, with pleasure and, though she had lost Vanity, just a *touch* of pride.

"The things that are in the bottom of the sea should stay in the bottom of the sea, and it's only nets and asking too many questions that gets them restless."

"Has anyone ever seen it?"

"Did you make potatoes?" Tom asked.

"Should I have?"

"I suppose I'm glad enough to be eating what doesn't spurt bladders."

"I'll make potatoes tomorrow," she said. "And if it's all right with you, I'd like to invite Jackie to have supper with us soon. I think he's missing his mother."

"Well, that's kind of you, Shan. But then what were you ever but kind, except for these past days when I was afraid you were crazy."

"Crazy?" she said, wondering what there had been in her behavior that was other than adorable, except for not knowing how to cook. For as Miles saying their romance was a comedy had offended her, so did Tom's characterizing as lunatic what was merely incompetent. Was it sanity just to do things exactly the way men wanted them? Was that how they assessed rationality? Oh, it made her so angry she wished she hadn't turned out such a fine chef.

Still, the food started to warm her belly, the lager her cheeks, and the nourishment made its way into her system like assimilated truth. She felt really cozy being there with him, by the candlelight, and the fire he had started in the grate.

"I don't think it was you, Shan, made yourself crazy, understand. I was afraid . . . meeting that princess . . . made you dissatisfied . . . and then . . . him coming back . . ."

"Are you talking about . . . *Miles?*" she said, with exaggerated disbelief, and when he nodded, laughed. It was the royal laugh, a little hollow with no regard for the feelings of the struggling, but it was the only laugh she had at her disposal. "You have to have more faith in me, Tom," she managed to say with more conviction than was in her laughter.

"Do I?"

"You have to have more faith in yourself."

"Oh, I have plenty of faith in what is faithful," he said.

"And you don't think Shan is a faithful woman?"

"You're a woman," he said. "So whatever happens isn't your fault. The victories nor the blame neither."

"I must say that's a pretty attitude," said Darcy, huffily. Much as she loved being excused before she did anything wrong she didn't like having the credit taken away in the event she was going to do something noble.

"I'm a man," he said. "My attitudes don't have to be pretty."

"Well, they don't need to be stupid!"

"Are you calling me stupid?"

"Not you. Your attitude!"

"Well, speaking of attitude," he said, "you ought not to be allowed out of the house, for you have but to trip into the chamber of a princess and you're all at once grander than she is."

"I am no grander," she said, furious. "But I am certainly as grand!" And throwing her fork down, clattering some lamb to the (not very fine) linen, she pushed her chair back and fled from the table.

Well, the terrible thing about being poor was there weren't that many places to hide. No lock on the bedroom door, so she couldn't seal herself in there, and, anyway, she had had just about her fill of being upended, which seemed to be Tom's way of closing every argument. Nor could she lock the door in the bathroom. In the end she had run down the stairs, and again down the narrow shallow stairway into the kitchen. She flung the casement windows wide, and took a whiff of evening, pressed her cheek against the fullness of the hydrangea blossoms to calm herself. Her heart was beating very fast, and she wondered if it was all the activity (although there were certainly more stairs to climb, and often, in the castle at Perq) or if it was just excitement at being allowed to make scenes. In Perq, of course, it was nothing a princess did. Even Darcy's distaste for Rodney had never been outwardly expressed, as the most she was allowed to do (it had been in premarital agreement) was turn away, and then while still smiling for the press.

Having had her half-day filled with the drama at the castle, with ghosts and incestuous longings and murders, she was really up for what was exploding inside her, Tom's not taking her seriously, plus her sense of personal outrage at hearing this great love she was on the brink of — and she was sure that was what it was with Miles, nothing less than a great love — characterized as comedy. Where was the Oscar Wilde for women? Why was it only *they* who had the love that dared not speak its name? Why couldn't women's sweet little agonies be so immortalized? The love that dared not seem too aggressive. The love that dared not look too eager. The heart that dared not be too open. And the legs the same.

Just then, she looked down, and saw that the second bud had come to flower. The light, though it was the whitish night of Welsh summer, was not so bright that she could make out all the details of the blossom without straining her eyes. Leaning down, she saw that, once again, it was the shape of a foxglove, but pink this time, with what looked like a cupid's bow where the top petals joined. As she moved her face closer, the lips widened into a smile, like a baby's, toothless but full of pleasure at being so attended. Touching it with the pinky of her left hand, for so tiny was the blossom that her fingers, delicate as they were, were too big to fit inside, Darcy thought she heard the tinkle of laughter, the being-tickled kind. And peering to the flower, she saw a little round belly, heaving gently, paroxysms of amusement shaking it up and down.

A sudden wave of appetite came over her, as during a goodwill tour when she felt in the grip of too many demands, she would wolf down a fistful of chocolate mints. So although she was not given to anthropophagy, she ate it.

A spreading elation from the region of her belly to her limbs and her lips and her fingertips suffused her. And she was laughing, and dancing in place, as though the world were indeed a merry spot, created for the pleasure of its inhabitants.

"Are you all right?" Tom was in the doorway, an expression of concern on his no longer placid face.

"But what could I be but all right?" she asked him. "What could happen in a kitchen?"

"Well, you could burn yourself or cut yourself, or as in this case go nutty."

"Oh, sweet Tom," she said, and flung her arms around his neck, and tickled him with her breasts. "Why must you be so dour?"

"Well, what am I supposed to be, with life being so hard, and nothing coming easy but sorrow. And the sweet, pretty woman

I love putting on airs and my not knowing what's happening to her, or to us, or to anything. Am I supposed to be laughing at all that?"

"Of course," she said, and rocked them both with her new-found laughter, which was not hollow at all, but came from the bottom of her heart. For she had eaten the flower that healed Taking Things Too Seriously.

And quite without meaning to, stunned by this outburst of merriment, Tom himself started to laugh. At first nervously, because he was sure she was crazy. And then because it sounded so good, he could not help but want to join in. For laughter is truly contagious, especially when it has just healed a disease, which in Darcy's case was terminal gravity.

"Oh, it's good to have you acting like my Shan again," he said, and squeezed her good-naturedly.

"Was I always this happy-hearted?" she asked him, not without a little twinge of envy, for although she was living the other's life and full to the brim, she could not help but covet the part that had eluded her. Having natural grace and beauty and all the privilege that had accrued as a result did not make up in Darcy's mind for what she didn't have. She was certain this other girl was contented all the time. Wasn't she?

"Why, you know full well there is not a gladder person on this earth," he said and hugged her. "That's the reason people want to be around you, and the man who has you is happy as a king."

"Well, a prince, anyway," Darcy said.

Now late that night, when the full humor of her humors was upon her, and Tom's rhythmic breathing was gently machine-gunning her ear, Darcy crept out of bed. Throwing his big woolly coat on, for the house was extremely damp, and the air felt chill, Darcy went down to the kitchen, an inexplicable gnawing in the base of her belly. Throwing open the casement window, she peered into the windowbox, hoping that another seed had flowered. For such had been the salutary effects of the two she had eaten thus far, that she had an absolute hunger for the next. A blossoming addiction, as it were. For it is not only the wicked things that hook us in this life, but the beneficent ones as well. More of those than the other, if we're lucky.

But alas, Grace takes its own time in coming, like the telephone company. No other bud had flowered. Disappointed and a bit famished, she gave the bud another slug of water. Then she drank from the watering can herself, holding the spout in the air and letting a stream of liquid arc into her mouth, as though it were a *bota* at a bullfight in Barcelona, where several bulls had been pledged to her and she was appalled to receive an ear.

Restless, she wondered what Miles was doing. The skies had grown somewhat dark, as it was nearly eleven, but there was still enough light to mark the progress of the clouds. They streamed in thick cumulus clumps towards the south, as though being sucked into a funnel, light gray just above where she stood, deepening into darker clusters as they moved towards the shore. She felt a sudden impulse to follow them, and putting on her slippers, purple velvet with soft soles, probably Shan's single extravagance, went outside.

On the cobblestoned street, all was silence. The tunneling clouds moved inexorably towards the horizon. The bay, moonless as the night was, shimmered silver. For such was the miracle of summer nights in the United Kingdom that you could see without benefit of lights, as some people do, passing through their entire lives without seeing anything.

As unused as Darcy was to introspection, there having been little reason to look inside, since what was on the outside had shown her such a glamorous time, she could not help noting that something wonderfully strange was happening to her. Besides learning to laugh at herself, and life in general, and not caring anymore about how she looked, she had a growing curiosity about what was going on. For a young woman whose entire young adulthood had been spent simply fulfilling obligations and being doted on, to be interested in things outside herself made her her own kind of pilgrim, off on an adventure there was no precedent for in any of her circles, which were by definition and shape, self-centered. Simply by being interested, she was finding the world more interesting.

Yet with all the excitement she was starting to feel, an aliveness that bordered on joy (well, she wasn't quite ready for absolute joy yet, since she wasn't sure what would happen with Miles), there was an undercurrent of danger, and she knew it. Something powerful and awesome moved around her, with the flow of the clouds overhead. Something glittered darkly beneath the surface of the bay.

Standing at the edge of the stone steps that led down to the pebbled shore, she grasped the metal railing, and looked out at the water. And a bubble of restlessness rose in her breast, and she wondered what she was doing there, so far from the safety of a really warm bed, and people who coddled and cajoled.

And a chill went through her, struck to the bone. She held her arms around herself, and shivered. She heard a terrible noise, which she thought at first was the sound of her teeth chattering. Then she realized it was somewhere out in the bay, a clanking, deep, sorrowful sound, as metal striking metal, like chinks in armor. And there was a fearsome howl, and from the depths of the water, a shudder that shook the very place where she stood.

And the clouds whipped black like a cloak round the shoulders of a man who was angry and unloved. And a funnel of darkness whooshed through the sky, and curled down into the bay, turning it to ink. And a flash of lightning split the air, and illuminated — No! Could it be? Were her eyes deceiving her?

For there seemed to rise from the depths of the dark, an ugly, horrible head, more dreadful than dragons, twice as grotesque as Gorgons, lion-faced with fearsome brows, sickeningly scaled, glowing dark green against the suddenly blackened night. And it opened its hideous jaws and bellowed, and its snakelike tongue licked the air. The long iridescent neck stretched towards the skies, the mouth opened, breathed in, and swallowed the clouds, clamped them inside the dripping teeth.

Darcy choked back a scream and raced through the empty

streets, ran inside her house, and up the stairs. She flung herself into Tom's chest, burrowed her face into the welcoming warmth of his armpit. "Huh?" he said, half-waking.

"It's true," she whimpered against the comforting, silky hairs. "It's true."

"What is?"

"There's something out there. In the bay."

"You're dreaming." He patted her head. "Go back to sleep."

"I'm not dreaming. I couldn't sleep, so I went for a walk, and I saw the monster."

"There is no monster." He seemed to come awake suddenly, sat up, and turned on the lamp by the bed. "You were out in the street like that? In the middle of the night?" It seemed a grievous accusation, since the nights didn't start until eleven thirty and the sun came up just after four. So to catch the middle of the night, a woman would have to be really ready for mischief. Suspicion chewed the edges of his lids. "You went to meet Miles!"

"Oh, for Heaven's sake. I saw the monster!"

"There is no bloody monster."

"It's got a long, scaly neck and its teeth are dripping venom."

"Well, I haven't seen him for a while, but that sounds like Miles, all right."

"You're impossible," she said, and went under the quilt, the coat still around her.

"No. What's impossible is your story. What happened to the sweet, truthful girl I married?"

"She's gone to Perq," Darcy said, sitting up. "I'm the royal princess."

6

JUST BEFORE SHE SLIPPED into unconsciousness, the patient etherized on the table, who was not part of a T. S. Eliot poem, or, in the strictest sense, etherized, asked that she be reborn with love in her heart. Babara, strangely spelled as everyone in Southern California enjoyed having their names, so the shops were filled with Joodis, had been heavily premedicated and given a shot of Brevitol in the IV in her hand, just before the surgeon directed the injection of the novocaine in her chest. In addition to the IV there were earphones in her delicate ears, to further anaesthetize her, into which was fed conversation from several recent Beverly Hills dinner parties.

The nurse attending the operation was not particularly impressed that Princess Darcy of Perq lay on the table. The surgeon had done many leading movie stars, the closest thing America had to royalty, and the nurse herself had been made over to look like Grace Kelly without troublesome children. Besides her newly aristocratic veneer, the nurse wore a mantle of secrecy, since the thing a plastic surgeon needed most, after good hands, was the reputation of confidentiality. So the nurse felt quite the insider, knowing how trusted she was, and was more impressed with herself than with the royal patient, who of course was not the royal patient but the girl who had been made over to look like Darcy. But the nurse didn't know that, so she wasn't as smart or as trusted as she thought she was. But what should she have expected in a plastic world, but two faces?

"They're going to be perfect," said the plastic surgeon. "Her crowning glories, if I may be permitted a pun."

"As long as it doesn't cost extra," said Adrian, who had flown to Los Angeles on Rachid's private jet, under cover of darkness (also Rachid's), with plaster impressions of the princess's breasts. Or so he thought.

It was an operating room tenanted by people none of whom knew who the others really were, including the plaster and plastic parts of them. And saddest of all was the girl on the table, who had no idea who she herself was, which was why, as little regard as she had for life, she asked to be reborn with love in her heart.

Surgeon, anaesthesiologist, nurse, and the toadying Adrian, who'd been introduced as a consultant, since it was clearly a violation of ethics to have an outsider present, were all dressed in their surgical greens. The surgery was taking place in the doctor's own office, as with the exception of tummy tucks and serious disfigurings, there was little that couldn't be handled there. It was amazing to Adrian how matter-of-factly the whole procedure had been handled, considering the fate of a nation hung, or in this case, lifted, in the balance.

Nor had the casual manner in which the surgery took place been lost on Babara, even floating in and out of awareness as she was. When the surgeon had done her eyes and her nose, reshaped her mouth and given her that little dimple of pleasure to the right of her lips, she'd been stunned in a Valiumed kind of way to hear him and his anaesthesiologist discussing stereo equipment as they worked. She had nearly cried out — or wanted to — for them to pay attention to her, the closest she'd felt to self-esteem since she'd looked in the mirror at sixteen and decided she wasn't anybody.

Although several years had gone by, that attitude had deepened, fermented, and solidified. So when the opportunity arose to become somebody else, she welcomed it, as those who dislike themselves imagine with a better nose the world will beat a path to their nostrils. Only afterwards do they discover, to their great disappointment, that a nose is a nose is a nose.

Still, when you weren't anybody to begin with, or thought you weren't and never would be, to become somebody else was extremely desirable. In like manner, after the initial impulse to preserve herself by asking the doctor to think about her face and not where he was going to get his new speakers, Babara decided that music and his enjoyment of it were more important than her life and/or possible mutilation. So instead of protesting, she simply salted away the information, and determined she would buy hers in the same place when the time came to switch over to compact disc, which she would soon be able to afford.

According to the arrangement she'd made with Adrian and whoever was bankrolling him, she would get increased increments to her original fee for every scandal she was able to generate in the guise of Princess Darcy. It was, as Adrian explained it to her, a variation on the old mode of explorers, who would arrive at a new place and say, "I claim this land for Spain!" Hers was to be "I claim this scandal for Darcy!"

Adrian had made it clear she would not have to sleep with anybody, since she did draw the line at whore, but only gain the reputation of slut. "Slut" was not offensive to Babara, either as a word or a category. Often she had been tempted to put it down on applications, next to the blank for "Occupation." For there was something romantic about "slut," really, when you got down to it, something eighteenth century and Moll Flandersish, full of portent of thieving, and being undone by the landowner's son. To the sentimental heart, which hers would have been, were it not so tight and strained, disappointment and lack of love having hardened and shrunk it to a walnut, "slut" seemed almost outgoing. Besides, the actual label would have nothing to do with her, because who would be the slut was the woman she was in the process of becoming, one for whom she had no particular esteem. Since she did not esteem herself, how could she esteem anyone else, especially as she was going to seem the person she didn't esteem either?

She did, however, feel the slightest bit of envy for Darcy, as her life, according to the evidence, was perfect and charmed. Like a number of people with low self-image, Babara spent a lot of time at supermarket checkstands, buying food she would chew and spit out into the toilet. Standing there, leafing through scandalpapers and magazines, she would read stories about how unhappy the people with everything really were, calculated to make people with nothing feel good, except that they were just as unhappy and nobody ever wrote about them. So she was totally up to date on every fashion statement and trip and excess of Darcy, every party in her honor, and her perfect romance/marriage. The only thing she did not envy her was her bone structure, which a beneficent nature had given Babara in kind. Fabulous cheekbones, high forehead, and a majestic jaw were gifts that, although she did not prize them highly, had brought her to the attention of Adrian's scouts.

She had had her features altered, and her name fixed, and just before this latest operation she had written to the Association of Astrologers to petition to have her sign changed, since she was sure that most of her sorrow stemmed from being a Taurus. Now that she was having her breasts augmented and was on her way to becoming a slut, she imagined, even with all the novocaine shot into her chest, that she could actually feel her life changing.

"They look great!" said the surgeon, who found it hard to believe how much ugliness he could stamp out in a single day.

"When will she be able to use them?" Adrian asked.

"Well, I'll take the sutures out in ten days. She can have sex after that, but gentle sex. Nothing strenuous."

"I'm not talking about sex!" said Adrian contemptuously. "We're talking about intrigue here. When will they look good?"

"I think they look good now," said the plastic surgeon. "But in a month she can run naked through the woods."

"Woods," Adrian repeated, and wondered if he should use that scene for the layout. "A month," he mused, and tried to figure the closing date for the *Playhouse* Centerfold. "The bellybutton, too?"

As wave by wave Babara drifted to the surface, with her low regard half-asleep, she felt little pops of self-preservation, like a diver decompressing. And she wanted to say, "Who are you people, and why have I put myself in your hands?" But doubt and fear and negativity came back so instead she said, "Who am I?"

"That's a good one," said the surgeon. "Most people say 'Where am I?' "

"I know where I am," Babara said, having been there before.

"Who's president?" asked the plastic surgeon, for once the amusing nature of her question had passed, he considered the possibility that something bizarre had happened under the anaesthesia, and was checking her out for *compos mentis*.

"Nobody," Babara said.

"I guess she's okay," said the anaesthesiologist.

Sensibility, far-off mountain peaks covered with snow that one has to strain to see, seeped back into her consciousness, and she began to feel pain. "Why do I hurt?" she said.

"Because you're alive," said the plastic surgeon.

"Oh," said Babara, disappointed. But all at once she saw Adrian, and something kindled in her. For one cannot ask, even under Brevitol, to be reborn with love in the heart, without risking that taking place. No prayer comes back unanswered. It's just that a lot of the time the answer is "No."

In this case, the universe had sent Babara a carom shot, giving her love in her heart for a flunky, a parasite, an ambassador without portfolio and in this case also without principle. But he did have very nice eyes, and she saw them above his spurious surgical mask, and interpreted the look of cupidity in them as longing. Imagining him to be one of the surgical team, her fancy filled with Pygmalion scenarios, she was sure that having transformed her into what he wanted her to be, he was in love with his own creation. Certainly its breasts.

"Hi," she said, very breathily, as though it were their first date.

"Who's she talking to?" asked the surgeon.

"You," she said, nailing Adrian with her cornflower-blues. "You with the hazel eyes and the very long lashes for a man."

"She means you," said the anaesthesiologist, a little disappointed, for his mother had had hazel eyes and if only her genes had been dominant this moment might have been his.

"Are my eyes hazel?" said Adrian, somewhat surprised, for he had spent most of his life being so busy looking at what other people had that he had not really noticed himself, except in what he was lacking.

"I would have said muddy brown with yellow flecks," said the anaesthesiologist, since that was how his eyes were always being described by people who were a little too accurate for his taste.

"Oh, no," breathed Babara. "They're hazel. Washed with green."

"Washed with green?" Adrian said, astounded.

"Do you kids mind waiting till you're alone?" said the plastic surgeon, who found displays of passion, even held in, disturbing, since they were too real for him.

"But who are you?" Babara asked.

Adrian untied his mask, and let it fall.

"You!" she said, and tried to cover her breasts. "What are you doing in here?"

"Don't touch those," said the surgeon, staying her movements.

"I was only making sure that everything was all right," said Adrian.

"And is it?" she asked expectantly.

"Better than all right," Adrian said. "It's perfect."

"Only one?"

"They're . . . magnificent," he amended, checking.

The surgeon looked from one to the other. "Remember what I said. You have to wait ten days."

"You understand we're in business together," Adrian said, as he drove her back to her apartment.

"I understand," she said.

"Everything I ever wanted is available to me if this works out. I've been months putting everything into operation, including your face. . . . And the rest of it."

"I understand," she said again.

"The fate of an entire nation and perhaps the arms business, which of course could affect world economy, is at stake here. So the feelings of two little people don't amount to a hill of beans."

"What kind of beans?" Babara asked.

"Don't get niggly."

"Well, I just wondered if they were lima, or something a little bit more costly, like soy."

"I make it a point never to mix business with pleasure."

"Oh, that's all right with me," Babara said. "I never mix pleasure with pleasure."

"How about pain?" he said, interestedly.

"Oh, pain's good. Pain's one of my favorites. That's one of the reasons I agreed so quickly to the surgery."

"Does it hurt?"

"It would if you touched them," she said, and looked at him.

"I never had anything," he said. "My parents were so poor my mother had to take in washing."

"A lot of women take in washing."

"Other women's husbands?" he asked.

"I'm sorry," she said.

"So was my father. And he told me if there was only one thing I learned from life it should be that women were here to be used."

"That's perfectly all right with me," said Babara.

"I don't mean sexually. I mean used for whatever it was you needed. A place in government. Glue."

"We don't have hooves."

"Maybe you don't. You should have seen some of my father's women."

"I'm sorry."

"So was my mother. But I've waited my whole life for a chance like this. Everything I've ever dreamed of and aspired to.

Power. Money. Influence. And it all depends on your doing as we planned. The *Playhouse* Centerfold. Scandal. Promiscuous sex with handsome strangers."

"You're handsome. And I hardly know you."

"Let's keep it that way," said Adrian. "The last thing I need is intimacy."

"Well, Tom," said the vicar. "And what brings you to the vicarage so early on a dark Criccieth morning?"

"I'm sorry to disturb you, sir. But I waited most of the night, and I can wait no longer without being so late I might lose my job."

The vicar had answered the door himself, dressed not in his churchly raiments, but a woolen nightshirt to the floor, not surprising since it was barely five o'clock. His pink toes peeked out from the tips of his brown leather scuffs, as his pink pate rose above the monkish gray fringe of his hair. His round cheeks were also of a very high color, setting off, by contrast, the paleness of his eyes. A cleft in his chin might have seemed more handsome had the chin itself not receded, becoming a part of the assortment of chins that waggled beneath. But he was, for all his lack of good looks, a most pleasant-seeming man, full of goodwill, even if it was early, and his wife was already angry at him because if she had married her other suitor, she would have been able to sleep undisturbed, since that man had died fourteen years before. "Come in, come in," he said to Tom. Much of what he said he had to say twice, people being not very receptive to good counsel.

"Thank you," said Tom, but only once, as it embarrassed him to seem too grateful. Still, he did put his cap in his hand, respectfully, as he moved inside.

The vicar indicated the more commodious of the two chairs in the parlor, the one with the cushions, for Tom to sit in, arranging himself in the high-backed dark wooden one, with only the slightest suggestion of upholstery on the seat. "Now, what can I do for you?"

"It's Shan, sir. Something terrible's happened. She's turned into the most fearsome liar." Even saying the word *liar*, Tom's voice shook, for accusations came hard to him, and he loved her with all his heart.

"She's a woman," said the vicar. "They're given to exaggeration."

"These are not exaggerations, vicar. Or even, accurately, lies. But delusions so grand and horrible that if she were anyone other than Shan I should think she was a madwoman."

"Really?" said the vicar, leaning forward with great interest.

"First," Tom said, with a huge intake of air, "she said she saw the monster."

"Darnall?" the vicar rolled the name in the base of his throat, so it sounded like a roar.

"Well, how many monsters are there, sir, considering there isn't even this one?"

"So she's seen Darnall," the vicar roared again, his eyes asparkle. For with all the evil in the world, it was pleasant to contemplate a genuinely odious adversary, one that was not in human or devilish guise.

"Says she's seen it, sir. Says such things as turn a man's heart to suet. For Darnall is not her tallest tale."

"She has others?" asked the vicar, excitement rising in him now, for Criccieth was a genuinely God-fearing community, where you could leave your door open, and your heart the same. So it was with a constant feeling of well-being that this shepherd herded his flock. But well-being in a churchman was not necessarily as stimulating as the occasional dose of dread, and he read with just the slightest edge of envy accounts of possession in various communities. Not that he wished any harm to Criccieth, or even a tadpole of anguish to spring forth. But a little genuine malevolence that he could fix (and he knew he could) would be something definite to tote up on the celestial scoreboard. Being a great reader of Milton, he had already justified God's ways to man, but was more interested in the vice versa.

"She says she is not Shan," said Tom, sorrow like wattles

weighing his cheeks, so he looked more a St. Bernard than the happy pup he had been only a day before.

"Not Shan?" said the vicar, his heart racing, for he could already hear his conversation with the Foul Fiend that had entered her sweet young body. "Who is she then?"

"She says . . ." Tom swallowed. "She says she is the Princess Darcy."

"Oh," said the vicar, terribly disappointed. He had in his mind swiftly reviewed all the fine names the demon might be called, the satanic opponent whom he could face with the righteousness of angels, something he had been practicing over the years in dialogues with his wife. Not that he had ever exactly accused her of being in league with Beelzebub, but it would certainly have explained a number of things, including the trials she had subjected him to, if all of it had been a preparation. For he was of the belief that everything in life happens for a reason, and the only reason he could think of that he was married to such a woman, was that God was giving him a dry run for arguing with the Devil. "Not Mephistopheles? Lucifer? Satan?"

"Ah, certainly not, Vicar. For this is nothing infernal, but very much of this world. It's delusions of grandeur she's having. Not being content with her life here in Criccieth, and with me, she's having uppity hallucinations."

"You think Darnall is uppity?"

"Well, work it out for yourself, sir. A thousand years and more there's been tales of the monster in Cardigan Bay, and no woman has ever seen him before."

"And lived to tell the tale . . . ," said the vicar eerily, eyes rolling, getting into the spirit, or more aptly, lack of it.

"You mean some have seen it and died?"

"Well." The vicar shrugged. "There are those tales, too. Women who've disappeared . . . in the dead of night . . . their footsteps echoing on the cobblestones . . ."

"On their way to being unfaithful to their husbands," Tom said skeptically.

"Is that what you fear, Tom?"

"I fear the loss of a woman whose very lips dripped integrity. Whose arms caressed the wonders of life. Whose hips —"

The vicar held up his hand, in caution.

"Sorry, sir. But there's no great phantasm here, other than the specter of a ne'er-do-well seducer, and a spoiled twit of a princess who turned Shan's head, and the brain inside it."

"You mean the actual Princess Darcy."

"Shan was fair mad to see her. I knew there was disaster ahead the moment she asked for the money for the lottery ticket."

"And what of Miles?"

Tom looked down. "I knew that portended disaster as well."

"Have they been together?"

"She went out to meet him last night. That's when she came back with her story. Darnall."

"But how do you know it's a story? Can you not give her the benefit of the doubt?"

"Doubt? Why I am in a sea of doubt. A veritable ocean of misgiving and suspicion and distrust."

"In which resides a monster," the vicar said, profoundly.

"I don't understand."

"Neither do I," said the vicar, for once in a while he had booms of inspiration, from whence, he knew not. "But I do understand that every man, and every woman, has terrible, dark depths. And maybe what's inside us all is . . ." He took a breath, like a bellows, and let it whoosh out on the air. ". . . Darnall."

"I'm an ignorant man, sir. I can only fathom what I see and hear."

"You're a Welshman!" exclaimed the clergyman. "Which makes you a poet and a dreamer! And you're a human being, which makes you a repository of all the wisdom in the universe, all the virtue and evil in the cosmos, all the spirit in infinity! Anything you can conceive of, you can understand, and be."

"Truly?"

"Truly!"

"Thank you, sir!" said Tom, and went to the door, his heart changed back from suet to his own sweet heart. A whole lot lighter now, because he understood how given the vicar was to practicing his Sunday sermons on whomever he could corner. So he figured the vicar had cornered Shan, and delivered that selfsame thought, that anything she could conceive of, she could be. Which would explain her thinking she was Darcy, and thus render her only half as false. So half his faith restored, if not in God or the vicar at least his wife, who was, after all, his personal angel, he went off to work in the dark and the cold below the ground.

Now Darcy awoke all filled with fear and trembling, because she had not only seen a monster but had risked losing her lovely new life. She had never told Tom except in that temper who she really was, the deception being so much fun, and the truth being she was afraid he might like Shan better, and want her back. She had hazarded his turning her in for the original model; her foolishness nearly overwhelmed her. Fortunately, he hadn't believed her.

Hadn't believed her. She sat up in bed. Who did he think he was, not to believe *her!* How could he not believe a woman with such impeccable credentials, whether or not he knew the credentials were valid? Was not every inch of her royal? Was not every word that fell from her lips sparkling with her specialness? Perking with her pedigree? "How dare he not believe *me?*" she said aloud.

And how dare he doubt she had seen the monster? To backtrack, why should the monster have presented itself to *her?* God only knew how long it had slithered on the bottom of the bay, waiting for its victims, how many sailors had jettisoned into these jaws, how many fisherfolk had been pulled into that gaping maw. But why should *she* have been the one to see it, and then be disbelieved? How could any of them treat her like that: Miles, making her sleepless to begin with, so she prowled the streets, the monster rearing its most ugly head, scaring the wits out of her, and worst of all, Tom, not believing. Not believing Darcy, whose word, since the wedding, had been as great as the law.

Whose words, even as a child, had made grown women tremble, at least her mother. For such was the imperiousness of her nature that she had had the lifelong advantage of making all those around her feel that their slips were showing, her superiority causing everyone to look down at their hems. How dare they now, then, actor, monster, miner, challenge *her!* "How dare any of them treat *me* like that!"

Furious, she slipped out of bed, into the cool of the summer morning, dainty toes scurrying onto their newly accustomed path, bathroom, stairs, stairs, kitchen. The casement window was flung open, and she saw, to her delight, that a new flower blossomed in the windowbox. Well, there was that, anyway. Something lovely and tasty to counteract all the insults she had received, all the body blows to her ego, all those people (and thing) so insensitive to *her* feelings.

Excited, she moved to the flower. Like the two that preceded it, this one was shaped like a foxglove, the bell of its petals sloping gently downwards, towards the stem. It was red, bright red, as love was in the beginning, before it lost its meaning and grew wearisome, like Christmas decorations left up too long after the celebration. Gently touching the flower, she tilted it back slightly, so she could see inside. No childlike face or belly awaited her this time, but only a little letter, a capital "I." It was a relief that it was only a letter and not a person or a seeming manifestation thereof, as she was extremely hungry, ravenous actually, the night having passed, and her digestive juices having combined with her rage at Miles, the monster, and Tom having so little respect for her. Then before her very eyes the "I" started dancing, so that its outer edges twisted down and around and upwards and it became a "U," exciting all kinds of wonder in her, and something akin to affection for the flower, which was very disconcerting. Oscar Wilde notwithstanding, and each man killing the thing he loved, it was hard, a woman eating that for which she felt affection. Still, hunger was hunger, and before it did anything more endearing, she reached over, plucked it, and ate it.

And a feeling like the easing of knots balmed the base of her belly. And a glow like a swallowed star spread through her whole being. And she realized everything that had taken place, though it was *her* adventure, was not really about her. That Miles was Miles and his attitude would have been the same towards any woman, or man for that matter. And the monster had made no particular assault on *her*, really: he had surfaced because it was time for him to surface, or he felt like surfacing, or who knew what monsters might be feeling. But whatever it was, it had very little, really absolutely *nothing* to do with *her*. And as for Tom, poor dear Tom, why, how could he believe her, or anyone, who said they were not who he had every reason to think they were? So his disbelief had nothing to do with *her*. A certain gossamer lilt came over her, a melody in lace. For she had eaten the flower that healed Taking Things Too Personally.

Smiling to herself, she gave a filled watering can to the thirsty earth in the windowbox ("Glub!") before rushing to the duchess's house to share her good news. It had been several days since she had seen her first and only true friend, the sole confidante she had, really, although the duchess hadn't believed her either. But then, that hadn't been about Darcy, but the duchess's hearing a different drummer, or, in this case, a different bell. Fifty of them, Darcy counted, as the duchess tinkled open her door.

"I've learned not to take things personally!" Darcy rejoiced as they sat in the duchess's parlor, with the cats arranged like cushions around the room, except for the one Persian on her head.

"Good for you," said the duchess. "That was hard to do in my case, since it always seemed to be about me when I was young. But as you get older you discover it isn't about you since there are so many better-looking, younger women. You're lucky to find it out early when there aren't that many younger, except for children who take *everything* personally. Tea?"

"Yes, please," said Darcy. "And I learned not to take things too seriously."

"That must be a load off your load," said the duchess, and poured.

"And the very first flower healed Vanity. At least, I'm humble enough to hope it did."

"Flower?" said the duchess.

"From the seeds you gave me."

"I gave you?" said the duchess.

"Very well," said Darcy, thinking she understood the game. "The guide that speaks through you."

"You've seen him?" said the duchess. "Did he ask about me?"

"Well, no . . . ," Darcy said.

"They're all the same. They never call. They never write." She handed her the cup. "It's going well for you, then. You're lifting yourself. I knew you would."

"But there are still so many things I don't understand."

"Good!" said the duchess. "Knowing that, you will grow."

"Mostly I don't understand about the monster. Why did he show himself to me? Not that I take it personally."

"You saw . . . DarNALL?" the duchess rasped.

"Last night," Darcy said. "In the bay."

"Darnall," the duchess murmured. "A thousand years and no woman has seen him and lived to tell the tale."

"Really?" said Darcy, feeling rather special and so pleased with herself, although she was not foolish enough to think it was about her.

"At least, none who's come forward." The duchess rolled her watery blue eyes upward, and the cat on her head licked his paws.

"You've seen him?"

"I'm not saying," said the duchess. "Did he ask about me?"

Darcy smiled. For one who did not take things personally, the duchess seemed a speck too sensitive about rejection, even from a monster. But then, Darcy knew a great many women who were the same. "But if no one has seen him and lived to tell the tale, or even come forward, how do they know there is a monster?"

"No woman," said the duchess. "There were a few men. Cowards and fools and drunks and reprobates, so no one fully believed them. And then of course, there are the mysterious disappearances. Fishermen and opportunists, obsessed novelty hunters, who have gone out in search and never come back. There was a day when the bay ran red, but that was with a particularly spectacular sunset, so it might just have been the lighting effects."

"Lighting effects?"

"The Lord works in mysterious ways," said the duchess, "and sometimes He's a Scenic Designer."

Just then there was a knock at the door. The cat sprang from the duchess's head, onto the floor, and ran towards the front door. "Bailey used to be my butler," the duchess said by way of explanation. "Old habits die hard, even with a new incarnation."

"Are you speaking of your cat?"

"Lower your voice," said the duchess, getting up. "He doesn't know he's a cat." She disappeared from the parlor, and in a moment Darcy heard her say, "It's all right, Bailey. I'll get it. . . . Why, Miles!"

"Forgive me for just barging in like this," said the bewitching voice. "But we have a break, and I needed to talk to you."

"To me?" said the duchess.

"It's about Shan," he said, and Darcy's heart leapt higher. As it was already in the base of her throat just from the sound of him, the report that he was there because of her nearly choked her.

"Well, what a coincidence!" said the duchess. "If you believe in coincidences, which I for one don't. For it is all a grand design," she said, leading him to the parlor. "Except perhaps for the furniture in here."

"Shan!" said Miles, on seeing her.

"That's what they call me," Darcy said. Although she had stopped taking things too personally, she could not help but feel this was about her, because even though it seemed to be about the real Shan, as Miles had not seen her in all those years, who he was drawn to right now would appear to be herself. And oh, she did take him personally, for every inch of her person was atingle from his presence, garbed so Hamletish and fetching, a black oilskin raincape draped about his broad shoulders now, a fine patina of rain on it, his reddish hair darkened to auburn with the damp, curling about his high forehead like conspirators, whispering their secrets to each other, one of them, she hoped, about her.

"I cannot go on like this," said Miles.

"Can they make a new costume before the performance?"

"I don't mean go onstage," he said. "I mean go on." And he was on his knees in front of her chair, his face bowed so his forehead pressed on her thigh. And she could feel the wetness of his hair through the thin fabric of her dress, the warmth of his face. "I have to have you or die."

"Well, then, flights of angels sing thee to thy rest."

He looked up, an expression on his face past surprise. "What's this? Sarcasm? Sophistication? So changed from the simple girl I loved?"

"Not enough," said Darcy.

"How do you know how much?"

"Actions speak louder than Shakespeare," the duchess said.

"Madam," said Miles, getting to his feet. "I came here to ask your aid in restoring my love to me. Not to have the two of you band together to mock me."

"You can't leave a woman like you did," said the duchess. "You can't touch her and lift her and then send her crashing to earth because of your own petty vanities. And what of her obligations? What of Tom? Now that she's found safe harbor, would you come like a whirlwind and disrupt all that?"

"Yes," said Miles.

"Very well," said the duchess. "You may use my bedroom."

"No," Darcy said, once they were inside, and alone, and he had her backed against the door, and his lips sought hers.

"Yes," he said, struggling for her mouth.

"No," she said, lips avoiding his.

"Yes." He turned his face with hers.

"No," she said, angling her head to the right, as he angled his to the left, so their noses touched.

"A hit," he said. "A very palpable hit."

"No."

"Yes."

"Well, all right," she said, as their mouths aligned. And their lips met, lush, and hungry for the other's mouth.

She expected him to take her then and there, against the door, standing up, the way the dreadful, common people did it. And she waited for the lifting of her skirt, and the rash intrusion. But all he did was succor and seduce her mouth and tongue, and gentle the edges of her face with his fingers, and hold her off as if she was a delicate treasure, and stare into her eyes.

"I have to get back to rehearsal," he whispered, softer than a breeze against her hair. "But I'll see you by moonlight. Meet me at the castle tonight, by moonlight."

"I'm not sure I can."

"You can and will," he said. "Or I don't know my Shan."

Now did the fair albeit aging Isabel sit at her toilette and try not to see the wrinkles. In the days when the archbishop had been still in charge of Perq's religious life, before worship had been outlawed, except of self and money and things, that eminent gentleman had spoken to her often of beauty. The beauty of the soul, the beauty of caring for other people, the beauty of the design of the Universe. Infinity, he had often pointed out, could have been constructed so flawlessly only by a mind that grasped Infinity, predating Einstein's. Isabel missed the discussions of beauty and infinity, for thinking in terms of the boundless, that which went on forever, her own span so far was terribly brief, even for its fifty-some years. But caught in the grip of her own small nature, the absence of the churchman, and passion for Rachid, her baseness triumphed, and the triviality in her coalesced. And all she could dwell on was her fear that she was aging and might lose him. Such was the pain of loving a younger pervert.

In her youth, oddly enough, she hadn't been all that pretty. Certainly she was lovelier than the run of the mill royal, but looking back at her pictures now, which she did when there was no chance of anyone catching her, and she needed reassurance, she saw that there was a vacuousness in that younger face, which time and experience and she hoped a modicum of wisdom had filled in. Hers was one of those looks that came together as the person did. Granted the eyes were always extraordinary, but where they had once been pretty but blank they were now full of interest and inquiry, glittering with curiosity about life, and humor at some of the answers she hadn't expected. High angularity of cheekbone from Hungarian forebears becoming more pronounced with time, combined with her generous mouth, to present to the discerning eye a deep sensuality. Just her luck, the most discerning eye had been Rachid's.

For oh, she did lust for him, and his vile, persistent ways, making her feel every inch the royal slattern. The mirrors on the ceiling of the hydrofoil had been but the beginning of her sexual fall. She had never suspected how much more exciting it was to watch yourself making love than simply to make love while not even daring to imagine watching. Self-censorship had been always a part of her makeup, since Perq had never sported a Bill of Rights, and everyone knew from the beginning they had no license even to think what was disgusting.

The red telephone by the mauve marble vanity by which she sat rang, or rather, insinuated. Isabel's throat closed, even as her blood pressure rose. For it was the phone Rachid used as a "hot line," literally.

Trembling, she lifted the receiver. "Yes?"

"I want to talk dirty to you," said Rachid.

"Who is this?"

"Don't get coy," he said. "I want to do it to you now, in front of the antique armoire."

"Then why don't you come in?"

"I want to do it to you now in front of the armoire with Junella watching."

"That isn't part of her duties," Isabel said, trying to keep her voice steady. "Besides she's Darcy's lady-in-waiting, not mine."

"I want to do it to you in front of the armoire with your lady-in-watching waiting."

"It's the other way around," said Isabel.

"That's right," he said, and his breath came heavy. "I want to do it to you the other way around."

"Can't you just come in here?" she said.

"Bitch!" he said. "Don't try to take control."

"Oh, I'm not," she said, trying to keep the apology out of her voice, because although humiliation was one of his favorites, he didn't like her too submissive to begin with.

"I want to take you the other way round while you're looking through a keyhole at an orgy."

"Oh, I couldn't," said Isabel.

"And I want you to suffer while I stick my finger in the keyhole so you can't see what's going on. I want you to beg me to let you see."

"That isn't like me," she said.

The phone went dead. Holding her heart she clicked the line. "Hello? Hello?"

Blushing, her color so high it looked like she'd spilled raspberry Jell-O into her cleavage, she looked at the phone, bereft. But in less than a flash, which he also enjoyed doing, Rachid came out of the bookcase, through the special hidden entrance he'd had built.

"Oh," she said. "I was afraid you were calling another woman."

"Get up!" he said.

She sprang to her feet and flung her arms wide for his embrace, but he seized her rudely by the arm and pulled her to the wall, standing her in front of a portrait of her ancestor.

"Take it off," he said.

"Really, Rachid, this is not a burlesque house."

"I meant the painting. Take it off the wall."

She did. To her surprise, there was a hole in the wall where the picture had hung. "Look through it," he said.

She did. On the other side of the wall the room had been redecorated to look like a garden. In it gamboled plump nymphs and overhung satyrs, lined up and circled around, naked and doing filthy things. "My goodness," she said.

"Yes, there's that, but we'll overcome it," he said and taking her by the hair, pressed her face hard to the wall, forcing her to look.

"Stop it!"

"You want to see. Your wish is my command."

"Don't make me do this," she said. "I am a queen. How can you degrade me so?"

"You love it," he said.

"No I don't," she whimpered. He pressed his hand in front of her face, and covered the hole in the wall. She turned, and looked at him with the contempt she knew she ought to feel. "Pervert."

"I know. Isn't it wonderful?"

"Oh, why?" she said. "Why do you affect me so?"

"Because you know what's good for you. And you're as bad as I am. Well, nearly." And he kissed her with all the technique that was in him which was unfortunately greater than that of an alcoholic king or indeed most of the nice men in the world. "You're mine," he said.

"Yes. Yes, I am."

"And you'll do what you have to do to stay mine."

"Yes," she said, weakly. "I'm afraid I will."

"And before we are done, you will be so much mine, you will denounce your own son's marriage."

"Never!" she said, drawing back. "You cannot force me to do that."

"I will not have to force you," he said, and turned her again, savagely, towards the wall, lifting her skirt, insinuating his vileness into her.

"What are you doing?" she started to say, but then said, "Oh, very well," and put her eye back to the hole. Quite eagerly, if anyone were to note it, which fortunately no one did, except for me, and you, dear reader.

"Before we are done," he said, thrusting, "you'll do anything I say. You will have sexual encounters with strangers."

"I won't!" she said, her protest around his rhythms.

"You will have sexual encounters with unknown men. I'll make you."

"I can't. You won't. I wouldn't."

"You will have sexual encounters with unknown men, and make love with another woman, with me watching."

"You can't ask me to do that," she panted.

"Very well, then," he said, and smiled wickedly. "I'll wait for you to ask me."

Afterwards, when they were spent, and the visiting players in the next room gamboled no more but lay exhausted on heaps of artificial moss mounded for their enterprise, when the passion that had so overwhelmed Isabel tickled rancid, she tried to hate him. But his black, curling hair looked almost innocent, dampened as it was by the effort of his own lusty labors, and she felt something so sweet, and — could it be, even with him? — maternal, she could not help fingering a lock of it, as uncorrupt as the gesture was, as much as he would hate it.

He did. He took her hand from his forehead, and put it somewhere loathsome.

"Why?" she said. "Why must your every gesture be so foul?"

"I like it like that," he said.

"Oh," said Isabel.

Then he arose and dressed, which was not that big a deal, since he had done nothing but unzipper his pants and loose his suspenders and take off his shoes, so his circulation wouldn't be affected, because he was a little bit of a hypochondriac as well as a lecher. Isabel was usually deeply offended by his failure to disrobe, as it seemed especially ill-mannered, being had by somebody with socks on. But the terrible truth was, she had been very excited by the scene she had witnessed, and by what was being done to her along with the witnessing. How dreadful it was to discover that like this miscreant she adored, she had all these seeds of debauchery in her.

"Degenerate," she said, as he zippered, and braced, and Guccied.

"I know," he said. "Aren't you lucky?"

"Yes," she said, and rose from her crumpled heap on the floor, not having to dress either, so unrefined had been his assault on her. "Yes!" she said again, and sighed, and swooned into his arms. He stepped back slightly, and let her slide to the floor.

"I'm getting tired of dependent women," he said. "I need someone who's a little feisty."

"I'll change," she said.

"Women don't change."

"Of course we do. You just have to give us a good reason."

"I'll give you the best reason in the world," he said. "Either you do as I say, or it's over between us."

"I couldn't bear that," she said miserably.

"Then before we're done, you'll denounce the marriage of your son!"

"Never!" she said. "Ask me anything, but not that!"

"Do you love me?"

"Yes," she said, abysmally, from the floor, which was appropriate. "God help me, I do."

"Then will you make love with another woman?"

"No."

"Will you have sexual encounters with an unknown man?"

"No."

"Then stop saying I should ask you anything," said Rachid. "And stop asking God to help you. There is no God."

"Yes there is," she said. "And He'll punish me for loving you."

"How boring you are," said Rachid. "Lucky for you, I love power."

7

BY THE ESTUARY that joined the flow of river descending from Perq's waterfall to the sea, maritime pine grew on a slant, tops brushcut by persistent winds, trunks twisted, as though beseeching a love who had lured and then repelled them. All the trees at that place were curiously angled, growing towards the sun, battered by the breeze, fed by the current of tropical Gulf Stream, so they were in their nature unique and slightly confused, at once oversized and bent, florid and scraggly, like big-breasted women with too thin ankles and scrawny necks.

Flowers had grown wild at their base, pansies in dark velvet hues with bright yellow patches, gazanias, open-faced in daylight, closed when the sun set, their purple centers flecked with gold, petals bright white like the common garden variety daisy they resembled. Rachid had had them dug up, decrying that what grew wild was too ordinary for Perq, not stimulating enough gambling juices. If people were going to go to a resort, they should not feel they were in their own backyards. So orchids were planted, cymbidiums, and gardenias, flowers the resident palace psychologist said stimulated insecurity, making people think of the proms where they hadn't had a date. So they would put more money on the pass line, trying for the windfall that life had not afforded them. Or, in the case of the really big gambler, who had won, but never enough, making them play more heavily at roulette or baccarat.

All the same, wildflowers are stubborn flowers, like children with the rebellion weeded out of them, their parents think, till the real trouble starts. So in certain places along the estuary, gazanias would reemerge, in clumps. And it was a patch of these that Shan found, and picked for her (supposed) mother-in-law, the queen, who had been looking at her with what could only be described as troubled glances.

Shan was guarded at the time by her faithful troop of irritable little boys, who hated forays into nature except where it included torturing frogs. Biology Lab was the most popular course in all of Perq's schools: if you got a good enough grade you could take it over again the next year, the attraction of the course being that the frogs were not simply dissected, but also alive. Needless to say little girls fainted, but the future of Perq, it was agreed and understood, did not depend on little girls. So with her hearty band of merciless protectors, Shan made her way along the banks of the estuary, searching for something that would make Isabel smile, instead of look at her sideways.

"Oh, how lovely," she said, when she found the gazanias. Having never seen that variety of flower before, she assumed that, like its simple cousin the daisy, it was as straightforwardly pretty as it seemed, never dreaming that it would close up at nightfall. "I shall take some of these to the queen."

"The queen likes jewelry," said one of the palace guard, his walkie-talkie hooked to the leather belt above his red velvet peplum.

"Rubies and opals," said the second palace guard.

"Diamonds and sapphires," said a third.

"But she has plenty of those," said Shan, getting down on her haunches, starting to pick the flowers. "These will be a sweet offering."

"She isn't into 'sweet,' " said the smartest of the boys. "Sweet went out with the king."

"What kind of man is he?" she asked, the innocence of flower-picking having blunted the edges of her deception. For since she had promised Rodney not to say anymore she wasn't who she was, she was careful to pretend she was who she wasn't. "I mean, from the palace guard point of view."

"He is our king, and so we respect him," said a little boy with wire-rimmed glasses and a machete. "We would never say anything against him."

"Daisies don't tell, and neither would I," said Shan, very curious, not out of any penchant for gossip, but because she was growing genuinely fond of Rodney and wanted to know as much as she could about him.

"These aren't daisies," said the wire-rimmed-glasses boy, whose name was Hayden, which meant, in the old English, "son of the rose-edged valley," the reason he carried a machete. To cut down either the roses, against which he bore a personal grudge, or anyone who might know what his name meant. "They're gazanias."

"They're lovely just the same, and they'll keep the secret," Shan said.

"It's no secret," said Hayden. "He's a drunk and a jerk."

"Not necessarily in that order," said the second palace guard.

"But what can you expect from someone whose name is Quirin?" said Hayden, contemptuously.

"I've never heard that name before," said Shan.

"Well, there's no honor to it," said Hayden. "It comes from a magic stone, found in the lapwing's nest. Also known as the traitor's stone. If you place it on the head of a sleeping person, they'll reveal their innermost thoughts."

"Is there really such a stone?"

"Nobody's sure. It's like the monster that supposedly lives in Cardigan Bay."

"You know about Darnall?" Shan said, rather astonished, since the monster was discussed only in the dread dead of night, and then, she had thought, only among Welshmen.

"'From the hidden or secret nook,'" Hayden said, proudly. "That's what Darnall means."

"Really?" said Shan, who thought she knew everything about the monster, or at least as much as one could know among people who pretended to know nothing. "You know a great deal about names."

"I know it all," said Hayden. "Because the man who said 'What's in a name?' was a true Farley."

"Which means . . . ?" asked Shan.

"From the bull meadow," Hayden said authoritatively.

"What's Engelbert?" asked Engelbert.

" 'As bright as an angel,' " said Hayden. "But we know better than to trust Germans, *or* their language."

"What's Hayden then?" asked Engelbert.

Hayden raised his machete. "Don't even ask," he said, menacing. "Don't even think it!"

This semipastoral scene, that is, the lovely seeming princess, her cornsilky hair flowing pale gold in the sunlight, picking gazanias she thought were the same as daisies, and her security guard of little boys in red velvet uniforms with peplums and conquistador collars and walkie-talkies, one of them with a raised machete, was being observed through the spread fronds of a dwarf palm tree. "We could take her now," said a sinister left-handed man, holding the frond with his sinister left hand, on which was a black glove with a tattoo on it.

"Too soon, Cesare," said Adrian. "The nipples haven't totally healed. Besides, we want no witnesses."

"We could kill the little boys."

"They only look like little boys," said Adrian. "In fact, they're the pride of the army."

"When, then?"

"As soon as I've done the layout," said Adrian. "We want the princess — or the girl they will think is the princess — with no demands on her time, completely free to disgrace herself all over the map of Europe."

"Why don't you use that as a background for the centerfold. The map of Europe." Cesare laughed, a left-handed laugh. "With the royal box somewhere between France and Italy."

In the gazania patch, Hayden turned. "Did you hear something?" he asked the other guards.

"What?" asked Engelbert.

"A rather . . . sinister laugh," said Hayden, his ears as sensitive as he was, because of his name.

"But this is paradise," said Shan, who had gathered enough gazanias to fill her basket. "There could be nothing sinister here."

"As Eve said to Adam," noted Hayden.

"That was a snake," said Shan, getting to her feet, brushing off the grass. "Snakes don't laugh."

"It depends how good the joke is," said Engelbert, looking around warily.

It was well past six o'clock when Shan was allowed in to see the queen. Never had it been the custom of Isabel to keep people waiting, as she was, for a late-blooming beauty and a sensualist, a very thoughtful person. But she had begun holding Darcy at arm's length, ever since Rachid had first suggested she would one day denounce her son's marriage. This was half out of fear that she would see something in Darcy that would sow seeds of dislike, and half out of fear that the girl would be totally winning. For when it came down to it, Isabel was willing to excuse Rachid anything, except the prospect of his leaving her. So it was more likely, horrid and impossible as the prospect seemed, that she would undercut the young royal marriage rather than risk losing him. It appalled her that the mother love that should have been unconditional, according to the resident palace psychologist, was subverted by a passion that would actually make her less loyal to her son than to a lover. Still, she loved Rodney dearly, and hoped that the bitch wouldn't do anything to offend her.

"Well, Darcy," she said, sitting on her throne, which Rachid's decorator had redone, insetting the gold with mother-of-pearl, a substance that by definition put Isabel on the defensive, as it was her mistressness that she liked to be reminded of, and not her maternity. So besides being on her throne, she was on her high horse, a design the decorator had also considered, having ordered a stuffed Arabian, which fortunately hadn't fitted over the threshold. "What is it that brings you here begging for an audience?"

"Your pardon, Ma'am." Shan curtsied, in the manner the duchess had taught her, before she remembered, too late, that the queen didn't want her curtseying. "I wasn't exactly begging," she said, a certain degree of pride even in her humility overcoming a natural reluctance to dispute. "But I do have a gift for you."

"Presents!" Isabel exclaimed, actually clapping her hands together, for she was as much a little girl as when she had been a little girl, except for the aspects lost with her innocence, and gained with her knowledge, which unfortunately did not extend to discrimination. "I do love presents!"

"These are the gifts of nature," said Shan, holding out the basket.

"Oh," said Isabel, hoping her disappointment didn't show, for she really liked jewels. She took the basket, opened the lid, and drew the flowers out. But the sun being just about to set, the petals drew shut, and the flowers shriveled on their stems, with a sound like a 'Thwup.' "Thwup," they went, in the queen's face.

"What's this?" she cried. "Dead flowers? Are you trying to tell me something?"

"Majesty. . . ," cried Shan, before she remembered the queen didn't want to be called Majesty. "Isabel," she tried to make it up to her. "They were fresh and fair when I picked them."

"And so was I once, is that what you're saying? That I am overbloomed, past my prime? Shriveled?"

"Oh, no . . . ," Shan pleaded.

"Do you know what the penalty is for insulting the queen?"

"No," said Shan, miserably.

"Neither do I," said Isabel, and turned to the palace guard. "Look it up."

"Right away, Your Highness," he said, and went to the computer. Besides wishing to take the prince out of principality, Rachid wanted to scuttle all that was traditional and inspiring, reminding people of the past. So the great quills and ink and sprinkled sand that had logged the history of Perq from time memorial had been declared archaic and obsolete, as had pens and even ballpoints and typewriters, replaced with word processors, which had driven off the scribes. ("Good riddance to bad rubbings," Rachid had said, pelting them with their erasers as they fled.)

"What would that be under?" asked the guard, a bit bent over from ducking and flinching, as Rachid had equipped the device to spit when an error was made, to wipe out once and for all the myth of user-friendly.

"'P,'" said Isabel. "Penalties. Punishment."

"But I meant no harm. . . ," protested Shan.

"Or perhaps it's under 'H' for Hanging. Or 'D' for Drawn and Quartered."

"Majesty . . ."

"And don't call me that. I'm not that much older than you are." She turned her face so she could see herself in the mirror at the end of the room, the clearest vision she had of herself without glasses, which she refused to wear. The palace ophthalmologist had called her presbyopic at her last examination. She had had him exiled under the new regulation that religion was outlawed, even as he tried to explain that it meant farsighted, from the prefix "presby," meaning aging. At that point she had his ticket taken away, so he had to hitchhike. Not easy from an island.

"Here it is," said the guard. "Insulting the royal family. The rack."

"But we don't have a rack," said Isabel. "Does anybody know where we can get a rack?"

"Spain, I would imagine," said the chancellor. "Or Hollywood."

"Please, Ma'am," Shan said, on her knees. For courageous as she was by nature, pain was a turnoff. "Mercy."

"And where was your mercy, giving me dead flowers? Make a call," she said to the chancellor. "Find out how soon we can get one here."

"Now look," said Shan, recovering her character, getting up from the floor. "I meant nothing but good. Beauty is in the eye of the beholder. So perhaps it is your eye, madam, that makes these flowers less than lovely."

"You dare . . ."

"I dare," Shan said. "For I respect and love your son, so I honor his mother. But I will remind you that I am as royal as you are, so the penalty that would apply to insulting the royal family is canceled out."

"Tell that to the computer!"

"I don't know how it works," said Shan.

"I knew he should have married a secretary," said Isabel.

"Ladies, ladies," said the chancellor, a tall thin bearded fellow in saffron robes and matching slippers. "Is this an example of our most high civilization? Have we not held ourselves out to the world as a shrine of courtesy and pleasant thinking? Is this not the Lourdes of luxury, where those with no joy in their hearts come to be healed, and lose money?"

"The old geezer spouts wisdom," murmured Rhea, into the queen's ear.

"I suppose," said Isabel. "Get up, Darcy," she instructed Shan.

"I'm up," Shan said.

"Very well, you're excused this time. But see that it doesn't happen again."

"You may be sure of it, Ma'am," said Shan, "for I shall bring you no more flowers." And seizing the basket, she left the room.

But one flower fell, and in the morning, when the sun had risen again, Isabel slipped from her sinful bed and found it, opened. "But it is the flower that was at fault, and not my poor Darcy," she said, under her breath. "How unfair I have been.

How callous. Without compassion or gratitude. I shall have to make it up to her." She caught a glimpse of herself in the mirror, and presbyopic or no, she saw. "When she's older," she said, because there was such a thing as being *too* forgiving.

What perfidy there was in Darcy's heart she tried not to dwell on or analyze, since the whole situation was so complex, she was sure she was blameless. For in order to be unfaithful to Tom, he would have had to be her husband in fact, which in fact he wasn't, being only her husband in fantasy. The fact that he didn't believe the facts, that she wasn't really Shan, made her even less guilty, she was nearly convinced. And taking into consideration what Shan might have done in this matter — for the truth was (fantasy aside), she was here only by the grace of her counterpart — Darcy imagined that Miles would be as irresistible to Shan as he was to her. More so, probably, since Shan had the buttressing of history to strengthen her passion. Darcy herself had never lost a love, having been snapped up on the slopes before she had time to find one. But she supposed that having lost someone, to find them again, and in costume, surely would have elasticized the boundaries of propriety. Quite convinced she was, then, that Shan would tumble into faithlessness as well. So fortified with the strength of both their convictions, she waited to be sure Tom was asleep, crept from her bed, and hurried to the castle.

What was all the fuss about adultery, anyway? Since religion had been outlawed in Perq, the Ten Commandments no longer pertained. Besides, like everything else, they'd been brought down from the mountain by men. Making adultery a taboo was to preserve the family unit, according to the royal sociologist. Not really all that wicked. Probably adultery had saved as many marriages as it destroyed, giving people another outlet for their dissatisfaction, besides divorce. Perhaps, Darcy thought, her own adventure giving rise to an originality of thinking that had never been called for before (or any thought at all, as a matter of fact), adultery, like the antibodies that fought off infection, was a built-in cure for the tedium of marriage. To keep the heart beating, partners from going mad, the anguished wife from suicide. Maybe cheating was simply a variation on turning the other cheek, so to speak, less sinful than nearly holy, if one imagined that spiritual things still counted. Why, if Darcy herself had been able to dally, which she never would have considered doing as a princess, it might have given whole new life to her marriage.

Her marriage. Rodney. Amazing she hadn't even thought of him, whatever guilt there was in her actions being related to Tom. Still, the truth was, out of all the men involved, the only one who really mattered to her was Miles. How strange it was that she, whom the world loved for having a romance, should have had to run away to find one. And what irony, that the first unbridled passion she should feel would be for one who played the prince.

She heard the soft fall of her velvet slippers (Shan's, really) on the cobblestones, felt the rush of summer wind, edged with just the slightest chill, through the fabric of Tom's woolly coat. Underneath, she was naked, baggage that she'd become, or couldn't wait to be. The moon, three-quarters full, missing just its lower left quadrant, glittered the bay silver, shone on the ancient, reddish stone of the gatehouse. She climbed the stairs, bounding up them, anticipation lending a spring to her step, an athleticism that hadn't existed in her before, for all the Jane Fonda workout tapes.

She could hear whistling above her, wind skittering around the four towers, sounding like sighs. "Miles?" she called out, into the darkness, finally, darkness. How long had she waited for there to be moonlight? How many hours had passed till she could come to him by moonlight? "Miles?" she called again.

There was no answer. No sound but the quiet lap of water bubbling to the shore, and her own measured breath, held, till she remembered to breathe. Her lungs felt close to bursting, like a swimmer's beneath the sea.

And she wondered if those who died of love had sometimes died from not breathing, holding their breath, waiting, strangled on expectation. She had no idea what time it was. As she had given her Rolex to Shan, to make her seem all the more Darcy, she had spent practically her whole time in the village not knowing the hour, monitoring her life by dark and light, instinct and errand: when she had to go marketing, when she had to be home to cook. So she had not the slightest notion of the time, except that it had to be well past midnight. The lights of the village, except for the streetlamps, were all extinguished. The houses were dark, the pale rectangular glows from flickering television sets no longer in evidence. "By moonlight," he had said. Why was the world so full of men you couldn't pin down?

She sat in the courtyard, on one of the wooden benches brought in for the play, wondering where he was, why he was so late in coming. Wasn't he as anxious as she was, more so, really, since he hadn't been sure of her? Or was he as sure as he said he was that she would be there? "Or I don't know my Shan," he'd said, and he didn't, but she was there anyway.

She did not dare to look out at the bay, for fear of what she might see there. Since she'd spotted the monster, he'd surfaced repeatedly in her memory, leonine face heavy with rage, dripping with enmity, smoke (had it been smoke, or breathed out clouds he had swallowed and spit up again?) seeping from his flared nostrils. The more she thought of Darnall, the more horrific he became. So she simply excised him from her mind, or tried to. It was better not to look at the bay. For having called him forth the first time, it was possible she could do it two nights in a row, even though, as she knew from eating the last flower, his appearance probably had nothing to do with her personally.

How freeing it was not to take things personally. How simple life became when you understood not everything was about *you*. How difficult it would have been for her, for whom traffic was always officially stopped, had she not been presently even more enchanted than when she was a princess. In some deep part of herself, she understood that even as she lost the privilege she was accustomed to, the rewards she was receiving were of the greater kind. So she was ashamed that in the petty part of herself, she was piqued. Past piqued. Where was he? What kind of man would long for her, beg her to come, and then be late? Oh, were women all seesaws in their souls, caught between an understanding of what was boundless, and their silly needs?

Above her she could hear melancholy whispers, ghosts more ancient than Hamlet's father, crossbowmen with weapons raised against those who would give supremacy to the English crown. How many dreams had been born and died in this castle? How many princes had stood on the battlements, waiting for more than love?

Footsteps sounded on the pale red stone, footsteps heavy as her heart, until she heard them. "Miles," she called into the lustrous darkness. "Miles?"

But no answer came. She shivered. Heard the footsteps again. "Don't tease me now," she said, annoyed, getting to her feet. "You have no idea how long I've waited."

"Yes, I do," said Tom. And there he was in the moonlight, his poor threadbare jacket all that came between the wind and his pajamas, Darcy having taken his coat.

"Oh," said Darcy, inanely.

"Come to see your monster, have you?"

"I can explain."

"I shouldn't be surprised. For you have become as fine a liar as ever lived in Wales, and that's a stretch of the mind to conceive of." He took her by the flesh of her earlobe, pulling her roughly out of the gatehouse to the stairwell, barely keeping her from falling as she stumbled after him, down to the street.

"Ow," she cried.

"Oh, you can do better. Anybody can say 'Ow.' You're more original than that."

"Tom, please."

"Please?" he growled, jerking her along the cobblestones. "You ask me *please?*"

"Brute!" she cried.

"That's what I am," he said, throwing open their door, pushing her inside, slamming it behind him. "A crude man, with no smooth edges, no feathers like your peacock. A brute, just as you say. But I'll tell you one thing I am not. I am not a dandy, or a fool."

"That's two things," she said.

He raised his hand to her.

"You wouldn't!"

"Oh, yes I would. But I won't just now. Because I know you're crazy. Or maybe I just prefer to think you're crazy, because it tears my heart to see how false you've become."

"I am exactly what I am," said Darcy. "There is not an insincere bone in me, that was not bred to be that way."

"Oh, Shan." He dropped to the couch, and covered his face. "What's happened to you? I went to see the vicar this morning. I thought you'd gotten so caught in his palaver that you actually fancied you could be whatever you could imagine. And that was why this madness with Princess Darcy."

"But I . . . ," she started to say, and then realized how much she stood to lose. Freedom and intrigue, romance, flowers in the windowbox. And this good man who stood ready to fight for her, with herself if need be. All of it gone with a word, if she could make him believe her.

But who was *he*, to think he could judge *her?* Where did he get the right, with his grimy hands and leathery brain? Who'd put him in charge, this common man with only one coat, which his wife had to borrow to cover her misconduct? And who was Miles, to keep her waiting like that, that smooth-talking popinjay. For all she knew, he wasn't even all that gifted, else why would he be in this roadiest of road companies. And who was *she* without the lure to bring a man to the castle by moonlight, when he himself had repeated the honeyed words, pleaded for the assignation? Were her own lips not sweet enough, her body, vanity aside, not soft? Her embrace not languid enough to tempt him? Had she lost all her charms? Or perhaps she had never really had them. Perhaps she was a victim of her own press, with nothing to offer but a dream for everybody else.

Tears filled her eyes. She ran down the narrow stairway to the kitchen, looked into the windowbox. Fed by the light of the ripening moon, a flower blossomed, another one beside it in the bud. She leaned forward and examined the bloom: pale green, shaped like a foxglove. Tipping the petals up, she saw inside a face that might have been quite like her own, except that she couldn't really tell for sure, since there was a blindfold across the eyes. Hunger snapped at her. And though she didn't like doing anything greedy, except perhaps fall in love, she broke it off at the stem, and ate it.

Peace, minty, like an unguent, soothed the burning in her brain, took the pucker from her mouth. And she knew better than to think badly of herself, or Tom or Miles, or anybody. Understood on the very deepest level that she didn't have to understand. That things were as they were, and had nothing to do with her lure or Tom's insensitivity. Now that she thought of it, he wasn't really insensitive, only bristling, because she had hurt him. He had seemed insensitive to her, but who was she to judge? In fact, he was a lovely soul, and so was she and so was Miles, though a bit (a big bit) of an egotist. But who was she to rule on his conceit? And she felt a burst of love for all of them, including Darcy. For she had eaten the flower that did away with Judgment, of herself as well as others.

"I've been a terrible fool," she said to Tom, settling herself beside him on the worn brown couch, tilting her head so it touched his, as though in a gentle intermingling of ideas.

"What's this?" he said, and looked at her as if he believed her change of heart no more than he did her other stories.

"Can you forgive me for thinking I was better than you are?"

"But you are better than I am," he said.

"I'll be the judge of that," said Darcy, and smiled at him.

Nobody was more a victim of the quest for fantasy than Rachid. Lout though he was, reprobate and libertine, he, too, had a soul, albeit a black one. And slithering through the corridors of the castle, he wished no less for a great experience than did the rest of our players. For even as Darcy's heart and mind were expanding in Criccieth, and she was learning not to judge, so was I. And, it would not surprise me, gentle reader, to find you were doing the same. Returning to this scoundrel, then, this cur, this (in the words of the king, who had a satellite dish, and watched MTV) scuzzball, greatly astonished was I to find him weeping, alone in the secret passageway he had built to the chamber of his lady love, connecting his room and hers. When people are devious and confused, and their whole existence is a maze, their life reflects that, as does their interior decorating. So he had had his iniquitous designer make a false back to his fireplace, linking it, via a hidden panel, to the bookcase of the queen. When he was really angry at himself, he would light the logs before going to visit her, so he could say, without prevaricating, "I've been through fire for you." For the basest of men now and then enjoys a gavotte with the truth, to better contrast the tap dance of his lies.

But he had burned himself in this particular excursion, his boot having caught in the sliding panel, and the fire giving him a hotfoot. He squatted in the darkness, weeping, partly from pain, partly over the ruining of his favorite boots, and partly from an overwhelming sense of loss. Because when he was a little boy running barefoot through the streets of his fly-ridden village, soles cracked and cut, his mother would soothe his scrapes and sores with her lips. Now that his boots were so costly — the most extravagant pair of them half-destroyed from his latest foray — she was not there to see it, or comfort him. Not that she was dead, but the last thing he needed in his life was another strong woman.

So he wept for himself, and his hurt, and his boot, and his mother, and the inequity of a world where the person you loved most, you had to keep at a distance. Which was probably why he had had the decorator build the secret passageway: besides being his dream of what a real adventure should include, a man needed a place to cry.

Wiping his nose on his sleeve, for good woman though his

mother might have been, she didn't know spit about manners, he pressed the joining, sliding and opening the panel into Isabel's bedchamber. She was sitting up in bed, candlelight softened by hurricane lamps in different darknesses of red mellowing the satin-ribboned spectacle of her cleavage.

A few renegade tears trickled down his cheek, as he tried not to hobble, his right boot having been left in the wall. "I've been through fire for you," he said.

"You should have used the door," said Isabel.

"This is an Arabian night," he said, and threw himself across the down quilt that covered her almost as puffily as her breasts. "Things mustn't be too easy."

"Including me?"

"Oh, my love," he said. "Easy would be the last word I would use to describe you."

"And what would be the first?" Isabel asked eagerly, for she was never so caught in a conversation as when it was about her. But we will not judge her, either, for she had been in as many articles as Darcy, in her day, and had a hard time believing it was over, in spite of the mailings she had received that very morning from Forest Lawn, offering a burial site right next to Clark Gable, who had, after all, been "The King."

"Magnificent!" he said, and thrust his finger into her cleavage. "Too much for just one man."

"I am a faithful woman," she said, her cheeks reddening so sharply that it was perceptible even in the rosy candlelight. "Or at least I was, until you corrupted me."

"What we have is not corrupt," he said. "Certainly not by Turkish standards."

"You are not a Turk."

"My enemies might argue that with you." He tweaked her nipple. "Do you know what tonight is?"

"My birthday?" she said, hopefully. Although she had stopped observing that occasion when she turned forty, she secretly longed for a celebration, especially if there would be presents.

"In a way," he said. "For as I have been through fire for you, you can now begin to prove your love for me."

"I have proved it a thousand ways," she protested. "Or at least three. Haven't I abandoned my troth to the king?"

"Not a good example."

"Haven't I done dirty things?"

"Dirty is in the eye of the beholder," Rachid said, and winked.

"Haven't I said I would do almost anything, short of denouncing my son's marriage?"

"*Almost* doesn't count," said Rachid. "Tonight we will begin to test your commitment. As you care for me, you will do what gives me pleasure. You will have a sexual encounter with a stranger."

"Never!"

"They're waiting in the secret room," he said, dragging her from the bed.

"Oh, you and your secret rooms," she said. "Why can't we go bowling like other couples?"

Veils, gauzy shrouds of dark lace twirled into streamers as at a prom for the perverted, hung from the ceiling, circling out to the walls. Music played at the wrong speed. Blue gels covered the slowly revolving lights set at angles in the floor, so the masked faces seemed even eerier than the masks alone would have made them. Bodies, seminude, breasts and an occasional flash of Little Elvis, as another once king called his genitals, moved in the cerulean glow, adding to the air of surrealism. Isabel could not believe she was really there, even disguised as she was, her own mask transforming her into a hawk, a bird of prey, she who was only beginning to understand what it was to be a victim.

Hands played against her breasts in the darkness. A strong-fingered stranger led her to an opening in the wall. He touched a button, and the wall closed them in. They were pressed to each other, hawk to field mouse. "This is my first blind date," she said, giggling.

He pulled off her mask, and traced her features, exploring them, his mouse mask implacable. "Can't I see you?" she asked. But he was lifting her skirt, taking her without a word.

He tweaked her nipple.

"Rachid!" she said, stunned.

"Did you think I would let any other man have you?" he said, lifting his mask, kissing her roughly.

So it was a test. Apparently, there were degenerate ones, as well as the spiritual kind, and those that funded character. Even as she felt relieved, Isabel couldn't help noting she was slightly disappointed.

"Move that reflector to the left," Adrian instructed Cesare, trying to keep the irritation from his voice. It wasn't easy having an assistant who was basically a kidnapper helping with a photographic session, even more frustrating that he did it all left-handedly.

Simply setting up the shoot had been terribly complex. Adrian had had to make sure that the official court photographer would be away, which he'd arranged with a series of false cables from the Continent, inviting him to be guest of honor at a photographic museum in Paris, sending him a ticket paid for out of Adrian's own pocket, because his deal with Rachid did not include airfare. Then he'd had to squirrel in, unobserved, tens of yards of green and pink satin to drape the floors and walls of the studio. This morning there'd been the task of secreting Babara from the apartment where she'd been healing to the royal studio itself, hidden behind her dark glasses, scarf tied tight around her head, raincoat covering her gloriously rehabilitated nudity.

Not to mention his having had to buy these *things*, lacy garter belts and brassieres, see-through pastel brassieres, patterned stockings, spiky heels for her to stand in against a photo blowup of the palace, so it would seem she was out there, *really* in the open, slipping out of her Victoriana. It had been so embarrassing, being in the lingerie store, with the salesgirl looking at him as if he were actually doing kinky things with a *woman*. Not that

Adrian disliked women, but as he'd told Babara right from the beginning, this was the turning point in his life, and the last thing he needed was intimacy. All the more mortifying, buying these items the salesgirl kept calling *intimate* garments, while he insisted what he wanted was lingerie.

And now she stood there in all her ameliorated glory, looking the image of Darcy from the top of her head to the tips of her tips. Really, he could not help thinking, she was lovely, if your taste ran to seminaked aristocrats, or their duplicates.

"There's a shadow across her eyes," Adrian said to the sinister Sicilian.

"That could be longing," said Babara, and looked at him.

"It's also on the bridge of your nose," Adrian said.

"I like that," said Cesare. "It looks like someone took a crack at her."

"This is not for distribution in Sicily," said Adrian, trying not to bristle. "Move the reflector to the left."

There were lights set up all around the studio that Adrian had arranged himself, as artistry was second only to secrecy. Because he needed someone to help him, as sparely as the session was being conducted, he'd had no choice but to have the criminal he'd brought in to help with the snatch, in a manner of speaking, of the real Princess Darcy. "Maybe if you took your gloves off, Cesare."

"These are like second skin," Cesare said, flexing his fingers so Adrian could see the backs of his black hands.

"Second skin," sighed Babara. "I used to think it was only an expression."

"You look . . ." Adrian paused. Though he wanted very much to avoid close personal relationships, he was a sensitive man, and he could feel her insecurity. Having spent all of his life wishing to be someone better, never imagining it could be himself, he was nonetheless awash in compassion for someone who had become someone else and still didn't like who she was. Or wasn't. "Fabulous."

"Really?"

"I wouldn't lie to you."

"You think a man could care for me?"

"I certainly could," said Cesare. "But I'd like you better with a smashed nose."

"Take off the gloves," said Adrian, not understanding why he should feel rankled.

"Okay," said Cesare, reluctantly, peeling back the one with the tattoo on it, to reveal the same tattoo underneath, on the flesh on the back of his hand. Then he moved the reflector again.

"That's much better," said Adrian, looking at her through a lens. "Drop your bra strap, Babara."

"My hands are cold," she said. "Can you do it for me?"

"I'll do it," Cesare said.

"Stay where you are!" said Adrian, and went to her, and tried not to touch her flesh as he lowered the strap. But his fingers, precise and delicate though they were, were still a man's fingers, wider than the flimsy, flowered band. And he felt the warmth beneath them, the silk that was silkier than the satin.

She stared at him. "Thank you."

"Anytime," he tried to say, but it stuck in his throat. And he was back behind the camera, using it as a shield, really trying not to be blinded by her, to see her as the piece of meat that she was, the portion that would nourish him, strengthen his position, change his life, giving him the power and money Rachid had promised if it all worked out. "Wet your lips," he said.

"My tongue is cold," she said. "Can you do it for me?"

His mouth was suddenly dry. "I have no spit," he said.

"I have plenty of spit," said Cesare. "Where I come from we learn to spit before we learn to speak."

"I wasn't aware you knew how to speak," said Adrian, hating the man.

"It's all right, I'll do it," Babara said, licking her lips with a pointed pink tongue, looking straight at the lens, and at Adrian.

He posed her in front of the blowup of the palace, standing

on tiptoe, in the spiked heels. And he could not help noting the musculature of her calf, and the graceful slope of her honey-skinned thigh. Even though God was no longer acknowledged or allowed in Perq, and Adrian himself wasn't sure what he believed, he allowed that, even counting the skillful practitioners of Beverly Hills, there was but One who was the Greatest Plastic Surgeon of Them All.

"Good," he said, as she smiled and flirted according to his instruction. "Great! Tilt your head to the right. Good. A little wider with the smile. Throw your left shoulder back. Okay, that's great," he said, clicking off, changing cameras. "Now you can lie down."

"It's really cold on this satin." she said, wriggling.

"Don't move too much. You'll spoil the line of the fabric."

"I wouldn't mind spoiling the line of her fabric," leered Cesare.

"Would you please keep your comments to yourself?" Adrian said.

Cesare covered his mouth, making a cup of his hands, whispering lewd suggestions into them. Adrian tried not to hear, but the words were foul, and his ears were acute. How disgusting that the only felons you could find were so base. Where were the elegant criminals, the ones with sensibility, perhaps even witty dialogue? Was it a world bereft of modish transgressors, cat burglars, jewel thieves, nothing left but child molesters and terrorists? Had all style vanished with Cary Grant?

"Don't you want me totally naked?" asked Babara.

"Would you mind?" asked Adrian.

"Would she mind?" Cesare mimicked. "What is this, a tea party? We're talking *Playhouse* Centerfold, you boob."

"Watch your language!" Adrian said.

"I was talking *you*, boob. Not her boobs."

"Please don't fight with him," Babara said, her eyes quite wide, with a look of concern in them, but not for herself. She moved her hands behind her back, and opened the snaps of the brassiere, freeing what Adrian had mistakenly thought was the subject of the dispute. "There," she said.

"The panties," said Cesare.

"Can't you call them pants?"

"It doesn't matter," Babara said, and whipped them off. "Don't be concerned about me."

"I'm not." said Adrian. "I'm not."

"Then why is your face all flushed?" said Babara.

"It's hot in here."

"I find it quite cold," said Babara. "Perhaps if you came and lay down on this satin . . ."

"I'm hot, too," said Cesare. "A lot hotter than he is, I bet you anything."

"Let's just take the pictures, gangster," said Adrian.

During the night, Junella, the princess's lady-in-waiting, had a stroke. For although patience is the reward of patience, according to Saint Augustine, too much waiting grits the teeth of the brain, and sometimes it bubbles. As Junella waited even while she was sleeping, her very breath on the edge, not even daring to dream, fists clenched apprehensively, jaws in a pit-bull grip, one of the bubbles exploded.

So she did not hear the creeping, creepy footsteps that passed alongside her chamber, or the squeaking door as it opened to the princess's bedroom. And as Rodney, passionately as he had begun to feel about his Darcy, still kept up the custom of sleeping in his own room, there was no one present to be alerted to the intruders, to hear the (presumed) princess's cries. There were not many, and those few muffled in the chloroformed cloth held over her face by Cesare, as her slender, splendidly peignoired body stiffened and then relaxed. He took the ring and watch from her hand, then slid the unconscious (purported) Darcy from the bed into the duffel bag he'd carried there, and flung it, with its insensate burden, over his shoulder.

"Psst . . . ," he hissed to Adrian and Babara, who huddled in the hall, where slept the drugged palace guard, soporifics having been injected by Rachid into their Smartees. Candy-covered pellets of chocolate fell from the bags they held in their slackened grasps. Cesare handed the watch and ring to Adrian, then moved down the hall.

"In here," said Adrian, taking Babara by the hand, trying not to notice how it felt in his, struggling not to be moved by the softness of her palm, the light coat of cold sweat on it. He hated that she was afraid, that he could feel her fear, and it bothered him. Cowardice had never been one of his character failings, as he didn't like himself well enough to be anxious about the consequences of risk. But he didn't want anything to happen to her. It would ruin his plot. That was the only reason for his concern, he was sure. His apprehension had nothing to do with the fact that he cared about her, other than as a means to power, he was totally convinced. "Don't be afraid," he said, softly, leading her into the bedroom.

"Why not?"

"Because it's all going to be fine," he said, setting her on the edge of the bed, slipping the watch on her wrist, the ring on her finger. "Tomorrow, when you get up, you'll ask your lady-in-waiting, Junella, to have the royal Learjet fly you to Nice. We'll have someone waiting there to take you to the next step."

"I can't quite hear you," Babara said. "You'll have to speak a little closer to my neck."

He moved nearer, trying not to see the outlines of her nipples in the nightgown. Somehow the suggestion of her body beneath the fabric was more inciting than the total nudity had been. Not that he was in any way aroused by her, for arousal was not part of his plan. His plan included only the rock singer in Monte Carlo, the drug dealer with the yacht in Saint-Tropez, and the ski instructor in Zermatt. The last would provide the juiciest scandal, since it was off-season; there was nothing more energetic and restless than a ski instructor without snow on his slope. "The royal Learjet will fly you to Nephew," he said, his mind not quite focused on the information, his heart beating in his ears.

"I thought you said Nice."

"I did, didn't I?"

"I'm not sure. I was watching your mouth," she said.

"You will know your contact when he says to you, 'Scum rises.'"

"I hate that. Can't he say something pretty?"

"Go to sleep, now," Adrian whispered.

"I don't think I can."

"Of course you can. You must be exhausted."

"I'm just coming to life. Haven't you ever wondered what it was like being dead?"

"No," said Adrian, which was a lie.

"Well, I can tell you. You feel like you're floating in a kind of gelatin. You see everything slow-motion and distorted. And you have no energy, but you can't tell you have no energy, because you have no idea what energy is. And there's no pain. But there's no pleasure either."

Adrian tried not to seem too fascinated, even though he was. He had several questions in his head about the afterlife, and reincarnation, which he hoped there wasn't any of, since this one trip had drained him sufficient to last several lifetimes. Still, it was exciting, speaking to someone who seemed to be an authority, who wasn't a movie star or a self-promoter. "How do you know all this?"

"Because it's how I was, till I met you."

"We're talking the future of a nation, and the arms business, with probable reverberations to OPEC and consequently the economy of the world. So the feelings of two little people —"

"You feel it, too?" she interrupted.

"I feel nothing," he said harshly.

"You said two little people," she said. "I'm only one."

"That's right. That's all you are. One little people. And you're not going to ruin the chance of a lifetime."

"All right," she said, and lay down. "But will you tuck me in?"

"Of course," he said, and drew the blankets over her, trying not to see how lovely she looked there.

"And will you kiss me good night?"

"Now, really . . ."

"I won't be able to sleep," she said.

"Oh, very well," he said, with not a little irritation, and brushed her cheek with his lips.

But she turned her face and caught his with her mouth. And for a moment he forgot the degradations of his youth, and the unlovingness of his history, and his specious hungers for power, influence, and unlimited credit. It was all he could do to pull away, but pull away he did.

"Good night," he said, getting to his feet.

"It really could have been," she whispered.

He switched out the lamp beside her bed, so he wouldn't have to see her eyes, with their lost, longing expression. And worse, the reflection of himself in them. Why, he'd looked absolutely handsome.

8

"BUT THIS WAS THE MOST AMAZING blossom so far," Darcy said to the duchess. "It took away Judgment."

"Then you must be very careful that you don't make foolish mistakes," the duchess said, and poured some tea. She had set an extra cup on the floor for Bailey, her former butler. But the rest of the cats, not understanding his exalted position, crowded around, licking it up with him, creamed as it was. So there was an absolute catlock around the fireplace.

"Not that kind of judgment. The judging that makes you judgmental about people. For example, if I had considered you eccentric."

"Don't you?"

"Not anymore," said Darcy.

"I'm sorry to hear that," said the duchess.

"And I'm not even angry with Miles, that's the most amazing part. Ordinarily, if he hadn't shown up, I'd consider him beneath contempt."

"Oh, no, he's too tall for that," said the duchess. "Contempt is very short."

Darcy smiled. "And I no longer consider myself superior to other people. Although of course I am."

The tea that the duchess poured overflowed the rim of her cup, onto the saucer, past the edge of that into the air, and thenceforward onto the carpet, a trickle that became its own kind of waterfall, as the duchess stared at Darcy. The cats left Bailey's cup, now empty, and rushed to the site of the new treat, licking at the puddle accruing near the duchess's feet. "Oh, my," the duchess said with some distress, as she saw what she was doing.

"Understand that that's not Vanity, which I lost with the very first flower, but simply a statement of the facts. As I tried to tell you in the beginning, I am not an ordinary person." Darcy took a towel from the tea tray, and actually got down on her knees to sop up the spill. As with the very first day she learned to cook and have it not be a disaster, there was a strange kind of satisfaction in something as simple as soaking up a stain, taking what otherwise would have been a mess and making it the way it was before. Well, nearly.

"I'm honored you're helping me," said the duchess, with what seemed the slightest bit of an edge.

"Of course you should be," said Darcy, on her knees. "Because it isn't every woman who has a princess cleaning up for her. But then you deserve it." She took the towel, soaked now, set it on the tray, and smiled at the duchess. "For that is who I am, as I tried to tell you in the beginning. Princess Darcy."

"Princess Darcy?" the duchess said.

"I told Tom, but he wouldn't believe me. It's really just as well. Because what would I do if he wanted his own Shan back, when I'm so happy here?"

"Shan . . . ?" the duchess said, looking deeply confused.

"She's in Perq. We changed places."

"And you don't consider *me* eccentric?" said the duchess.

"You don't believe me either," said Darcy, a little disappointed.

"This above all," the duchess said. "To thine own self be true, even if you're someone else."

"I shall have to remember that," said Darcy.

* * *

So it was clear to Darcy there was no point in looking for a confidante. What it was she had to be most confidential about, nobody believed. But she did not take offense at her inability to convince, since it was Shan they didn't believe, not Darcy. Clearly, Shan did not have as much of a reputation for integrity as one might have assumed, in spite of how virtuous a picture she had presented, good and sweet and straightforward and of limited wardrobe.

The wedding dress so severely soiled by the little wretches of security guards had been washed by Darcy, hung up to dry, and now, finally, was being ironed. Tea with the duchess and her cats, one of them reincarnated, had been concluded, with no real rancor. Having been healed of Judgment, Darcy couldn't pronounce the duchess less worthy for not believing her. Besides, the duchess had instructed her in ironing, apparently finding nothing odd or contradictory in this seemingly simple housewife's not even knowing how to plug in an iron. Rather did the duchess seem pleased at being able to help someone even more confused than herself.

So Darcy stood in the little house she was coming to love, shabby as it was, passing the hot metal over the sprinkled fabric, watching it become smooth, an even greater new satisfaction than cooking. For never in her life had she had the joy of immediacy, seeing some effort she made cause an instantaneous measurable change for the better.

As she ironed, Jackie, the sad little boy in red oilcloth slicker and Wellingtons, sat respectfully on a stool at her feet, watching. His eyes were oversized and chronically red-rimmed. Darcy knew little about children, having never been interested in them as a breed, her only thought of them being something she would have to bear, literally, one day as princess. Her own recollection of what it felt like to be a child was dim, blotted out by years of getting everything she wanted. Childhood was a time of insecurity and unfulfilled needs, according to the resident palace psychologist, a period of narcissism, before one discovered the better, higher self. Having been coddled from infancy, Darcy never had to make that transition. She'd had no reason to learn to distinguish narcissism from the higher self, or to make any kind of journey from the first to the second, assuming that where she was in the beginning of her trip was as good as it got.

So whatever pain there was in the little boy beside her was no more familiar to her than the bottle she used to sprinkle the fabric of her dress. But she did look on him rather kindly, since he had lost his mother and loved her, two things she could sort of relate to. Well, the second anyway.

"Why are you dressed like that, Jackie?" she asked him now.

"My mum said boys don't know when to come in out of the rain."

"But it isn't raining," Darcy said.

"It might. And she isn't here to tell me to come in. I don't want her ashamed of me."

"I'm sure she'd never be ashamed of you, Jackie."

"Do you think girls know when to come in out of the rain?"

"Certainly," Darcy said. "But it's not so much that they're smarter as that they don't want to spoil their hair."

"Oh, I think they're smarter," Miles said from the doorway.

Darcy turned. She could not help noting how fine-looking he still was, his hollow-heartedness having failed to transform him into the worm she might have seen him as, had she not eaten the flower that took away Judgment.

"No, they're not," she said. "Or they wouldn't love the wrong people."

"How can you say what's *wrong?*" asked Miles.

"Well, far be it from me to judge," said Darcy, going over the same spot again and again, killing what would have been left of any wrinkle that might have had the temerity to rest on that particular section of fabric. "But I would guess that if a fisherman lured a fish with a particular line, and the fish came up from the deeps of the water because it couldn't resist, and the fisherman didn't even bother to show up to catch it, the fish would know better about that man than certain women."

"What kind of fish?" said Jackie.

"Don't you have someplace to go, Jackie?" Miles asked.

"I'm supposed to go to school," said Jackie. "But not until September."

"You stay right here," Darcy said.

"You're angry," said Miles.

"A freshwater fish, or a saltwater fish?" Jackie asked.

"Why would I be angry?" Darcy asked. "Because I risk the love of a good man for a vain, empty bag of air?"

"A blowfish!" said Jackie, triumphant.

"A blowfish, indeed." Darcy ruffled his hair. "You're smarter than I am."

"I suppose you're not interested in an explanation," said Miles.

"I have things to do," Darcy said, and ironed. "I have clothes to iron and meals to cook, and a life to offer to a man who cares about the human heart."

"Don't you think I do?"

"Think?" said Darcy. "How could I possibly think, when I was up half the night on the empty ramparts waiting for someone with less substance than the ghost of Hamlet's father."

"I meant to come," said Miles.

"Was there a ghost?" asked Jackie.

"Not even," said Darcy. "Because in order to be a ghost, you would need to have spirit, and there are some people born without any."

It surprised her how much of a passion she was in. Never had it occurred to her that, should she fall in love, what she desired would be denied her. Having spent the past few years being everyone else's dream of romance, living the fantasy that most people wanted, it had been totally out of her ken that she could have wished for more, or different. Falling out of her cloud onto earth, daily discovering the wonders that earth had to offer on a simple scale, she was nonetheless still above and apart from other people, since she knew what they did not, and refused to believe even when she told them: that she was a royal princess. Royalty, as the few remaining royalists were always saying, carried with it certain obligations. But it also carried with it a certain superiority, since it meant, by definition, above and beyond the common and ordinary. (Darcy read the dictionary now for spiritual solace since Rachid had burned the Bibles.)

The fact that this probably ordinary actor (oh, how she wished she understood Welsh!) from the common clay was debasing her seemed more than an outrage. It was a contradiction in terms. For what was high could not be subverted by what was low, except in the case of revolution, which this certainly was not. He didn't have enough regard for anything outside himself to be a revolutionary. She knew that much about him.

"You think I have no spirit?" Miles said, looking more incensed than she felt.

"Well, it depends what you mean by spirit. If you mean essence, for example, the kind of perfume you wear, then I would say yes, you have spirit."

"It's not perfume," he said, blackly.

"Then if you mean intellect, heart, all we have seen is the reflection. That is to say, what you can remember of what other people have said. So, we can't really tell. But if you mean principle, soul, feelings, I would have to say most distinctly no, even though I don't judge anyone."

"I'm sorry if I hurt you," Miles said.

"Don't try and make me forgive you because you're so full of understanding. For there is only one thing you're full of, and as there is a child here, it would not be seemly for me to say."

"I could go," said Jackie.

"Go," said Miles.

"Stay," said Darcy.

"You're scorching your dress," said Miles.

"Damn." Darcy pulled the plug from the wall.

"Now take the iron off, before it burns through," Miles instructed.

"My only good dress!" Darcy started weeping.

"I'll buy you another."

"Do you imagine I have the heart of a shopgirl, that you can win me with a piece of clothing? And what would I say to Tom? Where would I tell him it had come from?"

"Why, you would not have to say anything. By the time you put it on, you would be on your way to London with me."

"If I could find you," said Darcy.

"Are you going to London?" Jackie said, stricken.

"Not to worry, my darling," Darcy said. "I'm not leaving you, or my brains, either."

"Coward," Miles said.

"It's true," said Darcy, wiping her eyes. "I'm afraid. Afraid of casting my lot in with a man who has only the strength of other people's convictions. Whose very life is a play, and that one with a weak-willed hero."

"Hamlet is not weak-willed. He is indecisive and doesn't trust women."

"Why?" asked Jackie.

"Because he has seen how spineless they are. How easily swayed. How disloyal."

"Not this one," said Darcy, closing the ironing board.

"And not my mum either," said Jackie, delivering a fine, sharp kick to Miles's shin as he ran past him, and out the door.

"Little prick!" Miles exclaimed, holding his leotarded knee up to his chest, so he could soothe his hurt.

"But a bigger man than you!" said Darcy. "For he knows how to stand up for what he believes in."

"So do I," said Miles, hopping.

"Then why didn't you show up?"

"Because if I am to have force in this role, I must bring truth to it. And as Hamlet has set aside his love for the sake of the action, so must I."

"What rubbish!" Darcy exclaimed, pushing him out the door. As he was standing on one foot, this caught him thoroughly off-balance, and landed him on his duff, which would have made her laugh were she not so angry. She slammed the door, and bolted it.

"Ohhhhhhh," she cried to herself, a great exhale of rage. And hands on her hips, she ran down into the kitchen. For all at once, she was starving, since love made people lose their appetites, and she had hers back, with a vengeance.

She flung open the casement shutters. There, in the window-box, a flower bloomed. Purple, this one was, and shaped, as the others, like a foxglove. She hardly took time to tip it up to look inside it, so ravenous was she. But tip it up she did. Inside was something that looked quite like a knot, but not one made of thread. Rather it was like the knot tied off on an umbilical cord. Dizzy with hunger, she broke off the blossom, and ate it.

And a roseate glow (a purple one, really) flowed from her belly to her breast to her brain. And she understood perfectly how anxious Miles was, and forgave him. For he was only an actor (not that she judged him) and all that he had for substance was his craft. Something quite past pity, even a soupçon past compassion sparked her sight, so she didn't look down at him, or apart, but simply saw, and felt, as he did.

There was a knock on the door, and she went to answer it. Bells were ringing in her ears. Not like the duchess's bells, for these had perfect clarity. She could hear to the absolute center of them, and, as a matter of fact, feel as though she herself were the sound. She opened the door, prepared to absolve Miles in person, now that she had compassion for him, and his limits, having them herself. But instead standing in the doorway was Jackie, with a lovely blue dress folded across his arms.

"This was my mum's," he said, holding it out to her. "Now you don't have to go to London."

"Oh, Jackie," she said, and knelt to embrace him, throwing her arms around him, and her love. Magically she felt the love come back at her, and the love he felt and the love he had lost. And she felt the loss, too, and she wept with him, and was a part of him, as he was a part of her. For she had eaten the flower that took away a Sense of Separation.

Well, it was the first time Shan had awakened since the start of her adventure that she felt other than cozy. Groggy as well as uncomfortable, she wondered if she could have drunk too much champagne. She had a burning in her nose, and a terrible headache, so was reluctant to open her eyes, for fear the sun would be too bright for them. But there was no sun at all, just a deep pervading gloom. And what she saw, instead of rose-petal drapes framing a window that looked out on the palace garden, were chains, hanging from a wall.

"But what . . . ?" she weakly exclaimed. ". . . Where?" Then she saw a withered, bearded man, tucked tight into a kind of slabby bed, and added: ". . . Who?"

"Quirin, you dodo," he said, sourly. "Have you forgotten your own father-in-law?"

"The king!" Shan exclaimed. "Am I in Switzerland?"

"Switzerland?" he said. "Does this look like Switzerland?"

"But aren't you in Switzerland, having a cure?"

"I am in Perq, having a disease," said Quirin. "And the disease is the lust and ambition of Rachid, wiping out all who are in his path, which now, apparently, includes you, Darcy."

"I'm not Darcy," she said. "But I don't suppose there's any point trying to explain." She herself was not tied, but on a cot adjacent to the king's, next to which was a beaker of water. She drank thirstily. "How are we going to get out of here?"

"Know any magic?" Quirin said.

"No."

"Then I guess we're stuck," he said. "I knew he should have married a sorceress."

"But this is dreadful!" she said. "How long have you been a prisoner here?"

"Two inches on my beard," said Quirin.

"And where exactly are we?"

"In the bowels of the castle. With no escape, save that trapdoor."

Shan got up unsteadily, and went over to it. For all the high-tech deco of the dungeon, the trapdoor was conventional and forbidding, having one huge metal ring atop rotting wood. When she pulled it, there was a sound quite like a groan. It shuddered, and lifted. Below, far below, was the pitch of nothingness, and a far-off lap of water, putrescent. "What's down there?" she said, wrinkling her nose in distaste.

"Sewers. Rats. A slimy slide to both. And no guarantee whether you'll crack your skull or drown or simply be caught there for the rats to eat."

"Well, at least we have alternatives," said Shan, who was beginning to understand about freedom. She let the trapdoor shut with a clang. "What's up there?" She indicated the wooden stairs leading up to the ceiling.

"The kitchen."

She ran up the stairs, and started pounding on the ceiling. "Help!" she called out. "Help!"

"No one can hear you. It's soundproofed. And even if you could make a stir, the only one who's likely to respond is that cursed Rhea."

"The cook?"

"Cook hyphen traitor," said Quirin. "For she is in league with Rachid."

"But there must be something we can do," said Shan.

"Do you play bridge?"

"No."

"Then turn on MTV," said the king. "They're doing a retrospective on Jimi Hendrix."

Who was it had said nothing that was worth getting was gotten easily? Babara wondered. For from the moment she had awakened in her role of spurious princess, absolutely everything that might have gone wrong did. To begin with, Junella, the lady-in-waiting, was dead, which was, Babara could not help thinking, a sign. Junella's was the only name she knew, other than Prince Rodney, and she could hardly ask him to prepare the royal jet so she could leave him. She'd had to deal with all that confusion, weeping besides, since it was a terrible shock, having her only contact expire before she could make it. Her tears came easily, stunned and frightened as she was, all at sea, or in this case, at island. No one in the palace suspected she wasn't really Darcy, weeping for a trusted servant, and all commented on her humanity. Even Rodney seemed sadly satisfied that she was who she pretended to be, kissing her several times on the back of her neck as she keened and moaned for poor Junella, when of course she was really crying for herself.

Once they'd taken the body away, and promoted her assistant lady-in-waiting to the now-vacated top spot, she'd had to decide what clothes to take to the Riviera, *and* Switzerland, she who'd never been anyplace more exotic than Lake Arrowhead. But Minette, the replacement, was exceedingly helpful, interpreting Babara's lack of fashion sense and indecisiveness as confusion brought about by the loss of her most trusted servant, which it was now Minette's distinct pleasure to have become, fond as she'd been of Junella. Together the two young women, security guards tight around them, made their motorcycle-escorted way to the airport, and onto the royal Learjet, which of course was less than royal, it being Rachid's.

Rodney had pleaded with the (he thought) princess to let him come along with her, but she had succeeded in convincing him she needed to be alone in her grief. He seemed quite devastated by her leaving, although he was visibly moved at how caring she had become. His prior princess Darcy would have wept for a servant no more than she would make aggressively loving love to him. So he was pleased with what seemed still another positive change in her, even though it meant a tentative separation.

The worst behind her, she certainly hoped, Babara zoomed towards the south of France, nervously checking the Rolex which had been wrested from the wrist of the true (everyone supposed) princess. The ring that had been on the unconscious woman's hand had also been switched onto her finger, a gesture that Adrian had made before leaving her the night before. She had imbued the act in her imagination with all the symbolism ring-placing-on-the-finger held, seeing him as her groom, fancying it as a kind of wedding between them, even though he refused to love her. The world was filled with married couples, neither one of whom felt anything about the other, so she considered the fantasy only half preposterous, since she knew *she* loved *him* and would for the rest of her days.

The rest of her days now had a livelier sparkle than before. She had a purpose. Besides making Adrian pleased with her, which she fully intended to do, enabling him to have his power and influence and all the unimportant things that men wanted, it was also her plan to make him fall in love with her. As little of a self-image as Babara had, she understood about insecurity. Seeing her on the arm of rock stars and ski instructors, which he had explained to her was his plan, he would have to feel some possessiveness, some jealousy, she was sure. Men were territorial, lifting their legs in their own way, pissing on something to mark it as theirs, even when they didn't want it.

"Oh, look, Highness: France." Minette pointed out the window.

Babara restrained her inclination to gasp excitedly, and looked indifferently down at the verdant coastline, tip reaching back on itself as though to scratch its own underbelly. Excitement rose in her throat, in direct inversion to the plane's descending, as her eye filled with red-tiled rooftops, sloping vineyards, terraced hills, and the deep, clear blue-green of the Mediterranean. Love, now that she felt it, now that it had been born in her heart, loaned excitement to all she perceived. The passivity that had been her nature was gone. In its place a spirit of joy and enthusiasm veritably pogo-sticked. Thrill after thrill at the visual splendor coursed through her veins, cushioned only slightly by the sad little knell of how much more beautiful it would all be if present were someone to share it with.

But she was ahead of most women who sang that sad anthem. At least she knew he existed, that the earth was not bereft of him. For the woods, and Rodeo Drive, were flooded with that breed: women who were sure he didn't exist, and had nowhere to go but shopping.

At the Nice airport, customs men in dark blue uniforms with matching caps respectfully asked to examine her luggage. Having never passed through customs before, much less as a visiting princess, Babara was discomfited from the outset by their perusal, polite as it seemed. Simply hearing their language put her on the defensive, filled as it was with erotic overtones. For we are all victims of the beginnings of our lives, and Babara had come from a home where genitals were called "down there." So although she had finally fallen in love, Babara was secretly pleased Adrian was so reticent, since anything straightforwardly sexual unnerved her. Hearing this amorous tongue, then — for wasn't French officially the language of love? — tightened her orifices. When the customs official asked in all innocence (as far as we know, for there is no time to examine his life or hidden thoughts) if she had anything to declare, Babara said: "I am not one of those women."

"*Pardon?*" said the Douane.

"Eager to tell my secrets," Babara huffed.

"*Je ne comprends pas.*"

"He doesn't understand," said Minette, not understanding either.

"Just because society's become so permissive doesn't mean we all have to bare our breasts."

"My feeling exactly," said a tall young man with yellow curls and carven cheeks, whose own breast was barer than those of any of the women nearby. His shirt was opened to the center of his rib cage, medallions threading through the gold hairs of his pecs. Curls hung to his waist. His pants were skintight black leather. Deeply tanned, his face slanted bronze at the angled cheekbones, beneath yellow eyes.

Photographers pushed and elbowed each other on the far end of the customs area, positioning themselves for taking pictures. Behind them, elbowing their way forward, and nearer, teenagers shrieked and pointed. "Nick!" they cried. "Nick Deamon!"

He seemed unruffled by any of it, apparently more accustomed to celebrity than Babara was, concerned only that the men handling the luggage be gentle with his guitar. "*Rien à declarer?*" the customs official asked him.

"Like the lovely princess, I have nothing," said Nick, as the customs inspector threw open a lid, revealing a suitcase filled with neatly packaged condoms. "Well, one can't be too careful these days," Nick said. "Scum rises."

"Oh, dear," said Babara.

So here it was then, the second leg of her journey, all encased as it was in black leather. Not knowing very much rock and roll, she had no idea who he was, except that he was apparently a celebrity on as grand a scale as Darcy, since the photographers were all over each other in their haste to snap the two of them together.

Outside the Nice airport, soft, end-of-summer winds blew the fronds on the long-necked palm trees, as Nick helped her into his white stretch limousine. Lady-in-waiting and security guards were dispatched to a second car, to be ensconced in the caretaker's cottage of Nick's villa.

Dressed for the concert that evening in the silver-threaded pantsuit Minette considered most appropriate, embroidered gold phoenix, national symbol of Perq, rising from her left breast, Babara tried to take genuine pleasure from the proceedings. But there was so much screaming and shouting even during his songs, she wondered how anyone could tell if he was any good.

"And now . . . ," Nick said, over the squeals and screeches, "I'd like to dedicate my next song to the loveliest woman in Europe. My special friend, Princess Darcy of Perq."

Prodded by her lady-in-waiting, Babara got to her silver-sandaled feet. Applause was reluctantly bestowed by resentful young women who knew they would be better for him, and would stand a chance were the princess not a princess. Flashbulbs exploded. Nick blew a kiss, tearing the epaulets from his shoulders, throwing them to her as matadors would a bull's ear.

Perhaps you are wondering, dear reader, as were the women

in the audience, why these magical things are always happening to someone else. Babara had often wondered the same thing, and now that this was happening to her, she wondered why she had ever felt envy. For she was terribly uncomfortable, and having no fun at all. The truth is, nobody should envy anybody, because we are all where we are supposed to be all the time, and not really missing anything. But it's hard to understand that until you get to the place you thought you wanted to be and then discover you were happier where you were.

After the concert, Darcy's security guards, in a united flank with Nick's, fought off the fans. The two managed to get away to a quiet café where they ate dinner unobserved, except for ten or twelve paparazzi.

"You're pretty real for a princess," Nick said to her.

"And you for a rock star," Babara said.

"Actually it's rhythm and blues. But I don't like to carp."

In the corner, in a candlelit booth, sat a dark man, handsome, slightly balding, with the angry eyes of one who has everything, but still can't keep his hair. He watched the two of them for a while through the hazy blue smoke spiraling from his gold-tipped cigarette, and then came over to their table.

"Franco Piccardoni," he said, bowing.

"The infamous drug dealer?" asked Nick.

"Import-export business." Franco presented his card. "May I join you?"

"I have a pact with my fans," said Nick. "I am not into substance abuse."

"What kind of abuse are you into?"

"If you will excuse us . . ." Nick turned away.

"For the moment," said Franco. "But I invite you to my yacht tomorrow morning. We sail at eight for Saint-Tropez."

"I think not," said Nick.

"I think so," said Franco, taking a deep breath. "Scum rises."

"Oh, I hate that." Babara covered her ears. "Why couldn't they have picked a nicer password?"

* * *

So there were King Quirin and the purported Princess Darcy, incarcerated in their bleak dungeon. Their palates had been slightly brightened by the gourmet slop Rhea had sent down for their dinner, with a guard wearing a turncoat. Much had our Shan pleaded with him for mercy and aid, pointing out to him what he ought to feel for his kingdom and his king, promising him all the rewards of the just, and those on the side of righteousness, even while the king offered him a bribe which he knew from experience worked better. But the guard had been deaf to them, since Rachid had long since punctured his eardrum.

Sitting in the pest-infested darkness, with the faraway scratching of rats in the sewers below, Shan could not help but feel remorse along with her anguish. For had she been content to stay who she was, even now she would be in the safety of her own sweet if undersized bed, a whisper away from her sweet if undersized castle. But instead she had longed to see a princess, and, with the princess's urging, had become her, making her a prisoner, as are all who choose not to be themselves.

Now she waited derelict in the dungeon of this perpendicular palace, rife with villainy of a kind she could not begin to understand or imagine. And even as the king brought together for her the little thread of Rachid's foul tapestry, explaining that smarmy villain's plan to overthrow the kingdom, she wondered how exactly Rachid would go about destroying the image of Darcy's marriage to Rodney. According to Quirin, such was his plot. In between puzzling over that, and how she would escape, and how to make up her infidelity to Tom (for which she was sure she was being punished), she wondered what would happen to Rodney. Was he missing her, tearing his hair in her unexplained absence?

"Turn on the TV," said the king, who had only a limited attention span for contemplation and self-absorption, even of the uplifting kind.

And there on the screen, on MTV, was the week's special Music News, filled with the latest gossip about rock and roll celebrities. Before their very eyes, rose the visage of Princess Darcy, smiling happily on the arm of Nick Deamon.

"So now we understand," said the king. "He's gotten some foul impersonator to disgrace you in the eyes of the world and the kingdom. For who's to know or believe the true princess is a prisoner here in a dungeon?"

"Not even me," said Shan, and sighed.

Now did the actual Darcy, whom all those around her thought was Shan, look out at the wonders that were Criccieth, which seemed to grow daily, as she did. Far along the curve of the pebbled, cobblestoned beach rose the narrow-windowed, light wood façades of Victorian rooming houses, top stories coming to a point below slate roofs, chimney pots belching smoke into the crystalline air. The water of the bay was a shade gray-bluer than the sky, reflecting it like a mirror. In a light wind, a lone windsurfer cut across the surface of the water, red and yellow and green striped sail brilliant against the cloudless day. From the place where she stood, Darcy could see Jackie playing by the water, bright red oilcloth slicker advertising his touching presence, as he filled his little yellow sandbucket with stones.

Her heart went out to him. So complete was her transformation from the self-centered, aloof woman she had been, that she could completely identify with other people, their needs becoming her needs, their hopes and desires something she hoped for and desired, too.

Especially the hopes and desires of Miles. Enlightened as she was obviously becoming, she was still a woman, and enlightenment had a hard time getting between the legs. The passion she'd felt for him, the rush she still experienced when she thought of him, the dizzying longing, were in no way abated. So she knew that one way or the other, it had to be concluded.

She stood now on the curve of seawall looking down at the shore, wearing the blue dress Jackie had given her, feeling the wind blowing in her hair, wondering, if Miles was rehearsing in the turrets of the castle, could he see her, far away as she was? Would he recognize her (or who he thought she was) in the dress she now wore? Was the slender figure so familiar to him that he would know her even from a great distance?

Naturally, the whole thing could have been easily settled simply by allowing herself to be part of Miles, as she was now part of everyone else. But were she part of him, how would it be to be him having her? Past incestuous, really. Past narcissism. It discomfited her even to think about it. Kind of psychosexual cannibalism, really, being yourself and eating yourself, too.

The reference to cannibalism, even in her most secret thoughts, brought to her mind a parade of the flowers she had eaten; the first that looked so much like her, and had taken away Vanity. The second, with its little round baby belly, laughing, healing her grave fault of Taking Things Too Seriously. The third, curing her of Taking Things Too Personally; the fourth, Judgment of herself as well as others. And now, this last, stripping her of a Sense of Separation. What a lucky woman she was to have grown such a garden. And what was in the other two seeds: what healing awaited her?

She could hardly bear to put it off another moment, she was so full of expectations. Yet there was a certain sadness to the thought of the flowers coming to an end. There was a sadness to the thought of anything she was experiencing coming to an end. For she had become greatly attached to all of it, Criccieth, and Tom, and Jackie, and the duchess, and the people of the village, and fish that didn't stare at her, and the castle on the bluff, and, of course, Miles.

What would happen if she did run away with him? Tom would be devastated at losing her. But he didn't have her now. Didn't have who he thought he had, and so would be unable to lose whom he thought he'd lose. Soon Shan would come back, Darcy was sure, for the royal life was a royal pain, which none understood so well as those who had to endure it. She imagined Shan would enjoy the charade for a while at least. But how could she stand it long, being with Rodney? Was she with Rodney?

Had she held him off as successfully as Darcy had done recently, or did she have to submit to him?

With her new five-sevenths illumination, Darcy put herself in Rodney's shoes, or, more particularly, his pants, and understood his longing for her. Not that she was vain about it, but her package was more or less irresistible. To Rodney, anyway, and now to Tom, even though he thought she was Shan. So how could Miles stay away from her?

Well, it was Saturday. Saturday at last. Tonight the performance would be over. Hadn't he sworn he thought about her all the time, except during *Hamlet*? And wasn't *Hamlet* all that came between them now, with the performance scheduled for that night?

Down on the cobblestoned strand, Samuel Stroll, with his pointed metal-ended stick, jabbed at the orange peels less caring souls had cast upon the beach, picked up beer bottles and sandwich wrappers, and put them in his sack. He looked up and saw her. For a moment an expression of puzzlement passed across his face. Then he smiled, came over to the wall atop which she stood, and shouted up to her. "I just had the oddest experience," he said. "I looked up and thought you were someone else. Dressed all in blue like that. You won't believe who I thought you were."

"Tell me."

"Princess Darcy of Perq. I hadn't noticed the resemblance before. But I was fortunate enough to have tea with that lovely lady, and damned if she isn't your spitting image."

"Thank you," said Darcy. "I take that as a compliment."

"A compliment to her," said Stroll.

Gathered in the castle courtyard that evening, on long lines of wooden benches, waiting for the performance, sat most of the citizenry of Criccieth, and visiting dignitaries from the Welsh Historic Monument Society. The curtain time (a traditional expression only, as there was no curtain, the action having been rehearsed and set on an open platform constructed for the event) had been announced for nine-thirty, calculated as twilight. Electric cables, run up the hill and through the gatehouse to support the klieg lights, were connected to the electrical system of the ice-cream parlor at the foot of the bluff. Everyone was counting on the full moon, and perfect weather, since there was in the nature of Welshmen the same fierce defiance of Nature herself as there was of enemies. Still, Nature seemed to support the endeavor, offering a clear, mild evening, and a huge yellow disc of a moon that climbed towards the towers as the sentinels did.

And soon the ghost of Hamlet's father walked the battlements. All the audience perceived that something was rotten in Denmark. But for Darcy, with Tom all rigid and tense on the bench beside her, the something that was rotten was in herself. For the truth was, this man who considered himself her husband was as sweet a spirit as labored on earth, and did not deserve the pain this evening was causing. It was clearly more than he could bear, seeing his rival sprinting about so smartly leotarded, elegant agonies dripping from his lips. Agonies Miles himself had reframed in his native tongue, giving him more importance than the too much he already had in Tom's and Shan's lives.

Were Darcy a better person, she knew for all her almost Enlightenment, she would never have asked Tom to be there. He had been edgy and reluctant, as apprehensive about attending as he was about letting her go by herself. But she had urged — in her own, learning-to-be-deferential way — insisting. It all had such symmetry, her having to decide whether or not to run off with Miles, Hamlet dealing with his dilemma, and Tom's predicament. Irresistible then, the temptation to make him a part of the evening, the theme of which, on every level, was being unable to make up your mind.

You can imagine, dear reader, having seen at least some production of this play, whether in high school, or at the Old Vic, or the film starring Sir Laurence Olivier which should be available on videocassette, what power the piece had, even in this provincial production. Building with the torment of the characters onstage was Tom's anguish. He understood full well what was at stake this full-mooned evening. Besides Miles's being a ranter and posturer, while bristling with charm and a certain undeniable magnetism, he could not resist glancing over at his old sweetheart from time to time to see how his performance was affecting her. So if Tom had been a moron, which he was not, he would have suspected what was afoot: that, as in the drama onstage, the fate of his own marriage was coming to a head.

So by the time the pitiful Ophelia had been weighted down by madness and her garments, and drowned in the weeping brook, Tom was in a quiet rage at women who loved foolishly. As the funeral procession bore her corpse to the graveyard, his fury built with that of her brother, Laertes. Because of the logistics of the scaffolding, the grave was down from the stage, and on the courtyard ground directly in front of the first row of benches on which sat Darcy and Tom. As they laid Ophelia to rest, Tom could hardly contain his anger.

As has been noted previously, the production this evening had been translated into Welsh. Since Shakespeare is difficult enough to appreciate fully in the language in which he wrote his plays — whether or not they were his, or Bacon's, or anyone else's that scholars and combative people looking for academic reputations will go on arguing probably till the end of Literature, the only thing generally agreed upon being his birthday, April 23rd — what was taking place at that moment onstage will be here re-translated into Shakespeare's own tongue, which was English, no matter what Miles or anyone else says. I have this on the highest authority, since along with the ghost of Hamlet's father, there are various other spirits afloat in the universe, one of them being Shakespeare, who is really quite disgusted with all this speculation about him and distortion of his product, Lears that take place on the moon, et cetera. He was, besides actor, playwright, and poet, an extremely hard worker, and for that alone he should be held at least a little sacred. So I will present his words the way he wrote them.

To the play, then, and Gertrude, the queen, scattering flowers on Ophelia's grave, and Laertes leaping into it, demanding to be buried with her. And Hamlet's doing the same.

"The devil take thy soul!" cried Laertes to Hamlet.

As the two men grappled in the grave, which as explained was just in front of the row of benches where Tom and Darcy sat, Tom turned to Darcy. "That is the difference between men and men," he said. "There are those who would jump into a woman's grave, trying to make her tragedy theirs."

"Do you mind?" said the woman behind them.

"And there are those," Tom continued, undeterred, "who would keep her alive. Who would say the words a woman needs, when she needs to hear them."

"Thou prayst not well," said Miles playing Hamlet to Laertes, his glance wandering, as Laertes choked him, to the place where Tom sat talking. "O prithee take thy fingers from my throat."

"Who would love her while she is quick," Tom said.

"For though I am not splenitive and rash . . . ," said Hamlet.

"And not be so caught in themselves that they wait till she is dead," said Tom.

"How rude can you get?" said the woman behind.

"Yet I have something in me dangerous . . . ," quoth Miles, teeth clenched, more against the disturbance in the front than the fingers on his neck.

"Who would give her strength and assurance," said Tom.

"Which let thy wiseness fear; hold off thy hand," said Hamlet.

"And love when she can still feel it," Tom said.

"Pluck them asunder," commanded the king.

"Hamlet, Hamlet!" cried the queen.

"Gentlemen!" said all onstage.

"And arms that would protect her, and not just carry her to ruin," said Tom.

"Good my lord, be quiet," bade Horatio.

"Amen to that, and to you, too," said the woman behind Tom. "We came here to see a play."

"But you are seeing several," said Darcy, turning and smiling at her. "You know the play within the play we just saw? Well, this is the play without the play. An argument of love pitched against the funeral of one who died of lovelessness."

"I see," said the woman, and tried to digest the idea, as attendants parted the players in the grave. "But it's confusing enough as is. So I could do without the extra."

"As could we all," said Miles, climbing up from the funeral pit, back onstage.

The southwest tower and the curtain wall had been added to the castle by Llewelyn the Last, about whose name there could be no dispute, any more than there could have been about Sir Howel of the Battle-axe, who had served as constable of the castle until his death in 1381. Darcy could hear them counseling constancy as she passed through the outer gateway to the ward beneath the tower, where a temporary tent had been raised to serve as shelter and dressing room for the cast. There underneath the *trebuchet*, ancient machinery for throwing stones, she could feel her heart like its own rock in her breast, no catapult to fling it forth. For she had wished upon the first foxglove with Miles, to do what was right. And unfortunately, doing what is right is seldom doing what is delicious or selfish or sexy.

Tom had declined to come with her backstage, saying he had seen quite enough of Miles, and would be waiting for her at home. There was a resignation in his tone as he said it, as though he knew she might not come.

Now, amid tube-shaped worklights and hurricane lamps, players disrobed and unsheathed their swords. Ophelia, head all garlanded, untangled fading flowers from her long flaxen hair. At a dressing table, taking off his makeup, sat Miles. His eyes caught Darcy's in the mirror.

There is a curious magic that happens with reflections, making images more powerful, more acute. Sometimes there are griffins in the sunset, great orange-winged creatures that seem a part of the clouds, but for dreamers and poets are simply high-flying evidence that it's myths and fables that are true, and reality that's the illusion. Potent as these visions are when seen directly, caught in a glass, reflected, they become hypnotic. So it was with Miles's eyes, so deep and dark they could unstring a woman's tendons. Mirrored now, leveled at Darcy, they had the intensity of laser beams.

"Are you packed?" he asked her.

"No."

"Just as well," he said. "We can get you everything you need in London."

"I'm not going. It would break his heart."

"What heart?" He creamed the makeup from his cheek with a swatch of cotton. "He has the sensitivity of a critic. Although the play's the thing, what matters now is *us*. My performance, his rudeness, the fact that he destroyed this entire evening, and even your opinion of me as an actor are beside the point. I cannot let you waste another moment of your life with that clod."

"He loves me," Darcy said, not bothering to explain that he loved who he thought she was, because we all love who we think each other are, and the confusion of identities doesn't really matter when it comes down to principle, which she was afraid it did.

"He is no more capable of loving a woman like you than a hound can love a Fairy-Queen." He got to his feet, and put his arms around her. "Not in the way you need."

A little of his cream smeared her cheek, and she could smell it, and him, and the two of them together. Her resolve grew faint. "He's a good man," she said. "They're rare. Not to be cast aside."

"And what about me?" he said. "And what about this?" He kissed her, his lips touching places on her mouth she didn't know she had.

"It was a lovely interlude," she said, managing to pull away.

"I'll be waiting for you in London," he said. "One day you'll be there."

She smiled. "Good-bye."

"You're really going to stay with him? I can't change your mind?"

She shook her head.

"Oh, well," said Miles. "So what did you think of my performance?"

9

ANCHORED AT DOCKSIDE in Saint-Tropez, with people on the *quai* staring at her as if she were a pastry in the window, Babara tried to take more pleasure from her imposture. How radiant shone the sun, blasting heat, though it was now September. How tanned were all the faces on hot2dock, the only thing deeper than their longing, the color of their skin. It was very like a reverse zoo, the caged animals those gaping at what they imagined to be total freedom: the people on the yachts. Lined up two and three deep the onlookers were, at the foot of the gangway, along the Quai Jean-Jaures with its trendy, open boutiques waving drastically reduced summer fashions into the air.

A little farther down the *quai*, what was left of the International Set, the month being past high fashion and the dollar being down, read their *Herald-Tribunes* and drank café-au-lait at the Café Gorille. Striped awnings shaded them from the glare, as white canvas over the rear of the yacht protected Babara, naturally honey-gold skin having been ordained by the plastic surgeon as dark as she was allowed to get. But that of course was on the outside.

Inside, she churned with guilt, reviewing perfidies, real and imagined, as she sat drinking champagne before noon with Nick

Deamon, and Franco Piccardoni, the scrofulous drug dealer. The scent of freshly baked croissants redolent of kitchens in homes she had never had, and probably never would have, mixed with the strong odor of coffee, and Grand Marnier for crêpes sold by fast-order chefs out of windows. Opening her nostrils and her consciousness wide, Babara could smell the fresh white-meat *loup* caught that morning in the Mediterranean, see it laid out on the ice in the stalls on the other side of the archway. Franco had described it to her, but had not let her see firsthand. There wasn't enough security even among his drug-dealing cronies to allow her to wander through alleyways. After all, the people on the dock thought she was really Princess Darcy, and would never let her pass unmolested, uninfringed upon. Saint-Tropez was loaded with jet-setty celebrities who had no peace, no peace, not even the most reticent and transcendental among them, such as the Collins sisters. Riotous Middle Eastern princes on the Côte d'Azure just for a rest, and the occasional arms deal, had flanks of bodyguards with bigger walkie-talkies than the real Darcy's own forces. Those little boys had been left behind with Minette in Nice, to allow the scandal to flower more fully. There was absolutely no way Babara could be allowed to roam free.

Her homed-in longing for Adrian mingled with the abstract yen to be someone other than who she was, even though she was supposed to be someone else. For what was the point of being in this gorgeous place with all these people parading with bare brown legs and chandelier crystals in their ears if you couldn't pass among them?

"How about if I put on a disguise?" Babara asked Franco. "Then could I get off the boat?"

"Ship," he corrected. "I labored all my life to be able to afford one this size. Don't call it a boat."

"Some labor," scoffed Nick. "Selling cocaine to schoolchildren."

"I don't sell to children. The only one who lives off acned adolescents is you."

"My audience is very mature."

"Overripe, I think you mean. Like the cucumber you wear in your pants."

"Pig!" said Nick, getting to his feet, flinging his champagne in Franco's face. Unfortunately, he was not very well coordinated, so the glass went along with its ingredients, cracking just above Franco's eyebrow, opening a small gash.

Blood flowed into the Italian's eye. "You fool! You've blinded me!" Franco yelled. "Aiuta! Aiuta!"

Four security men ran out of the cabin, bumping into each other in their panic, rushing towards him with towels, a gun, a telephone. One had a fire extinguisher, which he aimed at Nick and let go. Nick was covered with suds, only one angry eye visible in the foam, like a creature in a science-fiction film.

"Should I go for a doctor?" Babara asked, against the blaze of day, suddenly even more brilliant with the pop of flashbulbs from the dock.

"You stay right where you are," cried Franco, pressing a towel to his wound. He began talking in Italian to his security men, one of whom ran down the gangway. The other two stood arms crossed, one with his gun, one with the phone, on either side of Franco, as if protecting him from any more assaults and the possibility of no phone calls. The one with the fire extinguisher set it down, and started hosing Nick off with water.

"I can't believe that I've waited all my life to come to the South of France, and I'm stuck on a boat," whined Babara.

"Ship!" said Franco, bleeding.

"If you were any kind of man," she said to Nick, who was appearing from place to place behind the suds, "You'd at least take me out to lunch."

"You are out to lunch," said Franco.

"She's perfectly sane!" said Nick, from beneath his sousing. "You're the one who's crazy."

"Murderer!" cried Franco.

"Viper!" shouted Nick.

"I don't think this looks very good to the neighbors," Babara said, glancing nervously at the boats (ships) on either side of them, where the rich people were now lined up along the rails as the tourists were down below on the dock.

"Is there a doctor in the basin?" Franco shouted.

"How could this have happened to me?" Babara mused, holding out her long stemmed crystal glass for more champagne, which was poured by a wine steward, the only one on deck who hadn't lost his dignity.

"You?" said Nick, drenched to the skin, his white pants so wet and tight you could see the cucumber. "How could this have happened to *me?*"

"Scum rises," said Franco.

Now as she sat in her deco dungeon, the seemingly real Princess Darcy, who was actually Shan, tried to imagine some means of escape. She had thought about growing her hair, but that only worked in a tower, and there was not even a window in their cell. Not even a grate to the sewer below. Only that dreadful trapdoor, and the far-off screeching of the rats at the end of the deadly fall. Even if she could tear her Dior nightgown and peignoir to shreds (which they were already starting to be of their own accord, since couturier clothes were not fashioned for constant damp, or never changing out of) and reweave them into some kind of rope, it would not reach to the bottom of the pit, or hold her weight. She was sure of that just from listening to how far away was the lap of fetid water. Nor could she spin the straw with which her mattress was stuffed atop its poor palette into hemp, or, more traditionally, gold, since missing were both Rumpelstilskin and a spinning wheel. Oh, they did not give many alternatives to modern-day trapped princesses!

She went to the trapdoor, as she did almost daily, lifted the rusted metal ring in its center, pulled, and listened to the wood creak as it opened, counterpointing the king's snores. He slept nearly all day long, as much out of depression and cocaine withdrawal, she was sure, as weariness. In his ineffective way he was rather a sweetheart, and she was becoming genuinely fond of him. For at least he did not seem to feel self-pity, the only really offensive characteristic of weakness.

But he was not exactly a man of action, although even a man of action would have been hard pressed to do anything. Still, that did not stop Shan. Daily, she struggled to find some solution. Some escape. Now she took the roll from the dinner tray that had been brought the evening before, and held it over the opening in the concrete floor. It was heavy in her hand — Rhea was not too good with breadstuffs to begin with, and the damp of the dungeon crept only into bones and designer dresses: bread became stale as bread usually did. Calculating the weight of it in her palm, Shan held it for a moment before releasing it into the dark, and counted slowly to herself as she had been taught to do in physics class before Mrs. Thatcher cut back on aid to education. Shan listened to the plop as it hit, calculated the fall as at least sixty feet. Then she heard the greedy scurrying of rats, their shrill shrieking as, she imagined, they fought over the leaden morsel. What would they do with her flesh?

She closed the trapdoor, just as the ceiling at the top of the stairs started to roll open. Crouching in the shadows, she waited till Rhea was halfway down the steps, and then started up them, trying to run by her. But the turncoat guard who usually brought their meals was standing at the opening, sword and teeth flashing.

"Don't even try it, my pretty pretty," he said, as the ceiling closed. "Go back down and eat your lunch."

"Quiche, again?" Shan said, looking at the tray Rhea carried.

Rhea gritted her teeth. If there was one thing she couldn't stand, it was a spoiled princess. She had been ambivalent about taking part in this whole conspiracy, having grown rather fond of Darcy since her return from Wales, thought she'd detected in the girl some humanity lacking before, a quarter cup of compassion. Rachid had promised no real harm would come to the princess and the king, so Rhea had gone along with him, reluctantly. Now she wished she'd been ferocious, enjoying the villainy as much as he had. Her only regret was that she had fussed so over the take-out orders. "And what would you rather have?"

"Rat poison," Shan said. "Do you think you could get me some?"

"You would rather be dead than eat my cooking?"

"Oh, Rhea, you've got to help us. This is all part of a terrible plot to disgrace Prince Rodney's marriage."

"So?"

"Rachid wants to destroy Rodney. You raised him from a baby. You were his wet-nurse. His nanny."

"I never liked him," said Rhea. She looked over at the snoring king. "Or the big nose that sired him either."

"You're a good woman. I know you are." Shan touched the stocky arm. "You care about your country."

"I care spit about it," said Rhea. "They can take the island and shove it up the Gulf Stream as far as I'm concerned, along with the whole royal family. Except the queen. She's the only one of the entire bunch that I give a rat's ass about."

"What a . . . colorful phrase," said Shan, trying to turn up her nose or her ears at the offensive phraseology, wondering if there was some way to turn it around, and bring back talk of the poison. If she could get it, she could kill the rats, and take her chance with the fall. Maybe. "But if you give . . ."

"A rat's ass," Rhea prompted her, understanding royal sensibility, although she considered it bullshit.

"Exactly — about Queen Isabel, you must realize that the ruin of her son would ruin her."

"Not necessarily," said Rhea. "She loves Rachid. And he will be king."

The king stirred, snorted, snored.

"And abandon her," said Shan. "Make obscene phone calls to other women."

"He's called you, too?" said Rhea, who could not help feeling a little offended, since she thought herself his only telephonic infidelity.

That had been a lucky guess on Shan's part. For once she had picked up her phone (a princess) and heard heavy breathing. Very heavy. So heavy it had to be coming from the nostrils of a dark-haired man. As nearly all the male citizenry and intruders of Perq were blonds or redheads, she had surmised that the caller was Rachid, since besides sounding dark, there were little pauses, gasps, that had a Middle Eastern inflection. She had not even mentioned the dastardly communication to Rodney, since he already hated Rachid enough, and she wanted to make life pleasanter for him, not more conflicted. "Many times," she lied, whitely.

"The porker," said Rhea.

"So if you love Isabel, you have to help us. For Rodney's downfall will be hers."

"I have to think about it," said Rhea, her mind racing as though through a drawer filled with recipes.

"Think quickly," said Shan. "Time is of the essence."

"But sage gives a better flavor," said Rhea, starting up the stairs again, knocking on the ceiling till it opened.

"Lunch, Your Majesty," Shan said, tapping the king gently on the nose. She had discovered it was the best way to wake him without startling him, as his nose was his most imperial part, with the greatest resonance. So a simple tap with a spoon, as she was using now, set off a tiny drumroll in his head, making him wake up happy, since he thought he was back in court, with people still fussing over him.

"My loyal subjects . . . ," he said, half-springing to attention. That is to say, the top half of him sprung. For spring was in his heart. The rest of him was fall.

He looked around, a little disconsolately, and saw Shan. "But where's the parade?"

"I'm afraid it's passed us by," said Shan.

"They told me at boarding school that would happen," he said.

Darcy hadn't slept all night, for several nights. Although she had done the right thing, her stomach was leaden with discontent, her eyes strained with back-looking. For how often did a person, princess or no, have a chance to transmute her life? She had seized the miraculous opportunity to become an ordinary person, had experienced the ordinary life to its optimum. But the better nature she hadn't known she had had prevailed over her desires. She had missed her chance at a Great Romance.

Well you may ask, reader, didn't she know Miles was a blusterer, full of bravado, puffery, fanfaronade, offal? But we are talking about lust here. And if love is blind, lust is a cripple, deaf and mute, leaving us only with tongue to taste, nose to smell, fingers to touch, skin to be played upon and the rest of it, blood to run too hot and quickly, loins to be stirred. So what influence has the brain?

Now we enter into an even more fascinating area, because it is a scientific fact that testosterone, men's sexual hormone, affects the brain and makes hockey players more aggressive. There's a correlation in juvenile delinquents between levels of testosterone and the date of their first arrest. (Crime, one should remember, is committed by the brain.)

The picture for women is far less clear, since they are hormonally more complex and have fewer genetic defects than men. Being in general less deviant, they are also less often studied by science, since their troubles seem to have more to do with mood than anything else. Everyone knows about the Baby Blues, which is not a rock group but what many women get after giving birth. PMS, which I am loath to discuss here, as it has little place in a fairy tale, except that it often appears in *Cosmopolitan*, which as we know was one of Darcy's favorite magazines, is supposedly caused by an altered balance of women's main hormones, estrogen and progesterone. According to scientists, these two hormones are the reason for women's tendency to depression, besides their dreams not coming true. Probably they are also the factor in the so-called weaker sex not being more aggressive, except in the case of what certain men would label "ball-busters," being concerned about their genitals as aspirers are with the afterlife.

The absolute truth, objectively, and without sexual prejudice, is that progesterone induces calmness, while estrogen promotes a sense of well-being. Even if a book on the brain and sex were being written by women, which certainly some of the better ones have been, they would be forced to admit that those hormones connect to a woman's essential role as a mother.

But what of her role as ninny? For since individual females are the guardians of the Continuation of the Species flame, they have more to lose than men, who are natural gamblers, in reproductive roulette. So one would expect them to be hormonally safeguarded from impulse, and a misplaced or too-eager sex drive. Well, one would be wrong. For Nature has protected us from many things, but never ourselves.

Looking at the ceiling now, gazing out the window at the waning moon, trying to feel the same ebbing away, slice by slice from the upper right, of her longing, Darcy wondered why she hadn't just run off with Miles. Little "Ah, me"s escaped her, as if the play that linked them were *Romeo and Juliet* instead of *Hamlet*. Very sotto voce were her sighs, but even had they been a lot noisier, they would not likely have wakened Tom, who lay in a deep sleep next to her on the bed, a sweet smile of unexpected security on his face. It had come as the happiest surprise to him that his Shan had opted for home and hearth, instead of the glamorous lechery that the fly-by-night actor offered.

Still, pleased as she was that she'd brought such comfort to Tom, as with some bitter pill she'd swallowed, sugarcoated in the virtue she hadn't known she possessed, the loss had settled in Darcy's esophagus. There it mixed with lust, which, as we have already discussed, is mindless — and yearning, which is sentimental and self-indulgent, and lechery, which, testosterone aside, is not restricted to men. For she had seen him in his leotards, felt his lips and his hands, heard his voice burrowing to her core, smelled him, and let him have her feet. Now was the rest of her all lubricious, as wanton a word as had ever danced through a story of this sort. Certainly as wanton a feeling.

But, though Nature does not protect us, Grace does, especially if we are five-sevenths of the way along the path. Suddenly she was suffused with a different kind of hunger. She realized that so caught up had she been in her sacrifice, her reluctant rectitude, she'd been days without going to her windowbox. Even as she tiptoed down the stairs she wondered if she'd waited too long. The sixth flower might have already bloomed and faded. Oh, it was her hope to find a blossom of courage, abandon, action, something attaching mercury wings to the backs of her heels, so she could fly to him. Buzzing through her brain was the sick certainty that she'd missed the right moment, as women always fear they've missed everything, whether it be the best item at a sale, or the most attractive single man at the party, or, with the advent of the biological clock, the chance to be a mother, or, in the event that they are already mothers, the chance to live their middle years without wondering why it was they had been so eager to give birth to these creatures who now seemed hell-bent on giving them such a hard time.

She flung open the casement window, and there, in the windowbox, by the light of the waning moon, bloomed a flower so brightly orange, it seemed to be neon. Shaped like a foxglove, as had been all the others, it belled towards the soil, gleaming. Darcy angled it, tilted it backwards, and softly lifting its petals, peered inside. And there was something that looked like a butterfly, the same luminous orange as the flower itself, with white and black circles on its trembling, black-striated wings. Then it stopped fluttering, as though it was experiencing perfect peace, perfect calm, and had run out of cocktail parties it imagined were better than the place it was. Although she'd never eaten an insect, except for chocolate-covered ants from Fortnum and Mason's, overwhelmed by her hunger, she broke off the flower, and ate it.

And it was as sharp a taste as she'd ever had, but pleasant, like a zing of cinnamon to the tongue. And something that felt like harmony (could you feel harmony?) flooded her soul and her heart and, yes, even her brain, as she heard a chord that resolved itself. Every jagged, ruffled edge of impatience was smoothed. The crick in her neck that came from looking over her shoulder at what she might have been missing disappeared. A sense of euphoria — not high, understand, but that very real euphoria that comes from being on an even keel — came over her. And she understood, without thinking or analyzing, that the world was perfect as it was. That her life was perfect as it was. For she had eaten the flower that took away Restlessness.

"But I'm not restless anymore!" she cried to the moon above the kitchen window. "I'm not restless anymore!" she said to Tom, shaking him loose from his dreaming.

"That's wonderful," he said. "Why don't you go back to sleep?"

"Don't you understand how important this is? Number Six! It's an absolute breakthrough!"

"I'm happy for you." Tom pulled the covers over his head.

"You must be happy for yourself as well," she said, pulling the covers back down. "For there is no separation." She smiled at him. "That was Number Five. We're a part of each other."

"I know that," said Tom.

"Not just you and me," Darcy said, happily. "Everybody."

"Well, go wake *them* up," said Tom, and rolled over.

Fortunately, having lost Vanity, and Taking Things Too Seriously, or Too Personally, Judgment of herself as well as others, her Sense of Separation, and now (hoorah!) Restlessness, Darcy was able to smile and let him go back to sleep. Still, she was too excited to go to bed herself, so instead went back down to the kitchen. "Only one more to go!" she said, filling the watering can, and sousing the soil.

"Glub," went the earth.

"Oh, hurry and grow," she said to the last seed. "For I can't imagine what power you might have. But I know it will be beyond any I could even think of. And I just can't wait!"

"Well, you're going to have to," boomed the voice of the Afghan.

Turning, Darcy saw the duchess. She was dressed in a nightgown laced up to the throat, nightcap covering her pink-red curls. She was carrying her former butler. Her eyes were open but she seemed not to be inside them.

"Your Grace!" Darcy exclaimed.

"And yours as well," came the deep voice of the Afghan, from out the duchess's mouth.

It took Darcy a moment to realize the duchess was sleepwalking. But once she was over her initial shock, Darcy understood there was nothing to be alarmed about, since most of the people in the world are sleepwalkers: they just don't do it in costume. "I'll take you back home," she said gently.

"To the Khyber Pass?" said the Afghan.

"To your lovely little cottage in Criccieth." She held the duchess's arm, guiding her towards the door. "You must take better care of her, Bailey," she said to the cat.

"I know," the cat said.

Now there will be those among the stubbornly literal who, although they may have accepted the idea of the duchess's being a channel for a Spirit Guide, skeptical as they are about such things, will be totally unwilling to swallow a cat's being able to speak. Let me say quickly that what issued from Bailey's furry mouth was, in fact, a meow. But it was a meow of some refinement. Whether or not it was true that the cat had been her butler in a previous life, there was no question that he was highly evolved for a cat, so most certainly might have been a cat before, or even a dog, since he showed quite a bit of fondness and attachment for the duchess, and cats as a rule are independent and unemotional. Setting aside his being her butler or a reincarnated animal, it is still arguable that his meow was of a sufficient elegance to be heard and interpreted as "I know." Especially if one is gullible, which Darcy certainly was by this time, having gone through an absolute alchemy of spirit, or at least a sixth-sevenths alchemy. But for those of you who are less trustful and are tolerating this fairy tale only because it has certain things to say about women, and is occasionally salted with sex, your time is coming.

The advance proofs of the *Playhouse* Christmas Centerfold, featuring the Princess Darcy in her natural state, that is to say, in front of the palace of Perq, wearing only the royal stilettos, came back from the magazine in mid-October. Adrian rushed them to Rachid, who seemed quite pleased with them, and the attention the magazine was planning to give the piece. Already there was a full-out plan for an international television campaign hyping the issue and its majestic contents, guaranteed to explode into world scandal, not to mention incredible sales. True, gossip travels faster than light. But there was still a certain organized drumbeating needed to assure the issue's topping the sales of those that had carried Miss America in leather, and the new breed of Porno Queen: women who had brought down, to turn a phrase, evangelists and politicians, giving the girls, at least, new careers as foldouts. The world had had slatterns up to the eyeballs, so even a calumny of these proportions needed skillful shepherding to make sure it came out just right. Or, in this case, just wrong. The slyest hint that there was worse afoot than the princess's trolloping about the French Riviera with rock stars. The cleverest leak that there was something in the glossy works that would tumble an actual crown as earlier juicy layouts had tilted the one on Vanessa Williams.

Already the photos of the pretender princess on the yacht had zipped about the planet's wire services, getting her flashy headlines in the European press, and supermarket checkstands in the States. But the atmosphere created was one of fascinated disapproval, open speculation that Darcy had grown bored, that the royal marriage was in deep trouble. No one had yet pointed a finger and called her whore. It was such an ugly word, and the people of Perq, and indeed the world at large, still felt for the princess a great deal of affection, since blue-eyed blondes with that ability to wear clothes were not born every day. As we know from other recent times when our idealized, courtly women have shown themselves to be for sale, as long as they kept their figures and their second husbands died quickly enough, they were forgiven.

So it was the centerfold, finally, that would topple Darcy, and with her the monarchy of Perq. Like the Machiavellian mountebank he was, Rachid wanted to make sure the smut was handled impeccably. "You have the gossip columnists lined up to leak news of these?" he asked Adrian.

"They need no advance notice," said Adrian. "The world is already on alert that the princess and prince have gone their separate ways, and it's only the disapproval of the palace that keeps them from divorce."

"The queen's starting to understand it's not such a bad idea," said Rachid, going over the layout. "She has a fabulous *tush.*"

"Forgive me, Your Greatness, but there are some things I would prefer not knowing about my sovereign."

"I'm not talking about Isabel," said Rachid. "I'm talking about this sweet little dissembler here."

Adrian turned away, so Rachid could not see the heat rising in his cheeks. For it made him a little crazy to hear Babara's buttocks being bandied about. He didn't even dare to wonder what would happen in December, when everyone could leer at her. In a strange way he was starting to feel empathy for Prince Rodney, who according to reports had gone into a deep decline over Darcy's departure, more pained by her actual absence than any of the shabby communiqués about her activities.

The door opened, and Isabel entered. Rachid quickly gathered up the photographs, covered them with the sheafs contained in the envelopes, and pressed the pile of perfidy into Adrian's hands. "Thank you for showing me the royal Christmas cards," Rachid said.

"Oh, good, can I see them?" asked Isabel, eagerly.

"These haven't been color corrected," said Adrian, and, bowing, left the room.

"How will we even be able to send them out?" Isabel pouted, flouncing onto the couch beside Rachid. She was wearing her hooped diamond earrings that were always her signal to him that she was feeling like a gypsy, eager and pressing towards the next open-air adventure. Lately, he had been taking her in the woods, by streams, and rivulets, to try to underscore his assurance to her that what was going on between them was natural, and not just adulterous, although that was his favorite part. "It will look like such a travesty. Rodney and Darcy wishing joy of the season, when everybody knows she's all over the world with that rocker and his candy man."

"You never cease to amaze me," said Rachid.

"I don't?" said Isabel, perking up like a child who had been praised. She was looking particularly young on this occasion, gypsy diamond hoops notwithstanding, wearing a dress that could accurately be described as a frock, cut low on her still amazing bosom, which was deeply tanned and starred at the outside left with a beauty mark. The dress was a pale lemon yellow, with sleeves that were actually puffed, of a fabric that had once been described as dotted Swiss, but since Rachid's takeover, had been renamed spotted Iraqi. A summer material really, but autumn though it was, the brighter season still lingered in Perq. The same could be said about Isabel, who carried an air of tenacious innocence that contradicted her years. All the more remarkable in view of the corruption Rachid had tried to introduce her to, in between picnics. "I was afraid I bored you."

"Well, you do. But that doesn't mean you don't amaze me." Rachid pressed a button at the side of the couch, summoning the royal minstrel, who according to a palace memo had just returned from a workshop in Aspen where he had learned many new songs. That is, they were new for Perq.

"You buzzed, Your Highness?" said the minstrel, a laurel wreath on his balding blond head, the tips of the leaves coming to just above his dippy blue eyes.

"How many times must I tell you not to call me 'Your Highness'?" asked Rachid.

"Twenty-seven?"

"Fool!" Rachid said.

"I'm not the fool. The fool also has to know poetry and what to do when the king goes mad. I'm just the minstrel. I do music."

"Why can we never find you?" Isabel asked.

"I just got back from Aspen. But from now on, I'll be at your beck and call."

Isabel reached for Rachid's hand. She had grown careless in recent weeks about showing her affection, since Rodney was on retreat in the north of Perq, in a cabin specially constructed to house his grieving. She felt like a bad mother, really, not being with him at such a time, even though he was well past the age for mothering. But a sense of helplessness suffused her. Rachid was urging her to condemn the marriage, and she had to admit she was furious with Darcy. But in a terrible way, she understood how passion could undercut duty, even though she could not imagine Darcy's preferring that goldilocked ponce to the prince.

"Which shall it be?" asked the minstrel. "Your beck or your call?"

"Play, idiot!" Rachid said.

The minstrel dropped his instrument, and letting his tongue dangle from his mouth, fell on the floor and rolled about. Then he puckered his lips and made a blubbering sound with his finger.

"Don't you know nobody likes a smart-ass?" said Rachid.

"Hum a few bars," said the minstrel, picking up his mandolin.

"Hmmmm mmmm, mmmmmm, mmmmmm," hummed Isabel and Rachid together.

"I think I have it," said the minstrel, and started playing.

"Why do I bore you?" asked Isabel, snuggling up to the black silk of Rachid's shirtfront.

"Because you ask silly questions."

"Do I?"

He didn't answer her.

"Well, what would you have me say?"

"I'd have you say the truth. That the royal marriage is a farce. That the Princess Darcy has left your son to gad about with filthy characters. All the world knows that already. The marriage must be dissolved."

"But how can we do that? You've exiled the archbishop. There's no one to unpost the banns."

"There are still lawyers," said Rachid.

"Well, of course there are still lawyers. They're like cockroaches. Poison only makes them stronger."

"Have the palace lawyers draw up papers, and serve her."

"I can't" she said. "His heart is broken. Even now he's gone into the forest to try and find a lion and eat his heart, to give him back his courage."

"The liver is better," said the minstrel. "If you eat the liver, it gives you anger. Anger attacks and dwells in the liver. And with anger you don't need courage, because it makes everyone else afraid. Usually in their kidneys."

"Shut up and play," said Rachid, and turned to Isabel. "So you won't denounce the marriage?"

"I can't. Not yet."

"Then you'll do the other thing for me."

"The other thing?"

"Excuse us," said Rachid to the minstrel.

"Did you do something wrong?"

"Get out," he bellowed. The minstrel beat a hasty retreat. "Will you do it?"

"What?"

"Make love with a woman."

"I really like men better," said Isabel, half-hoping he might force a stranger on her, as he pretended he was going to do last orgy. Crazy as she was about him, she still felt a little cheated, to have missed that one.

"I want you to be with a woman," he said, breathing heavily, without a phone.

"Very well." She was sure it was just another of his tricks. Who the woman would be, in disguise, of course, was Rachid. Just like the last time. "If it will make you happy."

* * *

Now through the overgrown forest of Perq roamed Rodney, armed with his sword, sheathed in his belt with the golden phoenix of Perq on its buckle. The bird seemed to him as sorrowful as it was mythic, for the prince could not imagine anything rising from its own ashes, now that love had resprung from a place where love wasn't, and then left again. It was all he could do to get up in the morning and leave the cabin that sheltered him in his depression. Sometimes he spent the entire day underneath the covers, not even bothering to eat the soldier's rations that they'd stocked there for him. For he was neither soldier nor the sailor he'd been trained to be, nor the loving husband he'd become to his own and everyone else's amazement.

There was the real phoenix: love. Making a triumph of what had been disaster. Lifting the heart, straightening the spine, making the ears grow closer to the head, putting more calcium in the fingernails so they didn't splinter. Brightening the eye, and with it the brain, so that everything you saw had a glow around it, starting with the beloved. What to do when it again crashed to earth, and burned, consumed in the flames that had just been rekindled?

Why had she left him? What had he done? The entire miracle of their unexpected passion had raised him from the ordinary man he knew he really was beneath his title, to poet, philosopher, king in the truest sense. To have found this unexpected treasure, and then lose it had driven him nearly mad. Nearly, because he was sure he was not interesting enough to be genuinely crazy, or she never would have left him.

Besides the sword sheathed in his belt, Rodney carried a bow and arrow, and a rifle slung over his shoulder. It was part of the mythology of Perq that lions roamed these forests, and that eating a lion's heart would give a man the courage he needed to overcome any obstacle. But even if he found a lion — which he doubted he would, since he knew the island almost inch by inch, and had never seen an animal any wilder than a boar, if you didn't count Rachid — he wondered what the point would be in killing it. For the obstacle that could never be overcome, not even with a lion's heart, was to make a woman love you when she did not.

Perhaps if he could eat the lion's balls, then it wouldn't matter to him that she didn't love him. Then he could fly after her and reclaim her, and not be shattered by her indifference or disdain. Bring her back to the tiny kingdom and compel her to behave properly, not caring if she was unhappy or not. His mother had been after him to do that anyway. To go to the places where Darcy was making such a public spectacle of herself, and bring her back by force, if necessary. But he loved her. He loved her with all his heart, which was not a lion's, and he couldn't bear to face what would have to be her contempt. For why else would she have left him? God, there'd been all those mouthwashes and dentifrices and underarm sticks and after-shave lotions companies had been sending him over the years hoping to get his endorsement, which he'd never given. But he'd used them all. What had been the trigger? Their nights had been nearly Arabian, laced with splendor and affection and intoxication of the nonalcoholic kind, their days idyllic, filled with caring conversation, and music of the spheres, since they could never find the minstrel.

The exoticism of the forest, with its stunted, cigar-fronded Fescennine trees, gnarled branches of coral, alive with bright orange berries, the unexpected stately pine, and palm, and oak, so deep and green it should have soothed his spirit, only served to quicken Rodney's anxiety. For it was a panoply of things that did not really go together, and yet grew lushly side by side, reminding him of men and women. One particular woman: his beloved Darcy, and himself. So his heart, which was not a lion's heart, or, in his own esteem, that of a particularly special man, cracked like the sound of twigs beneath his feet, as he sought the adversary that he knew did not exist, the enemy who could save him.

From the time he'd been a little boy in boarding school, the same one his father had gone to, and hated, he'd known that in spite of the propaganda and the pap he'd been fed since babyhood (by Rhea, whom he didn't think really liked him), the only princely thing about him was circumstance. For all they spoke of the royal blood that flowed in his veins, it could have just as easily been the circulation of a beggar. Had he been born to a simple woman instead of one who dressed coordinated to her eye color, had he been schooled in the streets instead of a place where his roommate was the son of the king of Bahrain, he might have been a nobler person than he was. Always there had been in his mind some skepticism about the Divine Rights of kings, even before the foul Rachid had done away with the idea of Divinity altogether. Who was to say that royalty was other than an accident of birth? Certainly, the Buddhists (he'd studied Comparative Religion at University) believed that people chose their parents for the lessons they'd learn from them. Well, from his father he'd learned the senselessness of weakness. But it hadn't made him strong. And from his mother he'd learned the folly of being flighty. That had benefited him, at least. He'd become the pole opposite of that, in every corpuscle of his being steadfast.

But to what end? He'd been true to Darcy when she was selfish and vain, and it had given him little comfort. Yet when his very soul opened to her on her return from Criccieth, when she seemed so loving and changed, he'd been rewarded with this worldwide, world-press humiliation. So what did it all have to say about prudence? Was commitment its own punishment, as virtue its own reward? Oh, sometimes he wished he'd been born an ordinary man, instead of a prince who knew he was really ordinary. And often — more often than not now — he wished his Darcy had been born poor and common, so it was her own goodness that could have raised her, and him that could have spoiled her rotten.

There was still that in his nature, the prejudice that girls were delicate things, put in the world to be protected and coddled by men. But he was, after all, fairly illuminated about his role as royalist, so we must forgive him some duskiness in this area, especially in view of the failure of the Feminist movement to take root in Perq. Besides, there are still those among us who would like nothing better than the right man (or even the wrong one) to come along and whisk us away, convincing us to forget all our worries and cares, which are only societal and nuclear, telling us to cast our burden on them. The appearance of anyone vaguely like that could restore the balance of nature and the sanity of Blanche DuBois. But happily, for the progress of the equal rights and opportunity people, the chances of many like *him* showing up are virtually nil, so we are going to be forced to do it for ourselves. Still, it would be nice to think that there might be a prince or two who isn't yet out of the woods, who might be able to surprise us. Oh, well.

Now did he pause on the overgrown path, as he heard something stirring. On the other side of a thick, brambled hedge was motion he could sense. Cautiously, he unsheathed his sword, and spread the tangled branches. All at once there was a deafening roar. To his astonishment, he took not a single step backwards, felt not a quiver of fear in his heart, or a quickening in his knees, the rush of adrenaline that would give him the speed to run. For instead of the impulse to flee what arose in him was joy, joy of the highest measure. The enemy! The lion! His salvation! The heart that could vanquish all cowardice!

Elated, he slashed through the hedge, rifle at the almost ready, bow and arrow underneath his armpit. The leaves fell like foes in a battle, the branches snapped and opened wide. And there on the other side was an old woman with pink-red hair, in a safari suit, holding a cat in her arms. The cat opened its jaws, and a great roar came forth, like a lion's.

"Pretty impressive, don't you think?" said the old woman.

"Damn!" said Rodney. "I thought it was a lion. My enemy."

"Oh, your enemy is here, all right," the old woman said. "Come, I'll show you where he's hiding." And turning rather swiftly for a woman of her years, she made her way to a treehouse, steps carved into its giant trunk, so it seemed very easy to climb, even for her. Rodney followed, reaching around her to open the front door.

"Well, aren't you a prince!" she exclaimed.

"An accident of birth," said Rodney.

"Really?" she said, and looked at him with watery blue eyes."I'm not so sure." Leading him into her house, which was crowded with furniture, all of it carved, she took his hand and guided him to the dresser, and the mirror over it. "There he is," she said, and pointed.

He stared at his own image. "Myself?"

"Certainly. That's your enemy. Make him into your ally and there is no task, no feat you won't be able to perform. No victory you can't have."

"Without eating the heart of a lion?"

"Eating hearts is overrated," the old woman said. "Your own as well as anyone else's. For it isn't the vanquished heart that gives us strength, but the open one. It's love, really, that gives us the courage of lions."

"Who are you?" he said.

"Well, I'm one of a pair of twins who were separated at birth," said the old woman, who now that she mentioned it was a ringer for the duchess, which wouldn't have meant anything to Rodney, since he hadn't ever seen her. But it certainly came as a great relief to me, because I thought she looked familiar and wasn't sure where I'd seen her before. "But that is another story. Either that, or I'm an attained Spiritual Master, and can be in two places at the same time."

"I like the first explanation better," said Rodney.

"Then that's the one you can have. Now be off with you, and do what it is you have to do." She started towards the door. Just then a bird flew in the window, screeching, and circled the room. "Oh, get back to your nest!" she cried, beating her hands about her head so it wouldn't get in her hair, which could have passed for a nest if she hadn't advised him otherwise. "Silly lapwing!"

"That's a lapwing?" Rodney said, excitedly, as the bird settled into its nest in the open window.

"It certainly is. And a very stubborn one, too. She's been trying to hatch what she thinks is an egg for years now. Some kind of rock."

"A Quirin stone!" cried Rodney.

"Excuse me?"

"A magic stone, found only in the lapwing's nest. If you place it on a sleeping person's head, it reveals their innermost thoughts."

"I wish I'd had that with a few of my husbands," the old woman said.

"And it's my father's name!"

"King Quirin?"

He nodded.

"Then you are, in truth, the prince?"

"So it would seem."

"Well, appearances are deceiving," said the old woman. "But in this case I would say they are accurate. Here," she said, and, taking the stone from underneath the bird, placed it in Rodney's hand. "The heart alone can do miracles, but a little magic doesn't hurt."

"Thank you," Rodney said, and bent to kiss her.

And for a moment she was transformed into the young and beautiful girl she had been, a sparkle of radiance all about her, her clothes woven of gossamer and gold, her dreams filled with fresh beginnings, and the whole world ahead of her. "Thank *you*," she said, softly. And then she was old again, but the moment would keep her going for a very long time.

As Rodney started down the steps, he could hear the lapwing shrieking. "Oh, don't be such a spoilsport," came the voice of the old woman. "I'll get you another stone."

"Lunchtime!" cried Rhea, as she came down the dungeon stairs, carrying their tray. She had filled the princess's plate with baby vegetables, parboiled, crisp and brightly arranged, tiny carrots tented in the center of the dish, *petits pois* bright green along the gilded band of the china, trying to make it as delicate and appetizing as she could. Lately, the girl had been sending back much of her food uneaten. It worried Rhea, really, since she was not your basic villainess, and wanted no real harm to come to the princess. Still, she hadn't been able to do what Darcy wanted, and turn against Rachid, convinced his plan would benefit Isabel. But Rhea didn't want the girl starving. So she'd been making little cakes and irresistible pastries, which had been disappearing. But last night she'd peeked through a hole under her butcher's block, and who was eating it was the king.

"How lovely you've made it look," said Shan. "You're really very kind for someone who refuses to help us."

"I'm not in charge of this caper," said Rhea. "I am only a woman of limited brain capacity and a great gift for cuisine." She could not help noting how pale the girl looked, and that she seemed thin. It was a terrible reflection on prison cooking, Rhea could not help thinking. And she'd gone to such trouble. Maybe the princess was just trying to make her look bad. "Go ahead. Eat something."

"I'll try." Shan picked up her fork, and moved it around a little, rearranging the peas. Finally she speared one, and brought it to her lips, chewed wanly, and swallowed. But she turned nearly the color of the pea, and, dropping her fork, just managed to get to the tiny toilet behind the screen in time.

Rhea could hear the retching. My cooking makes her sick, was all she could think, and tried not to be angry. "My cooking makes you sick?" she shrieked, losing the battle.

"Oh, please, Rhea," Shan said weakly, coming from behind the screen, holding her napkin to her lips. "It isn't your fault. I've been like this for a while now."

"You've got to eat," Rhea said. "You're just being stubborn."

"I'm afraid not," said the girl, lying down, and putting her feet up. "How long have I been here?"

Quirin snored.

"Two more inches on his beard," said Rhea.

"What is that in time?"

"Eight weeks," said Rhea.

"Oh, dear," said Shan. "Then I'm in real trouble."

"You're a prisoner in a dungeon, the victim of a depraved,

pernicious shit, who without my intercession would probably barbecue you, without a very good sauce. If it wasn't for me, you'd be dead meat. But who would want to eat you, as skinny as you're getting? Still, you go on trying to make me feel bad, not eating my cooking. I'm going out of my way to make things pleasant for you, to come between you and any real harm he might do you. But I'm turning against you, Missy, and that way lies the torture wheel. What could be realer trouble than that?"

"I think I'm pregnant," said Shan.

"You have to let her out," said Rhea.

"I *have* to?" said Rachid. He was in his private chambers, all hung with burgundy and black, even over the windows, so no light could come in. "May I remind you that you are just an associate pawn in this game."

"But there's a baby, now. A royal heir. That changes everything."

"Yes, it does," said Rachid. "She must die."

"Over my dead body," said Rhea.

"You heard her," said Rachid to Cesare, who was standing at subordinate sinister attention. With that he moved forward, and struck Rhea on the back of the neck. She collapsed in a heap. Cesare took out his knife, raised her unconscious head, and held the blade to her throat.

"Not here, you dummy. There'll be blood. Throw her in the dungeon, and tonight we'll get rid of all three of them."

"It's my poker night," said Cesare.

"In the morning, then," said Rachid. "Take her away."

Cesare lifted Rhea's lifeless form, holding her under the arms, and started dragging her towards the door. "Use the secret passageway, dammit!" Rachid said. "You build these things and nobody honors them. I'm getting sick of being so unappreciated."

"Me, too," said Cesare, and pressing the white marble cherries on the mantel that opened the fireplace, disappeared into the wall.

“Darling?” Isabel stuck her head into the doorway from her chambers. “Did I hear something fall?”

“Only me,” Rachid said, holding his heart. “For you.”

“Flatterer,” said Isabel, cocking her head in the coy way she had that was not so much coy anymore as looking to see things from a different angle. For he had never loved her so much as lately, since she had gone along with his sickish wish. In truth, it had been the tenderest, most sensitive sexual experience she’d ever had, making love with another woman. Or, as she knew, really, a *seeming* other woman. What a master of disguise he was! But he couldn’t fool *her*.

10

JUST BEFORE SHE WENT TO SLEEP (or pretended to) Isabel hid the Quirin stone in the headboard of her bed. It amused her that Rachid, with so many concealed passageways he himself had constructed, had no idea there was this ancient, traditional hiding place for the royal family, fashioned by Quirin's grandfather, nicknamed the Squirrel King. It was the only secret she had kept from Rachid, since it was her conviction that love meant sharing, and also she didn't know how to keep her mouth shut. But some millimeter of self-preservation had alerted her unconscious that one day she might have something she wished she'd kept to herself. So much as she'd been tempted to show it to him, as part of their play, she never had.

Now she was frankly delighted, smiling to herself as he slipped into slumber beside her, hardly able to wait until she could see if the magic worked. Rodney had returned that afternoon from the forest, with a new, strange light in his eyes, and the stone in his pocket. He'd given it to her just before leaving in pursuit of his Darcy, whom he was determined to find and bring back to Perq. Isabel had never seen him with so much conviction and (could it be, in spite of his genes?) strength. Although he denied having swallowed the heart of a lion, she could feel something pulsing from within him that had never before been there. Radiated by an understandable pride that her fledgling was at last showing signs of taking manly wing, combining with her glee that she had an occult toy, she nearly glowed in the dark. The stone was occult in every sense of the word, for along with its mystery, there was also the fact that for once, just this once, she'd kept quiet. The surest way for magic to have power.

"Don't let yourself be used lightly," her son had said, as he boarded the royal helicopter, giving her the stone. In her naïveté she imagined he meant as a magician, as one would counsel a Ouija board.

She waited till the breaths beside her grew regular and deep, before taking out the stone. Then she placed it on Rachid's head, so he would reveal his innermost thoughts. At base (or more accurately, on high), she was hoping to hear how much he loved her. And in a way, that was what she got.

"Oh, my dearest Isabel," went his innermost thoughts. "Never have I hungered for you as much as when I watched you with another woman."

"What!" cried Isabel, but not too loud, because she didn't want to wake him. "You mean that wasn't you?"

"Seeing you with that redhead was the most sexually arousing moment of my disgusting history."

"I wondered how you did that, the redheaded part," went Isabel's dudgeon. "I mean certain things you can hide, but the color *did* look natural to me." Now was she furious that she had been used, as Rodney might have put it, lightly. She was tempted to wake Rachid, to hit him on the head with the stone that was on it, but it was probably not heavy enough to kill him. Besides, maybe there was more in there, something that would help her forgive him. Help her forgive herself, now that she was a pervert, too.

"I can't wait to claim you for my queen!" went his covert thinking. "In the morning when I kill Quirin . . ."

"Quirin?" Isabel could not keep her astonishment inside.

". . . and Darcy, and that interfering Rhea . . ."

"Darcy? Rhea?"

". . . skewering their innards like shashlik, throwing them all down the watery, rat-infested trap in the dungeon beneath the kitchen . . ."

"Dungeon?"

". . . I shall marry you in the cathedral that is now a jai-alai court, and make this kingdom truly mine!"

"Pig," she could not help saying, because her own great shame at having deviated sexually was now overlaid with a greater one. She had let this heinous libertine, this patent-leather villain, have his way not just with her, but with the great kingdom of Perq. Something like jingoism rose in her, because there was nothing like finding a man had betrayed you to make you love your country, where at least all the rules were clear. The fact that her poor, benighted husband was not in a sanatorium in Switzerland, but a captive beneath his own palace deepened her sense of disloyalty. How many people in life were there that really cared about you, even if you were a queen? And Quirin had always loved her, drunk though he was, incapable of showing his affection in better ways than slobbering, and occasionally singing "Melancholy Baby." But at his worst, his most ineffectual, he'd never done anything to harm her, or, for that matter, anyone. And Rhea! The last of the devoted servants, who would have done anything for her, and had, in exchange for an occasional cast-off Chanel, imprisoned beneath her own kitchen, worse than being hoist on her own petard. And even Darcy, Darcy for whom Isabel had little regard and no affection, did not deserve to be in a dungeon. Especially since the latest news was that she was in Switzerland. How could this be possible?

"And the false Darcy who is now slutting about the slopes of Zermatt will bring Rodney to ruin," went Rachid's thoughts.

"A false Darcy?" Isabel could not stand it another minute. She slid from the bed, careful not to wake him.

"I wouldn't mind having a little shot at her . . . , that sweet apple ass . . ."

"Warthog," she chewed, wondering how she could give him a

dose of his own filth. Well, revenge would have to come later. Right now, her job was to find them and free them.

Her job! Why, she hadn't ever really had one before, except to be there for disaster victims, to try to raise money for them, and console them, and to show up for court events, and be queenly. But it wasn't the same as having a task, an actual vista. To help people, in the truest sense, by setting them free. Starting with herself.

"Mommy, Mommy!" cried his innermost thoughts. "Why did you have to be so controlling?"

The helicopter that carried Rodney to Switzerland was painted with a gigantic golden phoenix, national symbol of Perq. In place of wings, however, it had been given the actual helicopter blades. The artist who had decorated it had smoked an entire frond of the Fescinnine tree before lifting his brush, which it hadn't been all that easy to do.

Rodney's heart was as heavy as it was open as he whirred towards his (he thought) beloved, since for all the courage that he had gained in the forest, he hadn't found optimism. He'd eaten a few trueberries on his way home, and as blueberries made your teeth blue, so trueberries made your eyes clear, and you saw things as they were. So much as he would have liked to see things as he wanted them to be, how they were was she was having a front-paged fling with a ski instructor in Zermatt. All the harder to bear since that was the place where she'd been found originally. Even harder because the first light snow had barely fallen, and she already had. To the sound of trumpets, or their modern-day equivalent, the newspapers.

Thus it was that he knew exactly where to find her, on the one patch of snow that was skiable, directly beneath the crumpled cap of the Matterhorn. He had wired ahead to the small hotel where they'd been introduced over hot chocolate, when their world was innocent as their beverages, asking for a suite of rooms, and no word to the press that he was coming. The suite of rooms he supposed was a hangover from another, richer time when he'd still thought of himself as royal. But there was little about him that was elevated now, besides his adrenaline level, and possibly his cholesterol, since monarchs lived off the fat of the land.

Beside him, in the helicopter, sat the chancellor of Perq, the tall, deadly boring man in saffron robes who uttered inanities that many considered wisdom. Rodney had wanted to go to Switzerland alone, without his security guards, or anyone. But his mother had pressed on him the uncomfortable fact that Darcy was very likely out of control, and some mediation might be necessary. No one capitulated as quickly at an arbitration as those who were anxious to leave because the people in charge were dull. Having run through a rock star, a drug dealer, and now a ski instructor, Darcy's attention span would probably be short, at best, or best at short. So the presence of the Old Geyser who spouted Wisdom, as they called him in the west of Perq where accents were flatter and somewhat Bostonian (though those in other parts called him Geezer), would probably bring things to a speedier conclusion.

As noted earlier, the one great democratic principle of Perq was that no one had to go where they didn't want to be. So the chancellor was most happy in his assignment, since he had never seen the Matterhorn except in pictures of Disneyland, where of course it was only a reproduction. As much as he knew that everything was an illusion, and it was the shadows on the wall of the cave that gave men his conviction, rather than the light that cast them, the chancellor preferred to see the real thing, even though he had cousins in Anaheim. For as Fred Allen said in a wittier time, California is great if you're an orange. But judging from the wonders outside the window, Switzer had to be a greater man than Disney, unless you came from Orange County.

Now so joyful was Darcy in her loss of Restlessness, along with the other five blossoms that had healed her, that her very day was aglow with the mere pleasure of being alive. Mere was hardly the word, but people do have a tendency to forget what a privilege it is to be able to breathe and taste and walk and look about even at the not-pretty things, until their eyes fall out or their legs buckle. Only the incursion of actual pain seems to bring them up sharply to how lucky they were to have had pleasure, which they didn't seem to notice at the time. Every moment for her now was chock-full of light, the elation of spirit that comes from knowing you are doing exactly what you should be doing, and that life always works out exactly as it should, though it doesn't always seem so at the time. For too much of our lives are spent cementing our brains, fixing them on how we want things to be, suffering over the fact that we seem not to be in control, which we're not, except for Rachid's mother.

Only one aspect of Darcy's life gave her even the slightest irritation, and that was that the seventh flower thus far had failed to bloom. It had been months now, and there wasn't a sign of a bud. She could hardly bear it because she knew that this blossom, whatever it was, would be the greatest remedy of all to whatever there was still inside her. One night she'd been so impatient she got up and rooted around in the soil to see what had become of the seed, but the duchess had been sleepwalking again, and stopped her just in time, before she rooted around so much that she killed it. "You can't push the river," the duchess-Afghan had said. "You can't hasten the harvest. Patience, and in the right season, you will harvest your Self."

But in spite of the counsel for patience, Darcy was too anxious for her total transformation not to be a little discontent at the time it was taking. Still, her days, as noted, were beautifully full, with longer walks and a little more ice cream and a coat Tom bought her as the days grew colder. So satisfied was she, in fact, aside from the corner of annoyance at being denied *her* timing for the flower, that she did not even read the newspapers: the news would probably be bad; she preferred to feel good. No sense of urgency or need propelled her. If, sometimes, the thought arose about where her life should lead in the long run, she was able to dismiss it, for she understood that the short run, the moment, was all she really had. Besides, she couldn't dream about going anywhere else or being something different until she'd had that flower.

But one morning, very early, as she walked on the rounded cobblestones of the beach, feeling them through the sole of her slipper, being aware of the sun, which seemed a little distant now, more a visiting relative than a member of the immediate family, she bumped into Samuel Stroll. He had his string bag for collecting garbage slung over his shoulder, and the point-ended stick for spearing refuse in his hand.

"I see where your look-alike hasn't been behaving like a lady, much less a princess," he said.

"What do you mean?" asked Darcy.

Samuel Stroll took from his sack several tabloid papers, holding them out for her, with their sordid headlines, "Darcy *Schusses*," being the most suggestive of them. There was the supposed princess, being helped up from a pile of snow by a handsome young ski instructor. "Doesn't she know how to ski better than this?" read the text under the picture. "Or has the princess lost her balance over Diedrich?"

"But this is insufferable!" Darcy said, reverting to her royalist diction, for never had it occurred to her that Shan would in any way disgrace the crown, much less her skiing reputation.

"There's worse," said Stroll. "A story that the princess has posed in the buff for *Playhouse* magazine."

"That's a lie!"

"It's supposed to reach the newsstands next week. I've had to order extra, everyone's so anxious to have it."

"I must do something at once!" said Darcy, running towards the stairs up to the street, leaving a rather confused Samuel Stroll staring after her.

Bailey, the former butler, was just inside the door to the duchess's house, licking his paw. "Hello," he might have said, if Darcy wasn't overinterpreting his "Meow."

"I have no time to talk to you now," said Darcy, rushing by him. "Your Grace?" she called out, tearing through the house.

The duchess sat in a chair by the parlor window, looking out at the sea, which had gone all gray and dark, like the air, like the season. Her cats, as well, seemed darker now, dressed in more lugubrious tones than they'd sported in summer and early autumn, their ginger stripes having faded into dull browns.

"Please, Your Grace," Darcy said, and fell to her knees in the middle of the pile of cats that curled at the duchess's feet. "You've got to lend me some money."

"Neither a borrower nor a borrower be," said the duchess.

"It isn't my style, believe me. But this is a real emergency. I've got to get to Switzerland. Shan, the real Shan, has gone mad with indiscretion."

"I've heard there was a lot of that going around," said the duchess. "You'd think with all the health warnings people would be more careful. What do you mean, the real Shan?"

"I tried to tell you," Darcy said. "We switched places. I am the Princess Darcy. And she is destroying my name."

"It still sounds like Darcy to me," said the duchess.

"I beg of you. The future of the kingdom of Perq hangs in the balance."

"It's a very rich country. They can pay their own freight."

"They will, I promise. I'll give you ten percent interest on the loan. Please. Just enough for a ticket."

"And where will you get the money to pay me back, a poor little girl like you, with a miner for a husband?"

"But I'm not poor. I'm the Princess Darcy."

"Saddest of all is to live in delusion."

"Twenty percent," said Darcy.

"I can't support you in this madness."

"Forty percent," said Darcy. "And the best cat food in Europe for all of your cats."

"Give it to her," they meowed in chorus.

"Oh, very well," said the duchess. "Though I hate to give in to community pressure."

Giving Rachid a little of his own medicine, literally, the sleeping draught that he always slipped into the desserts of visiting dignitaries, so he could go through their papers, Isabel made sure he would be out of commission for the night. She slid it between his lips in an eye dropper, and, for good measure, put some in his ear, so he couldn't hear in the event the escape made a clatter.

It occurred to her as she dressed under cover of darkness (literally, for her heart was too heavy to wear pastels, now that she knew the truth about him) that it would probably be wiser to kill him. But each man kills the thing he loves; women just write novels. Besides, murder was not part of her makeup.

Scurrying through the palace, she asked herself a hundred questions in her head: how could she have been such a fool? so blind? so innocent, except sexually? Reaching the kitchen, she saw the guard in his turncoat, asleep with his cheek on the butcher's block. Taking his gun from his belt, she held it nervously to his nose.

"Don't make any quick moves," she said. His lids opened. He saw the gun between them, and his eyes crossed. "Where's the dungeon?"

He got up slowly, and moved the butcher's block in a special way, so the floor beneath it opened. "Rachid and his secret passageways," she said, contemptuously. She hated him now with as much passion as she'd thought she loved him. "Quirin?" she cried, into the dank, as she made her way down the stairs, the turncoat guard ahead of her, prodded by the pistol at the back of his neck. "Oh, my poor Quirin," she said, seeing him tucked into the prisoner's cot. "Untuck him!" she said to the guard.

"I knew you'd save us," Rhea said, proudly.

"And you, poor Darcy. How I've misjudged you!" Isabel lamented. "A false impostor Darcy destroys your reputation."

"But she is not an imposter," said Shan. "I am Shan. The false Darcy is the true Darcy."

"Not even the true Darcy could be that false," said Isabel. "Rachid has placed an impostor in public to disgrace us, and the kingdom. Where could the real Darcy be?"

"In Criccieth, where we changed places."

"Then let us hie there," said the queen. "Quirin, are you up to hieing?"

"If you're with me," he said, somewhat sentimentally, his tiny brown eyes bright with reawakened hope. It had been a long time since she talked to him like she really cared about him, which is why a crisis is sometimes helpful for a marriage, especially a long one. The marriage, that is. Crises should be kept as brief as possible.

Soon they were skimming towards Criccieth on the queen's hydrofoil, the one that was all mirrored for the once-joyful debauches she had indulged in with Rachid. The very sight of the mirrors inflamed her to loathing, of herself, as well as him. But as she had not been the one to eat the flower that healed Vanity, she still could hardly keep her eyes off herself. Considering what a dupe she'd been, she didn't look that bad.

Quirin was at the helm, beard flying in the misty wind as they cut through the Irish Sea, imbued with a sudden, ecstatic sense of purpose. For never in his life, since his own early training for the Perquian navy, had he been called upon to do anything, really, except be a figurehead. And then, not that handsome a one. So to be rushing to the rescue — he assumed it would be a rescue — was the most elevating experience he'd had since his crowning. And, in truth, that hadn't been all that elevating. He had known he wasn't really the right man for the job, and was only getting it because his father had died, which was really depressing, as he hadn't been a very effective king either, but Quirin missed him. Now at the helm, he could hardly contain his feeling of near-elation, because he was needed, functioning, remembering how to drive this thing. And his enemies — it was so refreshing in a way actually to have them, and not just be undercutting oneself — would be defeated, and he would become a true and caring king.

But he didn't hear the sound of the motor, the slap against the surface of the water of a Cigarette, the fastest, most deadly of boats. And even if he had heard it, how could he imagine that it would be Rachid, in pursuit of him, with his associate villain Adrian? For hadn't Isabel told how she drugged him, gave him a powerful dose of sleeping potion? And hadn't they closed the turncoat guard in the dungeon? So who would have gone to wake Rachid, and tell him they were escaping? And even if anyone had tried to tell him, how could he have been roused?

Well, you know how they say Evil never sleeps? That isn't altogether true. It sleeps once in a while, but never for more than a couple of hours.

Even in the pre-season Zermatt had about it an air of festivity. Horses that would later draw the sleighs through heavy, banked snowpaths in the village cantered at their own leisurely pace through what was left of meadows. Only one light snow had fallen, and in spite of the mountainous altitude, bright sun had melted nearly all of it. So sparse patches of crystals glittered on the browned, frozen grass.

There was measurable snow only on one slope of Alp where the pseudo-Darcy practiced her ever-improving turns, as Diedrich, the ski instructor, watched her. She had a light blue wool knit cap on her head, with a tassel on the end, collapsed into itself at the same careless angle as the Matterhorn, which was just above her, so she looked like she was imitating that great mountain peak, or making fun of it, if she would dare.

Diedrich watched with a great deal of amusement as she labored on what most of his students did so effortlessly, the turns and responding to his blatant sexuality. In spite of all the publicity they'd been getting about their affair, he'd been unable as yet to set it into actual motion, which surprised the only part of him that was still capable of being surprised, a module in his right brain, which is the surprise side. (Scientists severing the corpus callosum in recent experimentation found modules in the brain that show certain propensities, for example, creativity. So in the autopsy that would later be performed on Diedrich after his being shot in the head by a jealous husband it was discovered that there was a surprise module, and in it was his astonishment that he hadn't been able to prong the princess.)

Diedrich was six feet three, with broad shoulders veeing down to narrow hips, and a bottom designed for ski clothes. The eyes with which he watched the seeming Darcy were a sea-green shade that could make any woman's heart do flip-flops, whether or not she was in the snow. He had white-gold hair and a dark gold tan, and a jaw so square it indicated character, which shows that genes can be deceptive.

As noted, there were not many surprises left for him, none in his mouth, which had tasted flavors from Bora Bora to Johannesburg (his favorites were in Jakarta, but with them had come dysentery), nor on his fingers, which had touched every fabric and kind of skin, inside and out. Certainly not in his penis. So the fact that this really not very unusual (besides her status) woman could resist him was a conundrum to him, even though he couldn't possibly have known that word. There is only one thing more spoiled than a woman whose looks and muskiness drive men mad, and that is a man who could have anybody and probably did. To make it as clear as the one icicle that hung from the evergreen tree near where Babara skied, he was the kind of man who, had he lived in Aspen, would probably have been killed by a celebrity wife who got away with it by sleeping with the prosecuting attorney. As it was, his fate was to be not dissimilar, but all that should concern us is whether or not the husband who would shoot him turns out to be Rodney. We shall see.

So there was Babara, joylessly practicing her turns, observed from behind various rocks by members of the world press who would use any excuse to get to a great locale, and this story offered one so good it wasn't even an excuse. Most of them by this time were so caught up in the romantic scandal they were reporting and photographing that they considered themselves sort of duennas, keeping the couple honest, much as they hated to think they were. One of them had gotten an advance copy of the *Playhouse* that featured the princess in the altogether, and hid it from the other journalists, and indeed, everyone but himself, secreting it underneath the carpet in his bathroom. He was representative of the overriding feeling of the network of watchers, all of whom were infatuated with her, though perhaps not in such a disgusting way.

Now it was getting close to noon. In their semihidden perches, they looked at their watches, and started signaling to Diedrich, pointing first at their watch faces, and then at the little inn near the funicular that served hot chocolate and Bratwurst.

"We should stop soon," said Diedrich, as she came up short in front of him.

"You're all alike," Babara said. "That's why I knew it was better not to start."

"I mean stop practicing," Diedrich said. "It's lunchtime."

But just then over the peak of the Matterhorn came the royal helicopter of Perq, its whirring blades flurrying the snow back into the gentle storm in which it had first descended. And from out the belly of the golden phoenix painted on the bulging aircraft stepped Rodney.

"Oh, dear," said Babara, who had not been prepared for such an eventuality. That is to say, she had been emotionally prepared, in a negative sense, from the time she was a child, led to believe by an undemonstrative mother that her only hope lay in finding a prince, which together with a rerelease of *Snow White and the Seven Dwarfs*, featuring the unforgettable ballad "Someday My Prince Will Come," had left a permanent mark on her. But she hadn't been practically prepared by Adrian as to what to do if Rodney showed up.

Now he was glaring at her, in the most loving fashion, proud in a very humble way, looking at her with all the neediness she herself felt towards Adrian. Surprisingly (for she, too, had that module in her right brain), she liked him.

"We must talk," Rodney said.

"Talk is cheap, you rich stiff," said Diedrich, who'd been instructed to make as much trouble as possible by Rachid, increments of the bribery increasing according to how many headlines he could grab. These days, scum doesn't just rise, it calculates.

"I wasn't addressing you," said Rodney.

"You want to talk to her, you have to talk to me." Diedrich stepped in between them, reaching behind himself and taking her hand proprietarily. "She doesn't love you."

"Do you love him?" Rodney said, craning his neck so he could see her, his eyes beseeching.

And even though she didn't even know this man, and he was certainly not her type, she felt such empathy for his love of the real Darcy that tears sprang to her eyes. "I don't know," she said, for that intelligence hadn't been given her by Adrian either. So the tears were partly those of understanding what he was feeling, and partly frustration, because if she had realized how complicated this all would be, she would have asked for a script.

"Can we go someplace . . ." Rodney looked around, suddenly, and saw a member of the press corps or two bobbing up from behind rocks. ". . . private?"

"She doesn't want to be with you," Diedrich said.

"She is a royal princess," said Rodney. "And no opportunistic idler is going to speak for her."

"You take that back!" said Diedrich, for the words were too big for him, and he thought he had been insulted, which he had been, but not in the way he supposed. He moved towards Rodney and struck out at him.

Now for all his once wimpiness, Rodney was not without certain boxing skills, begun in the boarding school he hated and his father hated before him, where all the little boys were privileged and rather puny, and so had to be taught to defend themselves against future handsome bullies, which Diedrich certainly was. Rodney caught the chop with the center of his left arm, blocked it, and counterpunched, landing an impressive right to the ribs. Diedrich let out a whoosh of air, and collapsed slightly in his midsection, resembling in his posture the overhang of Matterhorn above them.

Members of the press were unabashedly out in the open now, taking pictures, some of them waging bets on what would be the outcome of the fight that was starting. But seeing them, and noting how many of them there were, and with cameras, Rodney colored, and held up his hand. "If you have any decency," he said quietly to Diedrich, "let us take this someplace where these cormorants can't observe."

"What's the going rate for decency?" Diedrich said.

"Aboard, aboard for shame!" the chancellor cried, hobbling towards them from the helicopter, his saffron robes flowing about his long, skinny body like overblown imagery. "The wind sits in the shoulder of your blades."

"Who's this clown?" asked Diedrich.

"The chancellor of Perq, vermin," said the chancellor. "Look to your character."

"Why would I listen to some old creep in a yellow nightgown?"

"Give every man your ear, but few your tongue," said the chancellor.

"Is he making sick suggestions?" asked Diedrich, suddenly allied with Rodney, the enemy the old generation.

The chancellor, blown away as he was by the heat of his own air, was not completely unconscious. Sensing he was being closed out by youth, he looked at Rodney. "Beware of entrance to a quarrel, but being in, beat the shit out of him."

"I think it would be better if we went someplace else," said Rodney, who was wiser now than even the official wise man, since he had a heart full of love, instead of just a head full of sayings.

Now did the rascally Rachid throw the anchor of the swifter than swift Cigarette speedboat over the rail of the hydrofoil, and climb it. Like the monkey he was, he was agile as well as deceitful, and the feat was not difficult for him.

"Keep the boat alongside," he instructed Adrian, who was not very good at the yachtsman's trade, but had been taking lessons, since Rachid had promised him — along with a fortune in cash and a studio for his photography work and a bank account in Switzerland and charge accounts at Ralph Lauren — a speedboat of his very own, with a piece of Irish Sea for his bathtub. Boys understand the needs of other boys, and sailor though he didn't wish to be, Adrian still wanted the childhood comforts returned, and there'd always been strange men in the tub, so it had been hard to play with his ducks.

Arcing gracefully over the rail, Rachid came to rest on the deck of the hydrofoil, and padded in his soft-soled sneakers towards the cabin. He peered through the glass and saw Quirin at the wheel, Rhea standing near him. She looked up, screamed soundlessly, and pointed.

"Take the wheel!" Quirin instructed her, as his eyes and his courage steeled, and he went outside.

"Are you prepared to die?" Rachid asked him, pulling a dagger.

"I have no weapon," Quirin said.

"Nobody ever said it would be fair," said Rachid, and lunged at him.

Now for all his months of imprisonment, his weakness of body, and what had been, prior to now, his weakness of character, the king still had blood in his veins, and a few remembered dance steps. So he moved with surprising urbanity, parrying the knife thrusts with an old mambo. Then, as he was not a moron, he ran belowdecks to get something to fight back with.

The saloon where the queen had sported with Rachid was empty, except for the usual seraglio decor, pillows, soft beds, a most suggestive chair, and mirrors everywhere, walls and ceiling. Quirin started for the adjoining room, where Isabel and (they knew who she was now) Shan rested. But Rachid was too fast for him. He stood in the doorway, his black silk shirt opened all the way down the front, black pants and boots suddenly shading him into the pirate he was, teeth and greed gleaming, the blade of the dagger shimmering in his hand.

Quirin did a high, spectacular kick, from the season they'd all learned the can-can, toeing the knife out of the scoundrel's hand. It bowed through the air in a series of spectacular curves and circles, and came to rest in Quirin's open hand. "Are you prepared to die?" he asked Rachid.

"I have no weapon," said Rachid, sweating.

"You expect *me* to be evenhanded?"

"You're a king." Rachid shrugged. "How will it sound in the songs they sing a hundred years from now, that you killed an unarmed man?"

"There should be some swords around here someplace," Quirin said, going to the locked cabinet. But no sooner had he turned his back even an inch than Rachid was lunging for the chair, and raising it to smite him. Catching the villain's moves in the mirrors, Quirin stepped aside. The chair crashed into the wall mirror, smashing it into a storm of flying pieces.

"Foul fiend," Quirin said, turning. "No reason to be just with the devil!" He moved towards him with dagger poised.

But Rachid bent over and seized a shard of glass, the largest, pointed triangle of mirror, held it out, and ran it into Quirin's chest. The king groaned, and fell.

The door to the next cabin opened, and Isabel saw the king, blood gushing from the mirrored spear in his chest. The color drained from her face. "What have you done?" she said to Rachid.

"Now we can be together for always," Rachid said.

"In Hell." She raised the pistol she'd taken from the guard.

"You can't be serious," Rachid said. "Baby, it's *me!*"

She fired. But her aim was poor and she had had no real practice at revenge. So the bullet didn't get him. He bolted out the door, as she ran after, firing yet more shots at his fleeing form. She thought she saw him stumble. Then he was gone.

"Oh, my poor Quirin," Isabel said, rushing to his side, kneeling. "How could this have happened? What have I done?"

"Why, you've been the prettiest and sexiest," he said, smiling. "What more could any man ask?"

"What happened?" said Rhea, out of breath, standing in the doorway. "I saw Rachid jump over the side."

"Oh, Quirin, don't die," Isabel pleaded. "I'll make it up to you. Everything. Really I will." Tears started flowing from her eyes. "You mustn't die."

"We all have to die of something," Quirin said. "I rather like this way. For I have stood against a villain fearlessly. I didn't know I had it in me." He smiled at her, the weakness that had characterized his life, and his smile, suddenly transmuted into strength. No matter that it was ebbing. For the first time in the life that was ending, he was proud of himself. "So my life means something. And this . . . after all . . . this is only death." And he was gone.

"Oh, my poor Quirin," sobbed Isabel. "How I did wrong you! How you must have suffered."

"It's all right," said Rhea consolingly, her arm around the shoulders of her mistress. "His suffering had nothing to do with you. You didn't know he was imprisoned."

"But I hurt him. I wronged him."

"You didn't wrong him. He didn't know what you were doing, so it didn't really hurt him. Who you wronged was yourself."

Isabel's eyes darkened. Her shoulders squared, and anger ate at the corners of her mouth. She stood. "Rachid," she hissed. "We must get Rachid." Suddenly, she realized Rhea was with her. "Who's steering this thing?"

"Darcy," said Rhea. "Or whatever her name is."

The small hotel where Rodney and Darcy had first exchanged glances and, in short order, pledges, was set inconspicuously behind a number of more fashionable, better-known inns. It could be reached via a modest little walkway running between two streetfront buildings. This might have been unfortunate in the event of a great fire, but it served admirably for keeping out the press. A wooden horse had been placed along the walk, and the hotel's security guard, who was in fact its owner, stood out in front of it with a billy club, making sure the reporters stayed on the other side.

In the suite that Rodney had reserved, the hotel owner's wife set a tray of cocoa made extra sweet to try to balance the circumstances. Like most of the Western World, she more than knew what was going on, and was torn between her vested interest in the marriage's beginnings, and the fact that Diedrich, the interloper, was her nephew, and she liked the idea of having a princess, even a fallen one, in the family. So are most of us pulled between our romantic hearts and some form of nepotism, unless we can combine them by having affairs with our nephews, which she had from time to time considered. Incest might be the greatest taboo, but eiderdown quilts hatch the warmest fantasies, and there was no disputing Diedrich's attractiveness.

He seemed not to notice her as she set down the tray on the blue and white Dutch-tiled table between his chair and the quilted couch on which the prince and princess sat. "Will there be anything else?" she asked them.

"Are you hungry?" Rodney asked his (he assumed) wife.

Babara shook her head.

"That will be all," Diedrich said imperiously. The proprietor's wife curtsied and left the room, inflamed by his indifference. (It was she who later was to have the affair with him that culminated in Diedrich's being shot by her husband, for those of you who don't like loose ends, or ski instructors.)

"What do you want?" Rodney asked Diedrich.

"Why do you ask him?" Babara said. "Why don't you ask me?"

"Because I know what kind of man he is, and before you say anything that might embarrass you later, I want you to see how easily he can be bought off."

"What do you mean by easily?" Diedrich said.

But if the prince had a figure in mind, he did not have a chance to state it. For just at that moment a great uproar arose outside the hotel, a cry of such magnitude that even Diedrich, caught as he was in his first really major negotiation, rushed to the window. Through the ranks of the press, who were snapping their cameras, squawking like chickens, walked a woman who looked exactly like the princess.

"An impostor! An impostor!" cried the minions of the press.

"Forgive me, Your Highness," said the proprietor's wife, curtseying. "But there's a woman downstairs who says she's Princess Darcy."

Something churned in Rodney's belly. For love when deep enough, Shakespeare notwithstanding, is not that blind. It certainly knows *whom* it loves. And much as his heart was aching at the circumstances, it had failed to be moved by this woman next to him. "Show her in," he said.

"But she's an impostor!" Babara cried.

The door was opened. There stood Darcy, in her Welsh blue dress and velvet slippers, and sort of new coat.

"*Mein Gott!*" said Diedrich, getting to his feet.

"Impostor!" cried the chancellor, rushing in behind her.

"Who are you?" Rodney asked.

"Darcy."

"How can she be Darcy when I'm Darcy?" said Babara.

"I can clear this all up," said Darcy to the prince. "Just give me two minutes alone with you."

Rodney opened the door to the bedroom part of the suite, and, ushering her in, closed it behind them. In a moment the two of them reemerged.

"She's Darcy, all right," said Rodney.

"But how do you know?" asked the chancellor. "What did she do?"

"Nothing," said Rodney.

But what of the real fake Darcy? Darcy explained to Rodney during the helicopter trip about the switch, and what had happened in the little Welsh village of Criccieth. Even now they were winging, or at least whirring about the top, towards that place. Darcy wanted to say good-bye to Tom, to whom she hadn't even written a farewell note.

In the corner of the helicopter, Babara sat shivering, not

knowing what fate awaited her. The chancellor had read her the riot act, framed during Perq's last riot, calling her everything foul, although of course in very lengthy, boring sentences. "I am taking you back as hard evidence of Rachid's treachery," he said, as Babara quivered. "He will meet a traitor's end."

"And what about me?" Babara said.

"What about you?" said the chancellor. "We don't even know who you are."

"Neither do I," said Babara.

"So her name really was Shan," Rodney said to Darcy. "She was telling me the truth."

"Yes, she was," said Darcy, who had never liked him as well as she did now. For he had been much humanized by his romantic adventure, and if she hadn't had plans of her own, she might have found him a pleasant enough partner.

"And after you say good-bye to this . . . Tom . . . you'll come back to Perq?"

"I don't think so, Rodney. I don't really love you. It wouldn't be fair to either of us. You're a tenderhearted man. I see that now. You should search for true love."

"I had true love," he said. "I had it with you, but you weren't really there."

"Then go after her, and find her."

"She belongs to somebody else."

"Nobody belongs to anybody," Darcy said.

The last bullet that Isabel fired at Rachid had caught him in the fleshiest part of his buttock, which was thick enough to be considered a hide, as even those of you with suspended judgment must have recognized him by now as a horse's ass. Still, callous and unfeeling as he was, and now a murderer, a bullet was a bullet, and he couldn't stand the sight of blood when it was his own. So the Cigarette had slapped across the water to the closest port, which was Criccieth, where a local doctor extracted it and took a few stitches.

"Would you like to keep the bullet?" the doctor asked Rachid, as he dropped it into the kidney-shaped aluminum pan.

"What am I supposed to do, put it under my pillow for the Bullet Fairy?"

"Don't get mad at me. I'm not the one who shot you. Who did, by the way?"

"An angry woman."

"The worst kind."

"They're all the worst kind," said Rachid, for the poison in him was peaking now, and he no longer pretended for the sake of self-promotion or even his deviant sexuality that he had any feeling for them at all. He would have liked nothing better than a world empty of women, except for an occasional whore which they all were anyway. All but his mother, and even she would have probably shot him in the ass. Just because he didn't think she was a whore didn't mean he trusted her.

Outside the doctor's office, Adrian paced nervously, his pockets weighted with the money Rachid had given him not to turn back. He was on his way to being exactly what he dreamed, a rich and powerful man, the down payment in his pants. So why did he feel so wretched?

"Oh, look," said Babara, as she stepped down the helicopter gangway. "A castle!"

"This is not a pleasure trip," said the chancellor.

"But I've never been *anywhere*," she said. "Can't I just go and see it?"

"Let her go," said Rodney. "We won't be here very long."

"I'll come right back. Scout's honor!" Babara said, rushing fleet-footedly up the stairs from the beach in the direction of the castle, the whole difficulty of her position fallen away in the joy of the fact that she was finally being allowed an independent excursion. Why, she actually hummed as she made her way up the cobblestones. Hummed and sang and saw the day, cold as it was, as lovely. Saw the day, but didn't see Rachid, who, with Adrian, fell back into the shadows, at the sight of her.

"Which one is it?" Rachid whispered to Adrian as she went by.

"Babara," he said, his glottis closing around her name.

"You better slow down," said the chancellor, trying without success to keep up with her. "Don't try to run away. You're evidence of Rachid's treachery."

You would think with the king's dead body on the boat, and the queen's having seen him commit the crime, and all of his foulness and double-dealing now being a matter of practically public record, Rachid would have been above taking umbrage at a little accusation of treachery. But villainy has its own blind spots and stupidities. So out of control was he now, that he saw the only threat to him, really, as being Babara. So he followed after her, climbing the steps to the castle, Adrian close behind.

Now where Owen Glendower had led his uprising, and children had held streamers in the wind, and kites had flown, and lovers' hearts also, Babara looked out to sea. Standing high on the edge of the bluff, she stared past the stillness of Cardigan Bay to the Irish Sea beyond, the fact that she was finally allowed to look, making her able to see. Her mind all at once encompassed the vastness and beauty of the universe, forgot all that was petty and petulant, as she breathed in. And with her stance came some personal alchemy. For they say that monkeys on certain islands, having learned a trick, pass it on without direct teaching to all the other monkeys, and even monkeys on islands far away. So everything that her counterpart and *her* counterpart had learned in the course of their adventures was transmitted to Babara, and she understood that life was a thing to be happy about. That every day free of pain should be a celebration. That to exist is a privilege, and a joy.

But such is the irony of life that we often come to appreciate it just when it is being taken away. And no sooner was she rejoicing in her identity, confused as it was, than Rachid ran up behind her, and with the strength that is given to madmen, lifted her like a twig, and raised her above his head, preparing to send her crashing to the rocks and water below. And she was about to meet her end, just as she found her Beginning. For you see, dear reader, life isn't a fairy tale, even in a fairy tale.

But just at that moment, Darnall reared his ugly head. From the depths of the bay rose that hideous, scaly, leonine face, dripping with viridescent venom, long serpent's neck twisting. And out of its throat came a horrific roar. So stunned was Rachid by the monster's appearance that he drew back, and faltered. And in that split second, Adrian boosted Babara from his arms, and giving a powerful kick to the bulleted buttocks of that villain, sent him arcing off the bluff.

For a moment Rachid seemed to hang in the air, like disapproval. Then, kicking and screaming, he fell towards the hellish, gaping maw. Past the giant pointed greenish teeth, down the fiery, slavering tongue into the shrieking throat, echoes of rage all around him, as in a giant tunnel. As he twisted and tumbled, he could hear the monster wail, the preternatural cry of sorrow, for even in a beast was the awful grief of being alone, and without a philosophy.

And then he was sliding through the pink- and purple-veined esophagus, down towards Darnall's belly. He could see the monster's organs, and there was no heart, only a giant spleen. But there in the monster's entrails Rachid felt suddenly at home. For around him were rancor and fury, resentment, regret, ignorance, negative thoughts, fear and doubt, all the dark forces in his own nature, surrounding him, as in a womb. So, he felt totally comfortable. Because all his life he had expected the worst, and here it was.

"You saved me!" cried Babara, from her perch above Adrian.

"Don't get carried away." He set her down.

"Don't get carried away!" she said, and threw her arms around him. "But I love you. And now I know you love me!"

"That's no reason to get emotional," said Adrian.

Just after she said good-bye to Tom, and thanked him for all the good he had brought her (and he certainly had), Darcy went to the windowbox. And there by the light of an early winter moon bloomed the final flower. Shaped like a foxglove, as were all the others, it was white, luminous, its petals translucent. Tilting it up gently, so she could look inside it, she saw a tiny white balloon. And although she had never been given to eating things she could play with, with rare exception, she had waited so long for this blossom, she was faint with hunger. So she broke it off and ate it.

And a flavor that was the sweetest of any she had tasted glided across her tongue. Like white chocolate, only milkier. And she was suffused with a sense of lightness, as though her heart and her feet and her core of longing had all been given wings. And everything she was sure would happen, or was afraid might happen, she let go of. And a sound like a stringless harp flooded her soul. For she had eaten the flower that healed Expectations. And that was the most liberating flower of all.

For expectations are a leaden ballast, a weight on the mind, and the stomach, threads pulling on the spirit, more like burning ropes. Anchoring you to what you insisted on having, sinking you when you didn't get it, dizzying you with disappointment. To be free of expectations made you really free.

She stepped out of the little cottage into the street, where Rodney waited. "What will you do now, Darcy?" he said.

"I don't know," she said, with a smile on her face. "For I have no expectations. No attachment to outcomes."

"How about incomes?" said the duchess, leaning out her doorway, a grand parade of cats parenthesizing her comment.

"What are you doing here?" asked Rodney.

"I live here," said the duchess.

"Do you know that you have an identical twin in the forest of Perq?"

"You really believe that?" the duchess smiled. "Well, what about it? Are you going to provide for your princess?"

"Of course," Rodney said.

"You don't really owe me anything," said Darcy.

"Oh, give him a chance to be noble," said the duchess.

Now there was just the business of Tom and Shan to be settled. The living room was softly lit, with only the small pink-shaded lamp illuminated, because Tom had a sudden sense of shame, now that he knew how Shan had been living. That she had been captive in a dungeon was almost beside the point, because to be in the dungeon of a palace had to be grander than what his living room was, he was sure.

"Well, I hate to lose you twice," he said to Shan. "But as there were two of you, that makes it easier. Besides, I thought I lost you once already, and then to a jackass. It will not be as hard losing you to a really fine fellow."

"You like Rodney?"

"You love him. What can I do?"

"I love you too, Tom. But he needs me more than you do. And there's the baby."

"Go ahead," he said. "He's waiting."

"Someone will come along for you. You'll see."

He opened the door for her to the street, where Rodney and his retinue waited, by the lights of torches, to the sound of bells (the duchess's). "I'm coming with you," Shan said.

A great cheer arose, from Isabel, and the chancellor, and Adrian and Babara, and Rhea and the duchess and her cats. "Thank you," said Rodney, and shook Tom's hand.

"Well, isn't love really wanting the one we love to be happy?" Tom said.

"Fetch me my sunlamp!" Isabel cried. "I've found an honest man." And sidling up to his door, noting for the first time what a fine-looking fellow he was, she said: "Do you think you could be interested in an older woman?"

*　　*　　*

So everybody found everybody, and nobody really lost, not even Quirin, for he had died a brave man, which made Rodney very proud. And Rodney had found the chance to be noble with Darcy, and it is nobility that makes a man a king, once his father has died. And Adrian and Babara would be married and live happily once everybody forgot about the Christmas issue of *Playhouse*, and she taught him not to be afraid of intimacy, which she did by enrolling him in several California workshops. And Rhea found a recipe she couldn't ruin. And the chancellor and the duchess started corresponding, and when last we heard, they had a date for New Year's. So even the most down-to-earth and would-be hard-hearted among you ought to take some pleasure from a story that ends with as many lovers as *Hamlet* had corpses.

Now as for the only one who was left without anybody (including Rachid, who had found the perfect partner), what do you suppose happened to Darcy? Probably, dear reader, you were wondering if she was going to go to London and look for Miles. Well, frankly, I was wondering that, too. But I think (and hope, though I have no fixed expectations) that by this time she had gotten a great deal wiser. For she was an independent woman with an income, than which there can be no greater freedom. And it's freedom that makes a woman a queen, which is better than a princess.

So she went off into the glorious moonlight. And she knew a wonderful future awaited her.

As it awaits all of us, now that we have learned our lessons. And to love with a full heart.